ISRAEL POPE, MOUNTAIN MAN

A JOHN POPE WESTERN

G. WAYNE TILMAN

WOLFPACK
PUBLISHING
— EST 2013 —

WOLFPACK
PUBLISHING
— EST 2013 —

Israel Pope, Mountain Man

Paperback Edition
Copyright © 2021 G. Wayne Tilman

Wolfpack Publishing
5130 S. Fort Apache Road, 215-380
Las Vegas, NV 89148

wolfpackpublishing.com

Paperback ISBN 978-1-64734-655-3
eBook ISBN 978-1-64734-654-6

ISRAEL POPE, MOUNTAIN MAN

Appreciation is expressed to Denise Kearns
for her contribution as Beta reader.

CHAPTER 1

Springtime of 1834 in the Valley of Virginia, near the Wilderness Road, brought a cacophony of sounds and smells. Cicadas and Bob White quail sang and the aroma of honeysuckle was in the air.

Seventeen year old Israel Pope worked diligently in the vegetable patch. It was behind the family's cabin. His pa was taking the family and heading to Kentucky. Pa wanted to deplete the garden of the best vegetables to take on the trip. He did not plan on coming back.

Israel picked squash, onions, carrots, and other vegetables from the soil and slightly above on plants, and beans off the pole. Corn on the stalks was about gone. He put them in the only basket the family had. They would probably make the trip in the basket, covered with a muslin cloth.

"I was born to wander like Daniel Boone, not dig

the earth and pick vegetables!" he thought to himself.

"Kentucky was the frontier when Boone first went there. Now, most of it is just like here."

"Israel, you 'bout done?" his father, Jacob Pope yelled from the other side of the cabin.

"Just about, Pa."

"Maude will be around there in a minute to finish. I need you to hunt up a squirrel or rabbit for your Ma to fix for dinner," the elder Pope said.

Jacob Pope was not the first to leave the community around Linville Creek. Expansionism after the first war with England had grown to a fever pitch.

Boone led the way in the times before and after the war for independence. Israel knew of the Boones. They settled for a while in Linville Creek. Daniel left his wife and young ones there during one of his four month jaunts to open the west. Or, maybe to satisfy an itchy foot. Daniel and his immediate folk were gone, but others of his ilk had yet to leave Linville Creek.

The boy knew of more who headed further west for more land, less expensive land, or just the need to keep moving. Linville Creek native Tom Lincoln had eyed some Kentucky land. Then, he moved to Indiana. By 1829, he and some of his family had settled in Illinois. It appeared those with businesses, of which there were more than a few, stayed.

The cabin builders tended to move on. Boones, Lincolns, and Popes were cabin builders.

The boy went into the house and picked up the fowling piece. The shoulder bag accompanying it held shot, balls, a powder flask, some linsey woolsey cloth for patches, and a couple of extra flints. It also held a sparking steel and length of rope to hang a deer to bleed out. The bag was referred to as a "possibles bag." He got his knife and stuck it in his belt, the blade protected by a leather sheath he had made.

The fowler was kept unloaded. They would load it depending on the game being hunted.

"I'll see y'all later," Israel yelled. As he came around the cabin, his sister, Maude, made a face at him. He returned it.

Israel stopped and poured a load of forty grains of powder down the barrel. He put a patch over it and tamped it down with the ramrod. Next came a brass measure of small game shot. Another patch, wet with spit, and tamped down hard.

He primed the pan in the lock with finer ground powder and made sure the hammer was on half cock.

Israel headed up the hill as Maude picked the last of the beans.

He heard the chattering of a squirrel and saw one run around the other side of a tall maple tree.

Israel kissed the back of his hand with a loud "smack" and the curious squirrel reappeared. The single shot brought him down.

Fowler reloaded, he continued on. One squirrel

would not adequately feed a family of four. However, they'd had less for dinner many times. Too many times.

Jacob Pope was a poor planner and provider. He neither hunted nor farmed well. He kept looking for a new place, thinking it would solve all the family problems. It never did and he continued moving on. It was a vicious cycle.

He wandered like Diogenes searching for an honest man. The wanderer and his pup, Rataplan, never found an honest man. Jacob Pope never found the solution to a good life for his family.

Israel was a voracious reader. What he sought was his next book, almost as hard to find on the frontier as an honest man. He dared not tell his father about the allegory. There was no need hurting a man seeking to better his family's lot. Even though the boy knew he never would.

He was already a mile from the cabin, no other game in sight. He came upon some mushrooms on the side of a tree. Israel collected them and put them in his shirt.

Israel apologized to his mother for the slim pickings his hunt provided. She smiled her tired smile and said they would just have to do. Maybe Kentucky would have more game.

Her son smiled as he cleaned the squirrel for her. They were half a century too late for prime land in

Kentucky.

The squirrel was roasted. The pieces were put in a black iron pot with hot water. Mushrooms, and carrots were added along with salt. By dinner the family had a thin soup. It was not filling but would have to suffice. At least, simple bread made it more filling and palatable.

Israel's father addressed his family of wife, Adeline, daughter Maude, a year younger than Israel, and Israel, during dinner. He had arranged to trade the cabin and land for a wagon and one ox. He told everyone they would leave by the end of the week. Israel's mother rolled eyes, unseen by any but her son. She had moved so many times since marrying her husband. Their packing was a change of clothes for each, winter coats and boots, rudimentary iron cookware, and axe, rifle and fowling piece. These would be wrapped in a couple of blankets and some bear skins and carried in the rudimentary farm wagon.

The larger skin was from a bear Israel killed up on the mountain three years ago. He had been a very lucky young man. The buck and ball load of one sixty-two caliber ball and four buckshot was his deer load. He knew God was looking over his shoulder when a black bear charged him. If the only shot had not stopped the two-hundred pound bruin, it was going to be boy, butcher knife, and bear to the death. The weight and odds were on the bear.

"Pa, last time we went past Linville Creek and down to Port Republic, I met a fellow. He is called Ezekiel Boone. He's a distant cousin of Daniel Boone, whose family you knew long ago. His pa owns a sawmill there. We cooked up a plan and his pa approved it.

Mr. Boone said if we would cut the trees and haul them in, he would let us saw them into boards after hours. We would build a small flat boat or gundalow. He would provide the lumber for us to deliver up the river. Depending on what prices we heard from the watermen, we'd take it to Front Royal or Harper's Ferry. We'd offload, sell the freight, disassemble the boat, and sell the boat lumber.

Ezekiel would pay me my share of both, then we'd head home. I could leave from there to catch up with you on the road and go to Kentucky."

"I've heard worst plans, son. You'd have some cash money if you did not spend it in Hell Town," the father said, referring to the northern edge of Front Royal. It was largely saloons and brothels catering to boatmen."

"No worry about me going there, Pa. No way I would," the younger Pope responded.

Lots of young men on Shenandoah voyages said such things. This one meant it.

The day of the Kentucky move came. The young man had come down from the mountain with his family. Jacob walked beside the ox with a stick to guide him. The two women rode the wagon with the family's meager possessions.

The first sign of folks was Linville Creek, a bustling small town where the North River met the South River and formed the North Fork of the Shenandoah River.

The second was Port Republic, where the South Fork of the Shenadoah became navigable, which fit well into Israel's plans.

The meager procession parted from Israel at Port Republic.

Israel watched without trepidation as he lost sight of his family. Any sadness was overcome by him actually beginning his great adventure.

The other three went on towards the Cumberland Gap. His pa told Israel he would leave a letter for him at the first trading post on the Kentucky side of the Gap. It would have their direction of travel. The area had been settled over fifty years before, so there would be established roads.

The seventeen year old inherited his height from both sides of the family. He was already over six feet and showed no indication he would stop there. He was wiry. Yet he was also strong from walking long distances and splitting wood and working the fields. He enjoyed the axe work…. tilling the soil, not so much.

His horizons were far off. And, Israel had a plan how to reach them. He was finally beginning the plan.

The Port Republic area had mines, mills, and farms and was a small industrial hub.

Israel went straight to the Boone sawmill to find his new partner.

Using sweat to build equity, they began to cut tall trees and haul them into town. They used a logging chain and pair of mules. It took weeks of grueling work to amass enough raw wood to build a flat boat called a gundalow.

Ezekiel's father showed them the process of segregating trees by length and width. Then, they guided the logs through the race of the waterwheel-driven saw. Logs became planks. The final finish was done by hand with an adze. The work was grueling and extremely dangerous.

Working shirtless, their suspenders holding up dirty and tattered pants, they worked from sunup to sundown. Even though Ezekiel's father owned a sawmill, he was almost as poor as Israel. Both boys owned one set of clothes, worn boots and floppy hats.

Their knives were basically butcher knives. Knives with rounded points and thin blades. Better than a sharp stick for defense, but barely so.

"Israel, we both need to spend a dollar or maybe two wherever we end up buying some decent knives. A man has to have a good knife," Zeke said.

"Have you seen one of those Bowie knives yet?" Israel asked.

"Yep. A couple of the boatmen have them. They are what we need to set our caps to get. At least you got a gun. I don't even have one. I'm hoping Pa will let me take his fowling piece along like yours did for you."

"My Pa took the Bedford County long rifle with them on the trip West. I'm just glad for the fowler. It's twenty bore, which is about .60 caliber. I killed a bear with it while deer hunting," Israel said.

"How was she loaded?"

"Buck and ball. I had a .60 caliber ball over buck-shot. It had sixty grains of double F powder behind it. Did the trick on the old bear. Pa's .45 rifle will carry farther and more accurately. But, the fowler is quicker to reload and can be shot more before cleaning without rifling in the barrel. I don't know which I would want when I go trapping in the Rocky Mountains. There are hostile Indians, big-ass bears, buffalos, and panthers out there. Lots of things with either arrows or claws to kill a fellow."

"Won't a gun be better than a bow and arrow in a fight, Israel?"

"Maybe so, maybe not. I daresay an arrow will carry doggone near as far as my fowler and shoot twenty times faster. It won't leave a telltale puff of white smoke to tell me where the fellow is shooting from either. I will give away my position with every shot."

"I never thought of how fast an arrow can be shot…."

"Zeke, your Pa said he was going to talk to the boatmen to see how much more money we could make if we took our boat all the way up to Harper's Ferry. Did he share any news with you?" Israel asked.

"Yes, I meant tell you, but we have been so busy chopping, cleaning and dragging trees to the sawmill. He figures we can earn a hundred dollars in shipping from him. Since we are the boat owners, the only cut will be maybe twenty dollars salary for the third man. He says our size boat may bring eighteen dollars in Front Royal or forty in Harper's Ferry."

"Hmm....twenty-two more dollars for another several days of fighting rapids. It's a lot of money, but I just don't know if it's worth it," Israel said.

"Not to me, Israel. Because I am losing my sawmill salary every day I'm gone. I have an interest in the mill growing. It will be mine one day. Whether I keep it or sell it, I'd sure like it to be as valuable as possible."

"Any ideas on who our third boatman might be, Zeke?"

"I've been thinking about Arthur Calloway. He doesn't talk much. Some people think he's not real sociable, but they are wrong. Arthur just doesn't talk to hear himself talk. When he does say something, it's worth hearing, Israel. He worked several big jobs for my pa. I found he's real easy to get along with. He's a giant and stronger than an ox. His strength would serve us well fighting those front and back sweep oars in a big rapid."

"My worry is the timing. Will Arthur be available when we leave?" Israel asked.

"Probably. He does not have a regular job. Just does odd jobs requiring a lot of strength and endurance." Israel nodded.

The two did not finish with their needed lumber until the first of September. Finding the right trees for the two twenty-foot sweep oars took a while. Bow and stern, the sweep oars would provide locomotion in calm water and steering at all times. It also took longer than they expected to shape them and attach blades.

An experienced boatman helped them by drawing an outline of the finished shape on the two large boards for the paddle blades of the sweeps with a piece of charcoal.

Horseflies and mosquitoes were a major problem and both were covered by bites. Ezekiel caught a fever, probably malarial fever, his folks said. He was down for over a month before starting to build the gundalow.

Israel continued to work at the sawmill, this time in his friend's stead. A small operation, having a man down was a real danger to its continued profitability.

Their plan was to build a smaller gundalow than the usual sixty to ninety footers. While it would not carry as much freight, it would take less people to handle it. The reality was the two had neither the skill nor the time to build a larger gundalow.

The three would head to Front Royal when they left. Israel and Ezekiel already decided against the much further trek up to Harper's Ferry.

Up, because the fast-flowing Shenandoah River flows northeastwards. The reason is it flows from higher ground to lower ground.

Israel wanted to get on the trail and catch up with his parents and sister. He felt he owed it to his family to help build a decent cabin. His experience felling trees in Port Republic would prove useful in the project. His father built their cabin in Virginia. Israel had not been old enough to help. The one-man cabin was ill-constructed and drafty and often smoky. The new one would be appreciably better.

The accumulation of logs and their conversion to lumber for the boat was slowed by Ezekiel's illness. Even when he got up and about, he was weak for another month.

It snowed early in the Valley of Virginia. The river closed to traffic. It was low and had ice in spots along its length.

Israel reckoned his family thought he had died en route upriver. He had no way to tell them otherwise.

He took some money from the little he made at the Boone sawmill and bought an axe, some cast iron cookware and more powder, balls and shot.

An open-faced log shelter was quickly constructed. He put a roll-up waxed cloth over the opening and made a permanent fire pit in the front.

Israel rolled the front cloth up on cold nights and set a log reflector to direct heat from the fire into his primitive new home. He spent the winter dry but cold.

He thought about what he wanted to do with his life.

Israel hoped to join a fur trapping expedition heading further west. He would become a fur trapper. Beaver pelts were bringing a premium for hats. A few years of trapping should fund further travel.

He wanted to see places he had never set his eyes on. Big mountains, deserts, the Pacific Ocean. Seeing those should give him an idea of where he wanted to settle.

Israel gave no thought to finding a winsome lass and settling down to raise a family. Such an endeavor would keep him in one place and likely involve farming.

"I am not a farmer. Never will be," he thought to himself repeatedly.

Each day he planned more. He sat near their flat boat when work at the sawmill was done. It helped him plan by staring at their gundalow sitting on the ground beside the sawmill.

******

Spring came early and provided one benefit in having such a late start.

The snow melted in the Appalachians and the Shenandoah River peaked. While the rapids and their inherent danger represented a real risk, the trip would be faster. It would be faster, however, only if they avoided accidents.

Arthur Calloway, as suspected, was available for the trip. His pay would be the most he ever made. Since he did not contribute to the gundalow, his would be salary paid by Israel and Ezekiel.

Israel and Ezekiel supplemented their planned cargo with a one-ton pile of pig iron, and twenty barrels of corn. The shippers knew the Boones and knew they would treat them fairly.

A spit on the palm and handshake was the contract of the day. Trust and honesty were paramount. There was no way to reasonably perfect claims about lost cargo or accurate pricing.

They would set aside the cargo money for the shippers and pocket their money for the wood in the boat. They would split the latter two ways after paying Arthur his salary.

Once all accounts were settled, Israel would get on the trail after his family.

After helping his pa build the cabin and spending

the winter, he would head west into the frontier.

There was a warm period in late March of 1835. The three new boatman solicited the help of Ezekiel's father and several neighbors and two mules.

They dragged the boat to the edge of the Shenandoah, using two dressed logs underneath as rollers. Personal items, weapons, and provisions were loaded aboard before the long-awaited launch.

Once the hull hit the water, they better be ready on the sweeps. The race would be on as the boat hit the fast running current and headed for its first rapid.

They would have to constantly be alert for weirs, fish traps, and routes between rocks. Shallows where they might run aground in a rapid could upset the gundalow and they would lose their cargo. And, maybe their lives.

All three young men had heard the rushing sound of the river. On this day, they heard it in a totally different way.

With Arthur on the rear sweep oar, Israel on the front, and Zeke near him watching for hazards, they shoved off. The river caught them and they picked up much more speed than they had imagined.

A small crowd had gathered on the shore. The men cheered as they hit the middle and sped off. The three on the gundalow did not hear them. They were experiencing new feelings of apprehension as the boat rocked side by side. Waves smacked the wide splash boards which kept the flat boat from being just a raft.

At the same time, the blunt bow dove deep into the waves of the first rapid. Hundreds of gallons of water rushed in.

It passed, over knee deep on the boatmen, transited the boat, and emptied out the back near Arthur and the rear sweep.

Arthur let out a whoop, enjoying the ride. Israel was enjoying it when he could think about it. Mainly, he was steering away from rocks. Steering into the best line. Watching for V's in the water which signified hazards.

In the first hour, they hit their first small waterfall. The bow dove into the water at the bottom and popped straight up before regaining stability.

Zeke, bracing against the cargo, flew overboard.

"Ride with your feet first!" Israel yelled. "Better for them to hit a rock than your head!"

The two on the gundalow could see a shallow eddy behind a large rock.

Zeke could not see it from his perspective of underwater. Finally, his head surfaced for a gulp of air.

The gundalow swerved in behind the large rock and stopped instantly in the calm water of the eddy. The way it lay, Arthur was nearest the channel and Israel the shore.

"Arthur, throw your rope to him as he floats by!" Israel yelled.

The giant youth heaved a rope in front of Zeke. Zeke caught it. Or, rather, it caught him. Arthur pulled the rope in, hand over hand. Zeke was drawn rapidly to the boat.

Israel set the sweep in its holder and ran amidships.

He grabbed his friend under the arms and dragged him aboard. Zeke immediately vomited his earlier breakfast of biscuits and gravy.

Arthur appeared with a bucket and dumped a gallon of the Shenandoah on the deck, cleaning it.

Israel looked in the direction the current was taking them. He did not see any rapids for close to a mile. The boat was drifting out of the calm water of the eddy.

Israel readied his sweep and nodded for Arthur to do the same. Zeke waved his thanks to the big man on the rear sweep who saved him.

Zeke managed to assume a sitting position against a stack of the lumber they were delivering for his father. He checked the ropes holding it secure and held one as the current carried them on to the next fast water.

The boat moved and picked up speed once again. The three heard the roaring of a rapid in the distance.

Zeke stood and carefully walked towards Israel, keeping one hand on the cargo to maintain his balance.

"It looks like this rapid is in a wide spot on the river and I see rollers. There must be rocks underneath them. I don't see any sticking up, though," Israel told his friend.

"This may just be a fun, fast ride to the other side," Zeke agreed and yelled the prognosis back to Arthur.

They hit the rapid and literally flew through it with no problems. Beyond were several miles of fast-moving current with no rapids.

Zeke took the front sweep and Israel walked thought the boat and checked everything. The shelter they build amidships was still tight. It was little more than a tent.

Israel made sure their food, blankets, arms and powder were dry and secure. They were. He took out bread Zeke's mother made them and sliced beef. There was a jug with apple cider in it. He took all of it out and made sandwiches, using his nine-inch blade skinning knife. They had three pewter coffee cups. He filled each with cider and delivered lunch to his friends.

Israel took over the front sweep while Zeke and Arthur ate. The front sweep was sufficient to steer the boat in water as calm as this. He ate later and was refreshed for the next rapid.

The gundalow made good progress before dark the first day. It was too treacherous to stay on the river when darkness made the rocks and weirs invisible. They pulled over at a calm spot and tied the gundalow to trees. The sun had already dried Zeke's clothes. A fire on land finished the drying process. They finished the sliced beef and bread.

It was almost eighty miles from Port Republic to their takeout north of Front Royal. They covered ten miles on day one. Apparently, they realized, the normal five day trip was due to most boats having a larger crew on the sweeps, more length, and a lot more experience. All of which made the larger gundalows consistently faster. They had seen this first hand when two caught them and were out of sight within ten minutes.

They had bacon, flour for biscuits or fry bread, some apples and potatoes.

"Not much for another week of travel, boys," Zeke said as they sat around the campfire.

"I have some hooks and line. Maybe the man not on the sweeps can troll some grubs or worms and catch us some fish. Bass and trout are in the water all along the route, I suspect," Arthur said.

"We can try. Even one fish of any size is more than we have right now," Zeke rejoined. Arthur was shy and did not speak often. When he did, it was simple logic worth hearing. As Israel and Zeke treated him as an equal, he warmed up to them and spoke more frequently. They concurred he was a good companion and a good choice for the trip. In the morning when they shoved off, he had several handfuls of dirt with worms and grubs crawling around wrapped in a piece of cloth.

The boatmen got used to larger boats with more crewmen manning sweeps passing them. While neither of the three understood physics, they got the point and accepted it.

The passing boatmen waved, sometimes cajoled and made rude signs. The three young boatmen grinned and returned in kind. It was the way of the river, no matter whether Ohio, Mississippi, Missouri, or another.

With Zeke on the stern sweep, Arthur wet his bait. It was suspended from a green sapling pole. By mid-afternoon and several more rapids, they had gone another ten miles and had four trout for meals. Their speed was picking up as their prowess grew.

"No matter about those other boatmen calling us names, we are speeding up", Zeke observed loudly from the stern.

"Based on the distance to some of the towns we are passing, I reckon we might do twelve or thirteen miles today," Israel responded, as their large crewman pulled in a bass. A good-sized sunfish followed.

Three more days of progressively faster travel took them to Bentonville. It was close to ten miles from the take out at Front Royal. The take out area beyond the town was the part known as Hell Town.

They risked traveling at dusk to get past Bentonville and find a place to pull ashore and camp for the evening.

On this last night of the trip, they finished off a large mess of Arthur's fish for dinner.

"Well, Arthur, you've done well by us. Your time on the sweep and your good fishing have sped out trip and made it more delicious!" Israel said.

"I've enjoyed being with y'all for the past several days. What are each of you going to do once we deliver the cargo, break up the boat and get the money?" Arthur asked.

"I'm going to spend a couple bucks on a drink and a lady in Hell Town, then start the walk back to Port Republic," Zeke said.

"How about you, Israel?"

"I figure with all this cash money, we ought to leave together and hike back to where we started from together. I have been told there are robbers who haunt the roads along the river looking for boatmen bringing money back south. We have your strength, two fowling pieces we can load with buckshot and three knives. I figure we would be a bad group for robbers to pick on, don't y'all?" Israel asked. Both men nodded their agreement.

"But, to finish answering your question, Arthur, I will head from Port Republic to the Cumberland Gap. On the other side is a letter waiting for me to tell which way my family went. They are on the way to Kentucky. I will go there, help them build a cabin and then go west to join a trapping company. I plan to trap for a few years, then try to decide what I want to do the rest of my life. Maybe just wander, like Zeke's cousin Daniel Boone."

"Man, your idea sounds so good," the big man said. "I don't have any ties to our part of Virginia. I'd sure like to tag along, Israel."

"You are most welcome to join me, my friend. Zeke, you would be too, though I think you have an investment in the sawmill," Israel said.

"I do. I was born late in the life of my folks. Pa is old to have a son under twenty. He is slowing down. The sawmill is mine if I stick with it. It'd be a shame to let his twenty-seven years of sweat go to waste."

The other two understood and agreed.

******

They got underway at dawn and arrived in Front Royal late in the afternoon.

"Zeke, you got the letters between the shippers and buyers in your oilskin bag?" Israel asked.

"Yep, sure do. First one is a man who builds houses. I have to go into town for find him. Y'all want to look up the second man? He has agreed to buy the pig iron. His name is Gunderson and he has a shop on the edge of Hell Town."

"Any idea who we will sell the boat to for lumber?"

Arthur asked.

"Not an idea in this world," Zeke said. "I suspect we will just have to shop it around the landing. Every boat stopping here instead of going on to Harper's Ferry gets sold, so there must be a pretty active business."

Hell Town was rough, like many port areas. Boatmen had ample places to spend their money on bad whiskey, feminine charms, and minimal supplies before heading south again or pushing on to Harper's Ferry. They decided to leave Arthur to guard the boat and its cargo until the other two could arrange deals for sale or delivery.

His sheer size and the two fowling pieces he had on either side insured the safety of the cargo left under his care.

Zeke left for Front Royal proper. Israel began searching Hell Town for Gunderson's blacksmith shop. He found it and the owner. Israel showed him the letters between him and the mine south of Port Republic.

He acknowledged the deal and followed Israel back with a heavy wagon. Israel and Arthur loaded the pig iron onto the wagon. Gunderson gave Israel the agreed upon cash in return for the cargo and a receipt.

Israel noted several gadabouts watching as the gold changed hands. He would tell the other two and keep a close watch on their back trail on the way home.

Zeke returned with the buyer of the lumber in

his wagon.

Before darkness fell, the three boatmen had loaded all of the Boone lumber onto the wagon and money was passed in exchange. Zeke and Israel segregated the funds going to his father, and each of the boatmen. Arthur was extremely pleased with his salary. He was even more gratified with the respect and comradery they showed him from the very start. Because of his many contributions, they added a generous tip to his salary. He knew he had made lifetime friends in Israel and Zeke.

Zeke left the two guarding the money and eating a dinner picked up at a portside food stand. He headed into the middle of Hell Town and chose a one-stop shop. It was a saloon and brothel combined.

Four hours later, he had not returned. His friends began to worry.

"Arthur, you want to go looking for him? Or, want me to?" Israel asked.

"Leave me both guns and I'll guard the money, Israel. You go and make sure he's alright."

Armed only with his skinning knife, basically a thin-bladed butcher knife, Israel set out on his mission.

Despite the small size of the area he was searching, it took him half an hour to find his friend staggering around with a silly grin on his face. He had clearly consumed too much cheap whiskey.

Israel noticed his suspenders were on backwards. Which meant his pants were also. Apparently, Zeke dressed in a hurry somewhere.

Israel grinned.

He heard what sounded like a young girl screaming in pain. Israel knew his friend would be a hinderance in any sort of fight in his current condition. He pointed him back towards the gundalow and gave him a gentle push.

He rushed to the place where he heard the screams.

It was a wooden house with a wood frame rear. The rear had walls of waxed sailcloth and was divided into ten cribs. Each was for a prostitute.

The screams came from the fourth one. Nobody else seemed to want to find out why a woman was screaming in fear or pain or both.

Israel Pope wanted to know why. He ripped the cloth door aside. A large man was trying to force himself on a tall thin girl of perhaps fifteen. It was she who was screaming in dire terror.

Israel grabbed the man from the back by both shoulders and pulled him off her. He jerked the man outside the crib and spun him around.

The man was drunk but had enough presence of mind to draw a menacing knife with a blade a foot long.

Israel kicked him between the legs. The man let out a scream much like the girl's. Israel realized the man did not have any pants on and his rough boot had connected with bare genitalia.

The knife hit the muddy ground. Israel hit the man hard with a round house punch to the jaw. The blow rattled Israel all the way up his arm and into his shoulder. Growing up on the frontier, he had been in a lot of fights. But, he had never hit anyone as hard as this before.

The man went down. He was out.

Seeing the terrified girl on her back in a mangy cot, he turned and kicked the man in the side of the head. The kick was powerful enough to move him.

Israel did not know whether he killed the man or just sent him deeper into unconsciousness. Nor, did he give a damn.

He gently lifted the girl and held her up. She was not wearing very much. It was some sort of sleeveless linsey Woolsey shift which only came to a foot above her knees. She could not walk around in public in such an outfit. Or, rather, he thought, lack of one.

Israel ripped the rest of the sailcloth or canvas door off and wrapped her in it.

He saw a glint. It was the man's big knife.

Israel reached down and picked it up. He saw trousers in a rolled heap beside the cot. He retrieved the leather sheath and slipped the knife into it and tucked it into his own belt.

Israel led the girl back towards the water.

"Are you alright, Miss?" he asked.

"No! I think he was going to kill me! He slapped me around before he tried to have his way with me. I didn't want to be here! My folks died and my uncle hired me out to the owner. He and I thought I would be a cleaner. The owner had something else in mind for me," she said, the words tumbling out as fast as a rapid on the Shenandoah.

"He made me put this thing on and led me to what he called 'my crib.' I knew as soon as I saw it what he wanted me to become," she said.

"What's your name?" Israel asked.

"Hannah," she said, not volunteering a surname. "I hope you killed him!" she added.

"It might complicate my life if I did," Israel responded as much to himself as to Hannah.

"Miss Hannah, where is your uncle?"

"He went west. I don't miss him. He beat me. I knew what was coming next. The only thing saved me was the owner of the bar gave him some gold for me. Traded me like a slave. Now, I know how those poor souls must feel."

"I don't know what to do with you, Miss Hannah. For now, I think we need to lay low. If the man back at the bar is dead, the sheriff might get involved. I'm not so sure what kind of justice either one of us would get here. So, I'm going to take you back to our boat. My friends and I can protect you until we think of something."

"Just get me away from here. What is your name?" she asked.

"Israel. Israel Pope."

"Then, I will hide with you and your friends Mr. Pope."

"Just Israel, Miss Hannah," he said.

"Just call me Hannah."

They walked with his arm around her, helping to keep the cloth secure and hide how little she was wearing.

At the edge of Hell Town, they caught up with Zeke. He was urinating against a tree. When he finished, he promptly passed out and hit the ground.

"Hannah, you hold the material around you. This is one of my two friends. It looks like I am going to have to carry him," Israel said with resignation.

He bent over and scooped Zeke up and over his shoulder. They walked over to the boat with Israel carrying his friend and arm around his new protectee.

"What's this?" Arthur called out, setting the fowling piece down.

"We have an old friend who is too drunk to walk and a new one who needs our protection. Would you grab a blanket and my bear skin? We'll hang the skin on the roof of the shelter and make a room for Hannah to hide in for now. Hannah? This is Arthur Calloway. He's a good man. Arthur, this is Hannah.

A man was attacking her."

"Did you take care of him, Israel?"

"Yes, my friend, I believe I did," Israel responded. He thought one of his two companions needed to go into Hell Town tomorrow and keep an ear open. If the man was dead, they would be sure to hear about it. Israel did not care whether he killed the man, he deserved it for his actions. Israel's worry was having to elude the sheriff and get out of the county first and Virginia second would be tough. Especially with his gold.

With the big man on guard and Zeke snoring loudly, Israel spoke with Hannah.

"Hannah, what's your last name?" he asked.

"It's Winder. I am from Petersburg."

"How old are you?"

"Fifteen. I will be sixteen in a couple of months."

"Is there anybody kin to you who could look after you?"

"I am afraid I only have one person in this whole wide world," Hannah said.

"Where is this person, Hannah?"

"Squatting on the deck right across from me, Israel. You, silly. You are the angel God sent to save me from the horrible man. He would have killed me."

Israel looked at her pleasantly, thinking. Maybe she was right. He certainly did feel a responsibility for her. But, he felt less than angelic for a number of reasons related to her and her rescue.

Hannah waited to see what response she would get from her statement. She was pleased it was not horror or anger. She liked the pleasant expression as he formulated his answer.

"Yes. I guess I am. It is an honor, Hannah Winder. A distinct honor.

You may have a decision to make tomorrow. So, think about it tonight. I am leaving here tomorrow with my friends. We are going to Port Republic, down the Shenandoah. This time, we are going by foot.

When we get there, Arthur and I are going westward. We are going through the Cumberland Gap into Kentucky. I have to catch up with my mother, father, and sister. She is about your age, a year or so younger than me.

I will help them build a cabin. Maybe another for Arthur. Then, I will go further west and join a trapping party. I plan to trap for a couple of years and make my grubstake.

What will I do with it? I have no idea. I am not a farmer. I also am not a store keep.

So, what I am saying is we could look for a place for you in Port Republic, or you could go on to Kentucky. I am sure my folks would give you a place to live.

But, you need to know I won't be there all the time."

"I'm willing to chance it, Israel. All of those options beat what's facing me here. I have never been with a man. You saved me from it tonight. He planned to be my first, the drunk, smelly pig. I always dreamed it would be loving, gentle and wonderful. If last night was the way it always is, I want no part of it. I will be an old maid," Hannah said.

"Without any more experience than you have, I always thought of it the same way you do. If I might be so bold to suggest you and I might end up being each other's first. If so, I promise it will be gentle."

She gave him a smile which made him hope what he just said would come to pass. Really soon. It was not flirtatious. It was sweet and trusting. It was the smile of a good, kind person, who despite the rags, tousled hair and dirty face, appeared to be very pretty.

******

They had to keep Hannah out of sight until time to move her out of town. Israel knew from her the bar and brothel owner would be looking for her. He still did not know whether the sheriff would be looking for him.

He was pretty sure the man, if he lived, could not identify him. He was drunk when Israel destroyed his ability to have children, knocked him cold, and then kicked him in the head. His first and only look at Israel was through a drunken haze. He spent the rest of their minute together unconscious.

Zeke went into Hell Town to both listen for rumors of a murder and find buyers for the gundalow. Arthur stayed with Hannah, guarding her out of sight.

Israel entered the Hell Town area and walked south into Front Royal itself.

He found a general merchandise store already open and went in.

"Howdy, I just got in on a boat from south of here. My sister made me promise to bring her a dress back. You got any?" Israel asked. He had studied Hannah before leaving and memorized her height, width and foot length and width.

"We have some women's clothes. Do you want an everyday or dress-up?" the man asked.

"Everyday, please. And, I want to get her new shoes as a surprise. And, a hair brush."

"We have those, too. What is her size?"

"About this tall and this wide," Israel said, holding his hand up for the height and both hands apart for width."

The man brought out a blue dress and a green one the same size. He held them up to Israel's measure.

"I'll take both. She's a good sister."

Next were shoes. Israel took his best guess and they went in the sack. The hair brush was easy. He added hair ribbons which matched the dresses.

He got a new knife for Arthur and a bag of horehound candy for Zeke, hoping his friend would see the humor in the gift. His last purchase was a waxed tarp for a shelter.

When he got back, Zeke caught him on the shore and quietly told him there was no talk about any deaths in Hell Town last night. He also said he found a buyer for the gundalow. The man wanted to keep it intact for small cargo trips up to Harper's Ferry.

Since he was buying a boat instead of lumber from a boat, the price was greater. The two pocketed more than anticipated for the trip, as did Arthur with his salary and the bonus they added.

He stepped aboard the gundalow and went into the makeshift shelter with a wide smile. Hannah stood immediately in her ragged shift, looking expectantly at him.

He handed her the sack with the two dresses, shoes and hairbrush. He also brought a dampened scrap of material, along with a larger one to use toweling off.

"Oh! Nobody ever gave me two dresses before. They are beautiful. Pull the curtain closed and I will see if they fit."

He closed it and turned to leave, but she called him back and slipped her shift off. Israel Pope had never seen anything so beautiful in his life. She carefully washed and dried.

She put on the blue dress, then the shoes. Hannah brushed her hair and tied on a blue ribbon. Nobody in Hell Town would recognize this lovely young woman as the new prostitute in the River Bar.

Hannah ran to Israel and hugged him. She was tall for a woman of her time and her head came up almost to his chin. He looked down in time to catch a full-on kiss. It lingered. He would have been happy had it lasted forever. She stepped away and smiled. There was the smile again. It had a powerful effect on his mood and emotions.

"Hannah, I'm sure glad you are coming with me. My sister, Maude, and my folks will welcome you right into the family. Your being there will surely shorten the time of my trapping trips away from you. Right this minute, I seem to have lost any interest in going trapping at all," he said, less sure of his voice than ever in his life.

They walked away from the gundalow. The trip from Port Republic provided money in the form of gold coins, a new Sheffield Bowie knife confiscated from a rapist, and a new friend.

Israel looked at the young lady walking beside him. She was smiling so broadly. More than anything, the trip allowed Hannah to become part of his life and his future. He hoped she would be the most unexpected and treasured reward of all.

The three young men had their shares of gold hidden in small leather bags hung around their necks with a length of rawhide. What other meager belongings they had were rolled in their blankets and lashed closed. The blankets were worn over the shoulder with the tied end under the opposite arm. Israel had purchased a new blanket for Hannah, who had her brush and second dress carefully rolled in it.

The only other additions were a pair of Indian moccasins for each. Their leather shoes and boots were fine for anything except an eighty-mile walk.

They carried beef jerky, bread, a small jar of molasses, and cheese purchased in Front Royal and a couple of ceramic jugs with fresh water.

The day became hotter and their clothes wet with perspiration. Though all were used to walking as their only method of transportation, they were tired by dusk.

A copse of woods a hundred yards off the river road seemed a good place to spend the night. No fire was necessary.

Israel was glad they did not have to carry the cook gear and sailcloth curtains from the gundalow. Selling it had been a blessing. The sailcloth with its coating from the gundalow would have been a grateful addition to their shelter. Now, they would have one to share on the walk.

It rained. Rained in torrents. All four were soaked to the skin. Their first night on the road proved miserable. Even Hannah's spare dress was soaked under her blanket.

The sun the following morning was sufficiently hot

to dry their clothes in the first hour of hiking down the busy road. Wagons, horsemen and walkers filled it with traffic.

"This is making the trip through the mountains to Kentucky look pretty good," Israel commented to nobody in particular.

"I cannot wait. This is the big adventure of my life," Hannah said softly. He took her hand and squeezed it gently as they walked. He carried the fowling piece in his other hand. The new Bowie, with its twelve inch blade, was diagonally stuck in his wide belt at the small of his back. It provided him as much comfort as the gun loaded with birdshot.

They passed several shifty looking characters in the trees off the side of the road late in the afternoon. The three watched as they passed.

"I am thinking Arthur's size and the two guns are ruining their plan to rob us," Zeke said under his breath. The other two men nodded, but Israel was less convinced.

"I bet the big ole pig sticker stuck in your belt helped too, Israel," Arthur said. He had no idea, as they walked along, how many times a Bowie knife would save his friend's life in the future.

Late in the same evening, the three characters had their nerve supported by the cheapest John Barleycorn stolen money could buy.

Israel was sleeping on the right, Hannah in the

middle and Arthur and Zeke on the left.

Israel heard a twig snap. It sounded like a bigger twig than a small animal would break. Even more than a deer probably. He was instantly awake and reached across Hannah, who was sleeping soundly.

Israel touched Arthur's arm and he stirred and looked up. Israel put his finger to his lip for silence. They both heard leaves rustle.

Both silently rolled out of opposite ends of the open front tarp shelter, Arthur had Jacob Pope's fowling piece. Israel had the large Bowie. Both melted behind large trees in the pitch dark. Zeke slept on.

The three intruders split. Two came in on Israel's side, one on Arthur's. The quarters were too close to use the gun loaded with buckshot.

Arthur swung the butt and caught his man in the jaw. His jaw cracked loudly.

One of the men on Israel's side tried to hit him with a two-inch diameter stick.

Israel blocked with the blade of the Bowie. It cut the stick in half.

Israel moved in close and kneed the man in the groin. As he screamed and doubled over, Israel brought the coffin-shaped walnut grips of the knife down on the back of his head. He went down hard.

The last man grabbed Israel to grapple with him. He was an experienced fighter. Usually once he hit the ground grappling with his prey, the fight would likely be over.

Israel's knife hand was free and he slashed as the man jumped back.

The cut was long, but shallow and the man screamed out, awakening Hannah and Zeke.

Israel head-butted him, knocking him to the ground on his back. He straddled the man and placed the sharp blade to his throat.

Even in the dark, he could see the sweat of terror forming on the man's forehead.

He took the blade away long enough to punch him hard with his non-knife hand.

Hannah was awake now, her green eyes wide with surprise and fear. Zeke was beside her, holding his knife.

"It's alright, honey. You've got Zeke, Arthur and me. Nobody's going to hurt you.

"What should we do with these fellas, Israel. When they wake up, I mean," Zeke asked.

"I don't rightly know. Let's drag them out by the road and think about it.

They dragged them, taking no care towards being gentle.

Israel had an idea.

"Arthur, we don't have any rope we can give up. Let's use their pants to tie them up to trees facing the road for everybody to see. Maybe we can make a sign saying 'robbers,' or something."

The big man grinned evilly. He pulled the pants off the man with the badly broken jaw. Holding each pant leg, he gave a mighty pull and the pants ripped apart.

Israel tried the same thing but had to use the Bowie to get the split started before ripping them.

Arthur positioned each man against a tree. Israel and Zeke tightly tied their necks and waists around the trunk of their respective trees. The men were held completely immobile. The trees were large enough in diameter to prevent getting their hands around to the back of the trees in order to untie any of the knots.

"Hannah, will you break camp? We need to get going and leave these men here to contemplate their future in crime," Israel said. She nodded and started rolling blankets and taking the shelter down.

As the men regained consciousness, Israel had a short talk with them.

"My friend and I could kill you. Maybe we ought to. You deserve it. But we will leave you here alive to be found in your current trouser-less state by folks passing by. They are likely to notify the sheriff to come get you."

Israel took the small ceramic jar of molasses and poured a thin line between their legs. He spilled enough on them to ensure ants and other bugs would be attracted to the men, who were in plain view of the road.

The four travelers joined forces and found enough

rocks for Israel to spell out the letters "R.O.B.B.E.R.S" and make an arrow pointing to the three men.

Hannah walked over to the men as the three were leaving. She stopped and looked down rather pointedly.

"You fellas scared? Can't be you're cold. Maybe you are just unlucky."

She laughed at them and turned away towards Israel, Zeke, and Arthur.

"Let's get out of here. If I stay any longer with these little boys, I might bust a gut laughing."

"Damn, she's got spunk," Israel thought to himself. Both his friends were thinking the same thing.

They continued the trip towards Port Republic. The moon suggested it was around two in the morning. They always wondered what became of the three men, but never heard.

It took them three more days to reach Port Republic.

Zeke's mother made them a large bag of loaves of bread. They bought more cheese, bacon, and coffee, which was gradually replacing tea and cider as a preferred drink. At Port Republic, Arthur used some of his money to buy a used fowling piece. The ability to use shot for small game and a ball or buck and ball for larger made it more utilitarian than a rifle. Especially, if one were to own only one gun and use it around a farm or cabin.

Israel bought a Bedford-type long rifle. It was

forty-five caliber, long and slender and had a flint lock. The new percussion locks were getting popular. Many gunsmiths were converting flints to the percussions. Israel planned on being in remote areas where an adequate supply of percussion caps might not be readily available. He knew as long as he had powder he could grind finer for the lock and flint from the ground, he would not need to worry about how to touch off a shot.

Israel used half his money buying supplies for the long walk down the Wilderness Road to the Cumberland Gap and on into Kentucky. He bought several more waxed canvas tarpaulins for shelter, rope, an axe and some cooking gear. In view of the weight of these items, he purchased a young mule and a sawbuck pack saddle. He was promised the mule had been saddle broke and had also pulled a small wagon.

They were ready.

Just after dawn, the three headed southwest from Port Republic.

"Arthur, is this your first gun?" Israel asked.

"I grew up hunting around the farm with Pa's back in Charlottesville. But, it's the first one I actually owned," he said.

"Me, too. Just another sign we are on our way to the next big adventure."

"Well, depending on the lay of the land where your folks settle, I may stay there. I don't have your need to see new places. I like to grow things. I enjoyed being a farmer."

"It's all in what makes you happy, my friend. I have to walk this wanderlust out of my system. Who knows after I do?" Israel said pensively.

"How about you, Hannah?" Israel asked.

"I just want to make a home for you to come back to after each expedition," she said, smiling. Israel smiled back, thinking her plan did not clash with his at all. Not a bit. Boy, were his folks and Maude going to be surprised, when he showed up with a prospective wife.

They began the almost month walk between the Blue Ridge Mountains on their left and the Appalachians on their right. The route was down the Wilderness Road, soon to be called the Valley Pike.

The best purchase ended up being Amos, the mule. He carried the major part of the load without complaint. Hand carrying no more than a long gun made the long trip more palatable for Israel, Hannah, and Arthur.

Israel taught Hannah how to load and shoot the fowling piece. He had her braid some rawhide and made a sling for it. She walked with the gun loaded with buck and ball slung around her neck and one shoulder. Hannah was ready to help if a black bear or some two-legged varmints attacked them.

From the resolve she showed at every turn since

they met, Israel knew she would not hesitate to send a sixty caliber ball and six or seven buckshot pellets towards an adversary. No matter whether the adversary was man or beast. He became more drawn to this young woman daily. Hannah had felt the same about him from the second he pulled the attacker off her and she saw him.

Arthur opened up and spoke more. He seemed to adopt Israel and Hannah as brother and sister. The river trip up to Front Royal and the comradery with them and Zeke represented a major turning point in his life. He now had respect, people he cared about, and a direction in life.

They passed Staunton, Lexington, Wythe Courthouse, and Abington during their month of walking and leading Amos. The weather held well for them. They camped in open-faced shelters most nights and killed game along the way to supplement food purchased from stores.

"You know what I miss?" Arthur asked just after Wythe Courthouse.

"What do you miss?" Hannah responded.

"Bread. Biscuits. The fry bread we make over the fire is fine, but my ma made fine bread."

"You know….me, too. Let's see if we can buy some bread at the next village we pass. Maybe some more ham or other salted meat which will last?" Israel said.

"How about you, Hannah? What would you like?"

Arthur asked.

"Maybe some cider? Water and coffee are getting tiresome," she said.

All were easy and inexpensive things to find after they passed through the famed Cumberland Gap and stopped at the first trading post they saw.

"Howdy, my name is Israel Pope. Do you have a letter left here for me?" he asked as the other two shopped.

"I do. It's been here for quite a while now."

"My family left it. Everybody look okay?" he asked.

"Yep. They looked fine. Tired and hungry like everybody else who comes through here from civilization."

Israel unfolded the letter and read his father's hand.

"Israel. We made it through here and are on our way to Boonesboro. Told was pretty settled up. See you when you get here."

Hannah and Arthur were beside him as he scanned the letter and read a change in his expression.

"What is it, Israel?" Hannah asked.

"My pa is surprised things are pretty well settled here. I guess he didn't think about it's been fifty years since Dan Boone came through. You'd have to go to the Great Plains to get what he's looking for. Pa is better off living somewhere like this. He's not much at farming, or hunting, or trapping. He needs to get a job working for somebody who needs help with a business. Somebody like Zeke's pa."

"What are we going to do?" Arthur asked.

"Only thing we can do. We'll follow him and help him get set up. If you're limited in what you can do, keeping on moving does not accomplish anything."

"Why don't we take him to the nearest property office? We could ask about an abandoned homestead already perfected. Maybe it could be taken over for the back taxes?" Arthur suggested.

"What a great idea, Arthur. He does not have a pot to pee in. But maybe I can pay off a back tax bill. We have to get a nearby cabin for you and one for Hannah and me, which will take some of the grubstake."

"Did you just propose?" Hannah asked.

"Well, kinda. I'll do a better job when I have something worthwhile to offer you. But, if you are willing, we should consider it part of our plan."

"Nobody ever accused you of being romantic, did they," she asked.

"I guess not. But, I'll work on it if you want."

She leaned up and kissed him.

"You do it, Israel Pope. I'll be watching and waiting."

They headed towards the early pioneer town named for its founder.

******

When they arrived they found the old fort still standing. The village itself had a store selling general merchandise, there was a blacksmith, an eating establishment and an assortment of cabins and a few houses. It was obviously on a downhill slide.

It did not take too long to locate the Pope wagon and its single ox grazing nearby.

Israel, with Hannah holding his hand and Arthur by his side, hailed the modest camp. It was a fire pit and canvas shelter over the wagon.

Maude ran out and screamed "Israel's here!" The first thing she really saw though was a girl of her own age holding her brother's hand. She squinted her big green eyes and began an immediate appraisal.

"Maude, this is Hannah Winder. And, Arthur Calloway. Hannah is my intended. Arthur was a fellow boatman with Zeke Boone."

His folks came out in time to hear the introductions. His mother hugged Hannah first and Israel second. His father shook with his son and Arthur.

"How was your river trip and your trip over here, son?" he asked.

"The river trip was an experience. The one here was a grueling walk. I'm thinking it illustrates why God made horses and mules, Pa."

"Arthur, where are you from?"

"Port Republic, sir."

"And, Miss Hannah, how about you?"

"Petersburg, sir. Down south of Richmond."

"Well, welcome to our camp, such as it is."

"Ma, we have some grub to contribute. Loaves of bread, bacon, coffee, and corn meal we never had a chance to use on the trail."

"Those things will be real welcome, son. It's been sparse eating on the trail over here from Linville Creek," Adeline Pope said.

"Hannah, why don't you help Maude and me with cooking up some dinner. We can get to know you and Arthur better after we eat," she said.

Israel noticed all three family members had lost weight since leaving home. He recognized he, Hannah, Arthur had lost weight, too. Just not as much.

"Ma, you want Arthur and me to gather some more wood for your fire?" Israel said.

"You might have to walk a bit to get it, but it would be a big help."

Arthur had already taken the axe off Amos and the two young men walked off.

"Israel, I see what you mean. Your father's camp is a lean one, food and firewood especially. He needs our help."

"He does, Arthur. He's not a bad man and means well. Just a bad provider. He's not lazy, he just does not plan much. He would have been better off staying in Linville Creek. This town is dying. It's sure no improvement over where he was."

"Think about the idea of tax property. If it was anywhere, it sure ought to be here," Arthur said.

"You are right. We can bring it up after dinner. Maybe even during, though I suspect Hannah—the new Pope—might be the center of their curiosity."

"Haha. She certainly dropped right out of the sky as far as they were concerned."

"A wife was not part of my plan either, Arthur."

"She was part of God's plan. I reckon he smiled on you when he made it. She's smart and sassy. She will make you a fine wife."

Adeline Pope had been simmering a large pot of beans all day. Their meal was going to be pretty plain, nothing but beans and water. The addition of the bacon and some more salt and pepper made a big flavor difference. Bread to dip would help, too.

Israel made the coffee and contributed three more mugs.

He could tell his family was virtually famished by the way they attacked dinner.

Towards the end, Maude spoke up.

"Hannah, how did you and Israel meet?"

Israel, knowing how pious his parents both were, had known this question would come up and dreaded it.

"I came to Front Royal with my parents and uncle. My parents died. My uncle kind of indentured me to a man with a business. There were no papers of indenture, just gold coin. As soon as he indentured me, he took off for parts unknown.

The first night, a man tried to get too friendly with me. Israel came out of nowhere and beat the man senseless. He was a hero!

When he found I had no money or prospects, he knew he could not leave me alone, so he and his friend Arthur took me along with them to watch out for me."

"And, you became betrothed?" Maude asked.

"We did, sister. Our feelings for each other were strong from the first meeting," Israel answered for her. Hannah smiled and nodded.

"When are you going to marry?" Adeline asked.

"As soon as we have a cabin to live in and everyone here, including Arthur, is settled," Israel said.

"I just don't know how we are going to find a place to live here. The free land is all gone."

"Mr. Pope, I shared an idea for all of us with Israel," Arthur began. Israel nodded for him to continue.

"It looks like things are going downhill here. People leaving for somewhere else. We might be able to get land people abandoned. Maybe land with cabins on it already, just for paying the back taxes."

"But, it takes money to get abandoned land," Jacob Pope said.

"True. And, we might not have enough from our river profits. We each bought a few things and Israel got Amos," Arthur said. "But, we sure need to inquire and see what the lay of the land is before giving up on Boonesboro."

"There's a property office somewhere. We can ask tomorrow at the store to see where it is," Jacob said.

"Hannah, Arthur and I talked a lot on the way here. Arthur wants to farm. It would be perfect if we could all be close. If your and his land butted up against each other, he could expand his farm and pay you in crops for the use of your land. You and Ma would always have food. Or, food to barter.

I still want to trap for a while and build up some money. If we were close, it would make it safer for Hannah, too," Israel said. "Like Arthur said, though, this plan may not work if the tax bills are more than we can afford."

After dinner was cleaned off, Hannah motioned Maude aside.

"Why don't you bring your blanket and camp with me? Israel got me a tarp and showed me how to make a nice shelter. We should get to know one another, since we are going to be sisters."

"I'll tell my folks and get my blanket."

When she left, Hannah shared her plan with Israel.

"Your folks would be scandalized with me sleeping in the same shelter as you and Arthur. I will set up a shelter for me and let them assume whatever they want about how we camped on the way here," she said.

"I will miss having you beside me," he said in a voice only she could hear.

"Soon, my husband-to-be. Soon."

Maude walked out with her blanket and watched as her brother and Hannah efficiently and quickly erected a shelter. As it was early autumn, they put it adjacent to the fire pit.

Israel built a small reflector out of logs so the heat would gravitate towards the shelter.

"Good night, dear sister. I've missed you," Israel said. He hugged her, then Hannah. He gave Hannah a kiss in the dark. His sister saw, but his parents did not.

Arthur had already put up their lean-to and was snoring by the time Israel crawled in.

Tomorrow with the tax office would be a big day for the Popes and Arthur. Both young men and an older one went to sleep with their fingers crossed.

******

The three men went to the store the next morning. It had been a small trading post in the frontier days. Now, it was struggling to get by.

The owner said the property office was up by Lexington. They set out for what was the largest city in Kentucky at the time at around seven thousand people. It had been hit hard by cholera earlier in the year and lost five hundred people to the epidemic.

They found the property tax man.

"Boonesboro is failing. Folks have made good on their land claims, then walked away," he explained.

"We are looking for three pieces close, maybe even adjacent. My friend here wants to farm a bit. Pa needs to just establish a base. I need a safe place near them to leave my wife while I am trapping out West," Israel said.

"Hmmm…. the man said, "There's a place with a large cabin on it about a half mile north of the trading post. It seems, from the plat, to sit off the road. I'm betting you passed by it and didn't notice it."

"How many acres," Jacob asked.

"Appears to be twenty wooded and thirty open."

"Anything similar nearby?" Arthur asked.

"There's one butting up against it. Has a small cabin in the wooded part. It's open land butts up against the fields of the first property."

He told them what amount would pay off the taxes on both.

"Can you hold on to both while we return and give them a look-see?" Israel asked.

"Ha! They have been sitting like they are for nigh on to two years. I doubt there are other takers. It's not a risk to the county to hold them for you."

The three attempted to burn the plats into their memories as they did not have any paper. It was a precious commodity on the frontier. Lexington was a flourishing city, but they wanted to get out of the place as soon as possible in case some of the cholera cases were lingering.

"We'll be back as soon as we look at them and talk it over. Thank you for your help," Arthur said. They left and hurriedly began the trip back to Boonesboro.

As they found the trip was a good eight hours on foot, they stopped on the way out of town and bought some bread.

They stopped at a wooded area around dark. Israel used the twelve inch blade of his Bowie knife to cut some inch and a half diameter saplings for the frame of a shelter. His father gathered evergreen boughs and Arthur gathered loose wood for a fire.

They interlaced the boughs on the top of the shelter frame. The fire was built in front of the open shelter. It was going to be cool tonight and they had not thought to bring blankets. Only Israel brought a gun, something he was getting used to doing. It was a habit which could be the difference between life and death where he reckoned he would trap out West. Between hostile Indian tribes, bears, wolves, mountain lions and fur thieves, life was cheap.

They sat in the shelter, warmed by the fire, and ate the bread for dinner. Breakfast would be nonexistent.

"I sure hope these properties work out," Arthur said.

"What are you going to do, son?" Jacob asked.

"I figure I will pay the taxes for the bigger place based on the amounts he told us. I think there may be some negotiating room. They have sat for a while.

You, Ma, and Maude take the cabin. Hannah and I, with Arthur's good help, will build our own a piece off from yours."

"So, I won't own the property?" his father asked.

Israel held his temper. He was not sure whether his father was selfish or just plain stupid.

"Pa, I don't reckon you have the gold to buy it. Do you?"

"Well, no."

"Based on the earnings on the boat trip, Arthur and I can buy the properties. You can live on it and take vegetables as farmland rent from him, just like it's yours. But, the title will go in the name of the person who forked over the coins. Any way you look at it, you have a free home for life."

"You know, Mr. Pope, I have thought of something else," Arthur began.

"Boonesboro is still the first stop for folks coming through the Gap. You could probably sell your ox to one of them. Get a horse or mule to ride.

I am going to get a mule like Israel did. I can plow with him and ride him. We could also sell vegetables once I grow some. I'm sure pilgrims heading to Oregon or wherever would love to have some fresh food. I noticed a seed store and a farm store with equipment up in Lexington. If I have any money left, I am coming here to shop around. I might even look for a job to make some money to get started on. The tax purchase will take most of the upriver money."

"You boys are big planners," Jacob said.

"And, you never planned a thing in your damn life, Pa, which is why you failed at everything," Israel thought, but held his tongue.

They stoked the fire and went to sleep. One was planning his future, one was confused, and the other angry at an able bodied man who could not decide whether to pee or walk away from the tree.

******

The whole family, since Hannah and Arthur had quickly been accepted, explored the two properties the next morning. They were walking distance from the village, but remote feeling once at them.

"You know what surprises me? The trees around the main cabin. Most pioneers in the Boone days cut down anything which a brave with a bow or fusil musket could hide behind and ambush them," Israel noted. Arthur agreed.

"For our part, now Indian attacks are a thing of the past, the privacy the trees give is a positive," Arthur said as he squinted through the trees.

"What do you see over there?" Israel asked as he

pulled the long rifle up to a ready position.

"Let's walk over there. I think I'm going to like what I see. A lot," the big man said.

The whole group walked through the woods to a fast moving stream. It was too small to canoe but looked like a trout stream to Arthur Calloway. He beamed at it, and his friend smiled at his obvious excitement.

"I think we may have some fish meals to supplement venison, Israel."

They walked back to the cabin.

The cabin door was unlatched. The cabin was musty, but it appeared no animals had made a home in it during its period of abandonment. It had a large fireplace, its iron cooking swing arm to hold cooking and coffee pots was still intact. Even the rudimentary furniture was still in it. It had a table and four chairs. There were pegs on the wall to hang clothes. The bedrooms each had rope beds, but without the usual cornhusk mattresses. A little airing out, some cornhusks or spruce boughs stuffed into canvas mattresses and it would be habitable.

There was what had been a small garden outside and a split rail corral and open shed for a horse or other animal. There was a small supply of firewood, now well-seasoned. A privy stood out back. Jacob checked it. No snakes were visible, so Adeline was appeased.

They walked towards the open field. They could see

a small cabin. The property line ended somewhere in the middle according to the plat, but it was not visible.

The cabin for Arthur was newer and a bit fresher inside. It had one big room. The stone fireplace was in the middle of the rear wall and also had the iron swing arm still attached.

Arthur would have to make or buy furniture. Its previous occupants had taken their furniture when they moved out.

Arthur nodded his pleasure. He could turn this cabin into a home quite readily.

Israel walked back to the woods near the home his family would occupy. Hannah, no longer concerned about appearances, held his hand as they walked.

"What if we put a cabin here," he pointed. "It can sit in the trees, yet still look over both my folk's and Arthur's cabins. Such an arrangement where all three families were able to see one another from a small distance may be a good safety measure."

Hannah indicated her agreement by asking "Got your axe? You could start felling trees for our love nest right now!" He just grinned at her.

"I have to go back to Lexington and pay the taxes on it in the morning. Think about what we need and you can ride the mule and bring back what few things we will have enough money left to buy."

He looked at the delight on her face. "This married thing is going to be alright," he said to her.

Arthur, Maude, Hannah and Israel headed to Lexington the next morning. They took the ox-drawn farm wagon. Arthur drove it and Maude sat next to him so closely they were touching. She seemed to have laid claim to the big man.

Hannah rode Amos and Israel walked in front.

They paid the back taxes on the two properties, leaving both men with less than ten dollars. With Jacob's concurrence, Arthur traded the ox even for a mule. He was a bit older and larger than Amos but promised great strength.

Quietly, while the women were looking for cloth and sewing gear, both men bought rings. Israel looked questioningly at his friend, who shrugged and said "Just in case."

The wagon was half-loaded. It carried seeds for the spring planting, a few implements like an ax and shovel for Arthur and an adze for Israel to finish logs for the cabin. Arthur also bought five chickens.

"Some eggs would be good," he explained, chancing his last few dollars on something foxes would love.

Their final purchases were long-life foods such as sides of bacon, cheese as well as flour, cornmeal, salt and honey.

It was after dark before they made it back to their camps in Boonesboro.

"This will be the last night camping out for everybody but me, as long as you let Hannah sleep with you,

Maude," Israel said. His sister laughed and told him she knew exactly who her new friend would rather sleep with. No response was necessary.

"This is getting me ready for the real wilderness," Israel thought to himself after walking eighteen hours. He did not feel tired and credited part of it to his moccasins instead of wearing the typical boot. There was no such thing as a left or right shoe or boot. His moccasins molded to each foot.

He turned in and stared at the sky outside the shelter. Arthur was in his own cabin. Hannah was with Maude in the second bedroom of the cabin he bought for his parents.

All was not well in his world yet. But, it was getting there.

While the women made brooms, the men took axes and the two mules and chose trees for the new cabin. Once slashed with the axe to mark them, they began to clear a space on the edge of the woods for the cabin site.

Arthur once again proved his worth, having worked as a housebuilder in Port Republic as one of his many jobs.

"I think we have enough marked trees to start felling them tomorrow. If you want to fell them and have your father haul them to me with the mules and a log chain, I will clean them up with the adze. I did a lot of adze work at the mill and got pretty fast at it," Arthur offered.

In the work which followed, Israel was glad to find his father could be a hard worker. He just needed a project and supervision to keep him on track.

"Sure better than just being lazy," he thought to himself.

"Arthur, how much do you know about standing up a chimney? Our cabin in Linville Lake had no drafting of the fireplace at all. We had to open the windows and door in the middle of winter to let smoke out," Israel said.

"I know enough to know what I don't know, Israel. Building a chimney which will draft right is like an art. It takes a craftsman. Maybe the great source of knowledge who owns the store knows of somebody. We could mess it up so badly a chimney builder would have to knock it down and start over. There are lots of stones in the stream, but will they explode when heat hits them? We need advice on this, Israel," Arthur said.

The three took a break and walked over to the store.

"We bought the old Gulden and Cole places for the back taxes. Two cabins are built and fine. We still need one. We are alright on the building of everything except the chimney. Do you know anyone who can help with the chimney, Mr. Pollack?" Israel asked.

"There's a chimney builder up about halfway to Lexington. His name is Gideon Cross. Go see him.

Business is real spare now, so he'll cut you a deal."

They thanked the man and decided they needed to see Cross before putting the walls up.

While Arthur worked the adze and Jacob went back to his cabin, Israel saddled Amos and rode according to the directions they were given.

It took him almost five hours, but he found the man.

"The crick stones are alright," he said, pronouncing creek the local way. "For a small cabin like you are describing gather at least five hundred. You can use any leftovers for other stuff. Is there clay in the creek?" he asked.

"Yessir. There is."

"Good. We can use it to build the chimney and you can use it to chink between the logs of the house. Given man's tools and sweat, we can get by with what God provided."

"What would you charge to come down and build it with us having the stones ready and standing by to help?"

"Do you have real money? Not swap items?"

"A little bit left. Not much," Israel replied.

"How about four dollars in coin?"

"I could do it. Want to come down in two days so we can have the stones gathered and moved to the cabin site?"

"Wednesday, I think. Alright. Hold off on building

the cabin until I get there and see the best wall for the chimney."

Israel rode home, knowing his leather money pouch just got smaller by half.

He and Arthur spent two days collecting stones and moving them to the cabin site. Despite not eating properly, Hannah noticed he added visible muscle to his long, lean frame.

"You are looking right good, Mr. Pope. We need to hurry up and finish the cabin so we can get busy inside it."

"No argument there, Hannah. I'm thinking maybe you and Maude can help gather the clay from the creek and bring it up while we lay stones and chink them?"

"I believe our services can be arranged, dear. What do you think of your sister and Arthur? Seems like some sparks flying there."

"I get the same feeling. She's getting a better deal than you. She's getting a solid man who will stay with her day and night in one place. He will work hard and provide for her. Me? I'll wander some. You sure you can deal with me not always being around?"

"It is not my first choice, Israel. But, you are the one who saved me and looked after me. You are the one I love. So, I reckon it's settled. When do you plan to head to the trapping country?"

"Maybe spring. About five or six months. I'm

not sure. I don't have any way to earn a living for you here. I sure am not a farmer. Or, a craftsman or shopkeeper."

"Unfortunately, the things I love the most about you are the things which will keep you on some distant trail. The things which will keep you in harm's way," she said quietly.

Cross arrived mid-day with a mule-pulled small wagon. The wagon had camping gear and an assortment of iron buckets and tools.

He and Arthur laid out the perimeter lines of the cabin and spotted where the chimney, door and windows would be. Cross also suggested a design which would allow expansion in the future.

Hannah and Maude appeared with the first loads of clay from the stream. They were barefooted, with their skirts bunched scandalously above their ankles. Their hands, arms, feet, and legs as far as could be seen, were covered with gray clay.

From the spots on their aprons and blouses, it appeared a clay ball fight had occurred. The mystery of all the screaming and giggling heard by the stream was solved.

Gideon Cross turned out to be an affable and valuable old gent, who could still keep up with the young ones working. He had Israel or Arthur's next purchase. It was a big hand saw. They used it for door, window and fireplace openings.

When they stopped for the day, the logs and chimney up to the window line were laid and chinked.

Adeline made a group dinner with cornpone, potatoes brought from Lexington and fresh fish.

Arthur caught the fish in the stream prior to Hannah and Maude's escapades scaring the stream's trout all the way to the Kentucky River.

In three days, the men built a passable cabin. Cross checked the fireplace. The chimney drew well. No smoky interior.

"You'll need to make cedar shakes to cover the roof when you can make them and afford a hammer and nails. But, for now, the small diameter log roof with chinking, or daubing, as it is sometimes called, will work fine.

You should put some moss up there periodically. Your idea of using your waterproof sailcloth tarps as a liner was a good one and it will help keep you dry," Cross said.

He left the next morning, a sack with some food for the trip and four dollars in gold in his tool box.

They had a much better shelter than the open-faced ones. However, the cabin did not have a door fitted to the door opening. It also did not have window coverings.

"Greased paper would be good since we cannot begin to afford glass," Israel opined to the family. In the meantime, we will have to tack up some thin doeskin.

Since we need deerskin, buck or doe, and meat, I will go hunting early in the morning and see what I can kill."

He slept alone again tonight, this time with a roof over his head. Once he had a door and window coverings, he and Hannah could get married and live together. She was willing to move in immediately. Israel knew such a move would scandalize his mother and cause his father to break the truce forced upon them for the past week.

Israel took the long rifle out the next morning. He found some deer tracks and followed them silently in his moccasins. After an hour, he saw something in the woods ahead. It was a small buck.

The buck was moving between trees. It would be a tough shot with the branches interfering with the ball's passage to the animal.

The deer stepped through a clear spot for a moment and Israel fired. The flint hit the frizzen and sparked. The fire went through the touchhole and ignited the powder in the barrel. With a "boom," the rifle sent its round ball fifty-five yards and the deer jumped.

Israel knew from the way he jumped, the deer was hard hit.

He slowly reloaded his rifle and primed the pan with finer powder.

"If I go running through the woods after the deer

like a wild man, he will force himself to run and suffer. If I wait here and bide my time, I can likely find him dead close to where I shot him," Israel thought to himself. His thoughts proved correct. After a five minute wait, he found the buck dead within fifty feet of where he shot him.

Israel hung the deer from a branch with his rope. He knew a length of rope was a primary survival tool for a long hunter or a mountain man. He bled and gutted the animal.

One thing his father was good at was butchering. Israel slung the buck over his shoulder and began the hike home.

"Life has its turns. I never thought I'd build a cabin for a wife. A cabin in an area far from where I want to be. But, these are the cards I have been dealt. I have to play them.

I just have to figure out what I will do for a living. Can I leave a barely sixteen year old wife with my family and Arthur to look after her? Otherwise, how can I go trapping and make some money? I don't have anything to barter, so there is no other option," he thought as he carried the deer and the rifle to his parent's cabin.

"Meat for dinner!" he yelled out. There was no need to apportion the meat three ways. For now, communal meals were the norm.

"Here's the skin, like you asked, son," Jacob Pope

said as he began to cut the venison.

"I will walk over to the store and see who knows something about tanning to cover the windows," he said as he rolled up the skin and walked away.

An old frontiersman at the store shared a rudimentary tanning method with Israel. He immediately set out to tan the buckskin. After the tanning process was started, Israel cleaned his father's rifle barrel with lye soap and hot water, then oiled it. It was necessary each time the black powder was touched off, due to its highly corrosive nature.

Hannah sat and watched him.

"I reckon I will get a Northwest Trade musket when I get to St. Louis. I want one twenty-bore or sixty-two caliber. It will sling a big ball fast enough to kill a bear, but also allow me to use bird shot to kill small game for food."

"How is it different from the one you used today?" Hannah asked.

"It's got a larger bore. The barrel is smooth inside. It doesn't get dirty as fast as a rifle and therefore can load faster. But, not having rifling to true the ball, it is not as accurate and the effective range is reduced significantly."

"Do they look different? You rifle is kind of graceful," she said.

"Some of the Bedford County and other long rifles out of Pennsylvania are works of art. Mine is plain.

It's a poor boy's rifle.

A trade musket is generally fatter and shorter. It may stand up to abuse better. I want to get the old tried and true flintlock. In the wilderness, the new-fangled percussion caps are likely hard to find when you need them."

"Will you trade off this rifle on it?" she asked.

"No, I will leave it or Pa's fowling piece with you for your protection."

"I hardly know how to shoot it, and I only loaded it once or twice while we were walking to the Cumberland Gap."

"Honey, well before I go trapping, I'll have you shooting as well as Daniel Boone!"

"Not hard, Israel. Daniel Boone died when I was a young child. I heard my folks talking about it."

"How about 'I'll have you shooting as well as Daniel Boone could when he was alive?'" he asked.

"Any time you are ready, so am I," she responded.

The women made stew with potatoes, carrots, onions and the remainder of beef purchased in Lexington. The venison needed to age for a while yet to reach its peak flavor.

They ate the stew for lunch with cornpone and cider, again from the Lexington shopping.

Not having a plow, Arthur began preparing land for next spring's planting. It would be cold soon and the ground would harden. The cold ground would make working the soil with a shovel or hoe too difficult.

Hannah watched as Israel dragged a log to their cabin. It was not one he had cut, but a seasoned fallen tree. He removed the branches and used the axe to take the bark off.

"Would you hand me the iron wedge over there, Hannah?" he asked.

He used it and the axe to split the log into boards and the saw to cut them into lengths fitting the door opening on the cabin.

Israel laid the boards flat, then connected them at top and bottom with shorter boards. He used some iron nails Cross had left for him.

He put one more board across the center and affixed a crudely carved handle to it.

Israel used four of his nails to attach heavy leather from his worn out boots to serve as hinges.

"Hannah, darling, would you hold the door in place while I attach it?"

As she held it tightly inside the opening, he nailed the loose end of the leather hinges to the door frame.

He opened the door, took her in his arms and walked over the threshold.

"Finally. Can we do it now?" she whispered.

"Soon. Window coverings would help. But, very soon, dear Hannah. I promise."

They checked the fresh buckskin. It was ready

enough. They walked to the stream, whose fast flow had cleared it from the clay gathering.

"What's the water for? Are we gonna bathe?" Hannah asked.

"Not right now. We are going to soak the skin and stretch it across the window. I want you to help me hold it while I nail it.

The skin will dry tight across the openings. Once it's been there a couple of days, we can pry out the lower corner nails. We'll put a rawhide loop in the holes and a peg in each corner to secure the window cover down. Once I put in the loop and peg, we can roll the skin up for light and fresh air. We can lash it up with a piece of rawhide and roll it down for warmth and the very frequent privacy we are gonna need."

"Let's put the windows up now. No need wasting time," she said with enthusiasm.

"Help me cut the skin to fit both windows. Since we measured by guessing, they are probably going to be different," Israel said.

After measuring by holding the pieces of skin up and marking them with the end of a burnt stick, he cut them to fit with his Bowie knife.

"Alright, I have this one up straight, go ahead and tack it on," she said. Within minutes, they had temporarily non-opening windows. In a week, they would put the loops through the bottom two nail holes. The pegs to hook the loop around would follow. They would have two windows which would roll up, something they were unlikely to use until late spring in Kentucky.

The next morning at breakfast, Israel and Arthur talked about how they could make enough money or barter items to take them through the winter.

"I am going to plant my winter wheat now. I talked with the man who owns the mill on the stream downstream from us. He said he would charge a toll for any corn or wheat I brought in. His portion of the sale would be an eighth for corn and a sixth for wheat. He would then sell it and pay me my share. Seems pretty fair to me," Arthur said.

"Any idea about late fall and through the winter?" Israel asked.

"Not really. I will try to hire out, but it doesn't seem like much is going on. I may be able to ride the mule up to Lexington to find work and just camp outside of town. One idea would be to see if Mr. Cross wants a hand. He is getting pretty old for hard work like he does. I could learn a craft from him. Every house or cabin needs a fireplace and chimney."

"I talked to the man at the store. He said there is a real need for meat around here. It appears the long hunters are long gone," Israel said, tongue-in-cheek.

"He said he'd pay me for any deer or even rabbits and squirrels I brought in already butchered. I reckon I could hunt and haul the meat back on Amos. Pa could butcher it and we'd split the money. Pa, how does it sound to you?" Israel asked.

"Seems pretty good. I don't have any other ideas. I wonder if I could help at the store?" Jacob responded.

"Sure worth checking, Pa. We don't really know how cold it gets here yet. And, for how long," Israel said.

"What could we do?" Hannah asked.

"I wonder if there's any call for sewing around here? There are probably a lot of single men who need stuff darned. Maybe even washed," Adeline asked.

"See if Mr. Pollack at the store will let you put up a sign," Arthur suggested.

"All we need is some paper and ink for a sign. I'll look for a turkey for dinner and some quills to write with," Israel said. "I will buy the paper and a small bottle of ink and bring it home. Pa, you have a readable hand. Why don't you let Ma tell you what it should say, then write up a sign? Then, y'all can go to the store tomorrow and talk about helping part time and putting up the sign."

"I feel like I haven't made any contribution," Maude said.

"Honey, you can sew better than I can. We'll do it together. You, Hannah and me," her mother said.

"Looks like we have a plan. Or, plans. Arthur, are you riding up to see Mr. Cross, then maybe on to Lexington tomorrow?" Israel asked. The big man grinned at him and nodded.

"Good! Then, I'll hit the trail for game meat to sell when you leave. Hannah, do you want to walk with me over to the store to buy the paper and ink?"

They walked, as always, hand-in-hand.

Israel bought three sheets of writing paper and a small bottle of ink. He picked up a quill pen for a cent. He saw Hannah eyeing the liquorish and bought a string for everyone.

"Honey, I will promise you to be a good provider. I don't like being this poor. We are not alone in our financial situation here. We are probably better off than many.

I am putting a lot of faith in the fur trapping to make money. The risks are having a season's furs stolen, getting an arrow somewhere it hurts, or being breakfast for a big grizzly. I don't aim to have to deal with any of those things. I plan to work hard and be careful."

CHAPTER 2

Israel became the primary hunter for the village. Some men hunted on their own, others did not for a variety of reasons. Age, inability, or another occupation were at the top of the list.

Since he was spending the most time and money for powder and balls, he gave his father one third of the profits for his butchering. It was probably generous in view of the disproportionate contributions he made to the effort.

He used the first profits to get another oiled canvas tarp for a shelter as well as a tomahawk. Israel did not need a large axe on the trail.

Some folks did not have money for the meat and he took foods properly put up for the winter in barter. As a result, the Popes and Arthur had a healthy diet during the winter. Everyone was always a bit hungry, but it was the way of the frontier.

Arthur planted winter wheat. The field was small because he had to turn the soil with nothing but a shovel. A plow would come later.

After planting, he spent a fair amount of time away. His idea of working with the chimney builder was quickly accepted. He was pleasantly surprised at the amount of work during the winter. It was almost all repair work instead of building. Nonetheless, Arthur added a craft to his growing list of talents. It was apparent to all Maude missed him on his nights and days away. A double wedding was becoming a generally accepted fact.

The sewing and washing business was sporadic, but as Hannah analogized, "it chinks the cracks in our financial logs."

Israel and Arthur both made sufficient money by February to proceed to the next steps of their plans.

Arthur proposed to Maude, who said "Well, it took you long enough, big boy! Of course I'll marry you. Hannah is warm at night, but you have to generate more heat."

"My heat is the only reason?" he asked.

"Oh, no. Just one of hundreds of reasons you'd be my ideal husband. Can you imagine how beautiful our children would be?"

"Even if they looked like me?"

"Walk down to the stream and look into a pool there. Study the reflection. If you are honest with yourself, you will see a very handsome man staring back at you. He's the man I see every time I look at you, Arthur."

Nobody had ever told him he was handsome before. He was at a loss for words. He took Maude and hugged her for a long time.

"And, the answer is yes!" she said.

There was one church in town. Jacob and the women went to it most Sundays. The two young men were too busy trying to earn enough to get by. No day was their day of rest.

They arranged for a double wedding following the Sunday service. It was done without much ado.

The meal after was excellent and, for once, there was enough food for everyone to eat as much as desired.

"Israel, I have waited so long to be able to lay here in your arms like this," Hannah said.

"Me, too, honey. Are you okay after….well, you know?"

"I am more than okay. I will spend every day waiting for night with you. By the way, I have a surprise for you!"

"What?" he asked.

"You married me on my birthday."

"I did not know. But, happy birthday, Hannah. I will remember it next year, now I know when it is."

"I didn't mention it. I was fearful it would get in the way of this. Wedding first and birthday a distant second," she said.

"After wedding night?" he grinned.

"Way after." She snuggled up closer and kissed him. It appeared they were not going to sleep much on their wedding night.

******

Things went much the same at the Calloway cabin across the field.

Arthur got up at dawn and had coffee, bacon and fry bread. He was going to check his winter wheat seedlings today and meet Gideon Cross fifteen miles north for a chimney repair job tomorrow.

As he was saddling his mule, he saw Israel several hundred yards away riding Amos across to the woods. He whistled and Israel saw him and waved. Seconds later, he melted into the trees.

There was a light layer of snow on the ground. Much of the snow last night had been caught on the branches roofing the ground with green and now white.

"Let's find some deer tracks, Amos," he said to the mule.

They walked almost soundlessly though the woods for an hour. It was strangely quiet. The country he was in was increasingly hilly.

Amos let out a loud bray. Israel heard something

big crashing the brush between the trees on his right. He swung the Bedford county long rifle over Amos' head to point it towards the oncoming noise.

He was too late. A six-hundred pound black bear charged into him and Amos, toppling the mule.

Amos got up while Israel was still stunned. The black bear came at him and received a two rear leg kick for his trouble. The bear paused in pain and surprise, giving the mule time to run off between the trees.

Israel was shaking his head and looking for the rifle he dropped.

He found it in time to shove the muzzle into the male bear's chest.

The full weight of the bear pressed against the muzzle as Israel poked him hard.

Still lying flat, he fired point blank at the bears massive chest. The bear moved back and shook.

The rifle was now no more than a slender stick, so Israel drew the twelve inch blade Bowie for the next attack.

The attack was less than a second later. The bear growled and attacked in a blur of speed.

Israel, on his back, partially blocked a sweep of the bear's claws as they swung. He knew killing a bear this size was improbable, but he was determined to go down fighting.

His coat and shirt had been ripped open by the

bear's first try. He felt a raging burn across his chest and knew he was bleeding badly.

Israel managed to get up on one knee. The bear came in to grasp him and use his teeth to end the fight.

Israel held the Bowie up in two hands as the bear came down on him. The bear's own weight pushed the blade into his heart deeper than any stab Israel could have made.

The bear made an odd, almost screaming sound and rolled back.

Israel rolled over. He could not get up but knew this was the last chance he would ever have to live beyond this day.

He jammed the big Bowie into the bear's throat so deeply he could not remove it in his weakened state. This would be his end, he knew.

Israel did not know about things like spinal cords. But, he severed one and an artery. The bear was making gurgling sounds and appeared to be unable to fight further.

"I'm so sorry Hannah," was the last thought as Israel lost consciousness.

He woke up an hour later.

He was shocked to still be alive. Israel looked at the bear. It was dead.

Nobody knew where he was. He did not see Amos, nor blame him for leaving.

The wound had bled a lot. So much he was weak

and dizzy. It was still bleeding some. He knew he had only won the first fight to live. The second one was stopping the bleeding and the third was getting back to civilization. The fourth one would be staving off infection.

Fighting massive pain, Israel shook the tattered coat off. He removed what was left of his shirt and folded it as well as he could. He tied the shirt around the eight inch gash.

He could not tie it in back, so he did the best he could with a knot almost under his arm. Struggling to put the coat back on, he called and whistled for Amos.

Presently, the mule appeared. He approached with hesitation.

"Amos, you are the most beautiful creature I ever saw," he mumbled.

He crawled over to the bear and tried to withdraw the live-saving Bowie. It was still lodged firmly. He knew, if he could even get on Amos, he would have to hang on with both hands. Bringing the rifle was a not an option.

It took him fifteen very painful minutes to get on the mule's back. He screamed so loudly with pain once, the mule moved away.

Israel enticed Amos back and on his tenth try made it up on his back. The activity had restarted the bleeding from his chest. He was unaware of bleeding on his biceps and his back from when the bear hugged him.

"Home, my friend. You are on your own," he mumbled to Amos. The mule could probably not hear the request. Israel was not sure whether he said it aloud or in his mind.

Instinctively, the mule began to walk. His pace was similar to the walk through the woods while Israel was cutting sign.

They made it to the village first. The bloody man unconscious on the mule, his face laying in the mule's mane drew immediate attention.

Israel was lifted off the mule, who having done his job, walked off in the direction of home.

"Send somebody over to the Pope's. Tell them Israel has been ripped up bad by a bear or panther. They are going to need a wagon."

The mule, his saddle and hair covered with blood, made it to the cabins minutes before the messenger.

Hannah took one look and screamed as if her heart was cut out of her body.

Maude and her mother were with her. Arthur came running across the field as Jacob came out of the cabin and the messenger arrived.

"Israel has been attacked by a bear or panther. We don't know which, but it's bad. Real bad. You better bring a wagon to get him back here. We don't have no doctor, so you will have to do whatever needs to be done."

Arthur heard the last and nodded to Jacob to

harness the wagon with the remaining mule. Amos looked like he was on his last legs.

Jacob drove the wagon. Adeline had gathered all the linen she could to make an initial dressing. The two young wives rode in the bed of the wagon. Arthur sprinted ahead.

When the family arrived, Israel was stretched out on the store boardwalk. An old lady who acted as a midwife was cutting the bloody shirt off.

"I'm hoping his self-done bandaging saved him. But, from his color and the blood everywhere, I'd say he lost a lot. Maybe too much. Won't know for a few days. He'll need liquid poured into him like there's no tomorrow. And, dressings changed and wound examined several times a day. I'll come by every day, if you want," the woman, Sadie Peters, said.

Hannah hugged her and said, "please," through her tears.

"Can we move him?" Arthur asked.

"I don't think you can hurt him any more than he already is," Sadie said.

Arthur gently picked up his friend, now brother-in-law, in his arms and set him in the bed of the wagon.

"Let's take him to Maude's old room. More space for coming and going," his father said. Israel's mother looked on, horrified at her son and his dim prospects.

"Take the linen and boil it several minutes in water,

then when it's cool enough, wash the wound and put clean, dry linen on it. I got me plenty of linen from midwifery, so I'll bring you some extra tomorrow."

Israel came to for a few seconds in the wagon.

"Arthur, the bear and my weapons are in the woods an hour's straight ride from my cabin," he said and passed out again.

"One of the fellas in the crowd is an old tracker. I'll get him to ride back with me today and get the bear, rifle, and Bowie knife. We have plenty of daylight at least for the trip out. May have to come back in the dark. I'll ride back and look him up as soon as I carry Israel in and put him in the bed," Arthur told the family.

It took them mere minutes to reach the cabins. The women rushed in and while the girls changed the linens on Maude's bed, Adeline began to boil water with sufficient linen in it to clean Israel's wounds.

Arthur came through the door with Israel in his arms and placed his friend on the bed.

"I have to saddle up and get the old tracker. We need to move fast."

It took the two men until dusk to find the site by reverse tracking Israel, using both tracks and blood spots.

"Sweet mother of God!" the old tracker said. "The boy killed the biggest bear I ever saw with one shot and a big knife! I never seen the likes."

It took Arthur's tremendous strength to pull the knife out. The two used it and the tracker's knife to skin and dress out the bear.

"This here is a lot of bear meat, Arthur. We need to build an Indian travois to get it back tonight."

He left Arthur and returned with two long saplings he had cut with his tomahawk. He also had an armful of cross pieces. They made a tall, slender fifteen foot triangle. The top was "mule-wide" open as the tracker called it. They used the bear's own hide to cover it and piled the meat and rifle on. Arthur carried the Bowie. "What a killing machine this blade must be!" he thought.

With such an experienced guide, they made it back to Boonesboro just after dark.

After checking on Israel, Arthur got the senior Pope outside and pressed him to bleed, gut and hang the valuable meat so it could be butchered for market. A bear approaching six hundred pounds could provide much needed income for several months. The skin, properly tanned would be an asset to have or to sell.

With Jacob busy, Arthur went inside to observe. The midwife had immediately followed them home.

Israel was laid out on the bed, having been checked all over for wounds. He was clad only with a sheet from waist down.

"He had wounds we didn't see at the store. See his

arms? He has some on his back. It looked like the bear got him in a hug and dug in to squeeze him," Hannah said.

"We bought the bear back. Tom, the tracker, has been killing bears for forty years. On the way back he told me this was the biggest he's ever seen in Kentucky. He calls it Kaintuck.

It took me all the strength I had to pull the Bowie knife out of the bear. I cannot imagine where Israel got the strength to stick it in so deeply. It must have been a superhuman rush of power or something.

I brought his knife and rifle back. One lesson here is the rifle is good for squirrels and rabbits with a light load. Fully loaded it will knock down a deer, maybe even a small bear. But this kind of bear and the kinds of grizzlies they have where he wants to go would take a bigger ball and a lot of powder," Arthur told the women.

"I put a poultice of spider webs on the wound to draw out impurities. Once we stop the bleeding, we will put some honey on it. It might help keep it from getting infected.

We tried to stitch up his wound with thread and a needle, but its still seeping blood. I fear the only way we are going to save this young man is to seal it shut with heat. It will be a horrible thing. But, we don't have a choice. He cannot keep bleeding. I worry he has lost almost as much blood as he can. You are a big man and we'll need every bit of muscle you have. You are going to have to hold him down, if his wife here approves. Missy," Sadie turned to the mother. "Get yourself a butcher knife and heat it up in the fire 'til it's red hot. Wrap a bunch of skins or wool around the handle while you are handling it. The heat will come right up the handle and get you if you don't."

Sadie turned to the man and two young women.

"Miss Hannah, it's your call. Have him go through the most horrible pain anyone can suffer for a few minutes and hope it works and his chest and the deep claw marks on his back get sealed up and any impurities killed off. Or, let him lay here and pray a lot as he dies."

It was a rough choice for a sixteen year old newly-wed. But, he was hers now, not his parents. She had to make it.

Through new tears, she said "Do it, Miss Sadie. And God be with Israel and all of us."

Adeline was already heating the knife. Maude went out to warn her father what was going to happen.

"Arthur, get your friend a soft stick to bite on for the pain. Please do it fast," Sadie ordered.

Jacob and Adeline chose to stay outside after she handed the red hot knife to Sadie.

What they heard was almost as awful as what they would have seen had they been there when the bear mauled Israel.

The old lady put the superheated blade flat along the gash. His skin burnt and looked like it was sealing with a horrible red glue. It took every muscle in Arthur's body to hold his friend's shoulders down on the bed. Hannah held Israel's hand and Maude his feet.

When the blade touched his chest, his back arched up and he emitted a cry which would terrify any war chief. The room was filled with the strong smell of burnt flesh.

"I'll get the windows for some fresh air," Maude said, shaking with tears running down her cheeks.

Hannah held her husband's hand throughout the procedure. While tears streamed down her cheeks, her face was resolute and determined. If she had the power to will Israel to live, they would find out now. She squeezed her eyes together and concentrated.

Her concentration was broken as she heard Israel mumble something.

She leaned close.

"Say it again, my only love."

"I didn't kill the bear for me. I killed him for you. I had to come back to you. If for just a short while," he said before passing out again.

"He sounds like his mind is fine. It's a real good sign. The next week will be telling. Keep him flushed out with as many liquids as you can pour into him. Like I said, change his dressings a couple times a day. I put enough spare linen on the table to cover until I return. Any changes, you let me know."

Sadie patted her patient on the leg, almost the only thing a gentle touch would not hurt. She went outside where the parents waited. She turned back to the door for a second and caught Arthur's eye. Sadie mouthed "damn cowards" silently. He nodded and looked her in the eye with total agreement. The bravest one here had been a sixteen year old. He would be civil with his father-in-law. It was his way. But, he would never, ever respect him. Not one damn bit.

Arthur went back in.

Sadie had said not to cover the burned area for several days, but to watch Israel all day and night long until he was fully conscious and she returned.

"We better set up a schedule with the paper, pen and ink Israel bought. It's five of us. How about shifts every…." He paused as he figured. "We could do four or four and a half hour shifts. Maybe somebody on the day shifts can add a few hours to give more sleep to the ones at night. The night shift ones have to work the next day."

Hannah nodded. Maude said "I'll tell Ma and Pa."

"Yes, honey. You tell them, I'd just as soon not," he said with a harder edge to his voice than she had ever heard. Maude and Israel had talked privately many times. She knew her husband had figured out her father was honest, but not to be trusted with anything unless supervised with a strong hand. She did not know where her and Israel's steadfastness came from. It must have been a generation back. Maybe on their mother's side. She smiled sweetly, but with resignation at her husband of several months, and walked out the door.

"Hannah, I believe he'll pull through. He's tough. Nobody less than a real tough fella could have killed a bear the size of his with a Bowie knife. His Bedford rifle was not up to killing an animal this size and this enraged. Israel did it with his knife. When word spreads, he will be famous. I bet the meat from the bear will command a premium because of the legend.

While he's healing, I will carefully clean the knife and his rifle and sharpen the knife. It's really sharp now, but a sharp knife doesn't slip and is safer. It's one of the many things Gideon Cross taught me", Arthur said.

"Arthur, he's gonna have a real scar across his chest, isn't he?" Hannah asked.

"No, Hannah, he will have a lifetime badge of courage on his chest."

Israel stirred and groaned. Hannah tried to give him some of the Sadie-mandated water, but he was not alert enough to take it. She blotted a soaked piece of linen on his lips. Hannah took the first shift and stayed by him almost six hours. Maude took the next one, lasting until daylight. Adeline came in for six hours, then Jacob for four.

Arthur went part way to Lexington and worked with Gideon Cross on a chimney repair job. He reckoned he could take over the business for a share of future earnings when Gideon's age and climbing ability prevented him from continuing. He and Gideon talked about it.

Gideon said it was a lucrative half-time job. Arthur knew it would provide money or barter goods to support his farming efforts. Nobody much in 1833 Boonesboro was farming, repairing chimneys, or providing meat. He knew he and Israel could just keep doing what they had been and make a better living than most in the area.

Arthur Calloway did not consider the possibility his friend may not survive his wounds. He knew how tough he was. The only fear he had was the fever which accompanies many wounds.

"The fever could take him no matter how tough he is," Arthur thought silently. This person had become the brother he never had. He just could not die before his time.

******

After a week, no fever had set in. After two weeks, Israel did not require an all-day watch. He stayed awake most of the day and slept a normal amount at night. At the end of the second night, he moved back to their own cabin, something Hannah was very happy about.

"What was it like?" she asked of the bear charge.

"Fast and furious, honey. It happened so quickly. He charged on the side away from the muzzle which prevented me from shooting before he knocked Amos and me over. Then, I had to find the rifle. I was dazed on the ground. Amos gave the bear a hard hind feet kick. It slowed the bear and gave me time to get my one shot off. Pa tells me from cleaning out the bear and butchering it, I got him dead in the heart. Looks like a .45 ball in the heart takes longer to kill a big bear than I had.

Then, it was him, me and Mr. Bowie. He closed in on me. I knew the bear hug and resulting bite on the head was going to be the last of me. I was on my back, not a good place to be, so I stood to a knee level as he charged. I held the Bowie, but against my stomach as he came down on me. His own weight pushed the knife in.

I pulled it out and stabbed him in the throat. The jab stuck in so deep I could not pull the knife out. I passed out for a long time.

Using a tree, I made it to my feet and whistled for Amos. Bless him for being the best mule alive. He came, though carefully since the bear was still laying there.

It took me some tries, but I got on his back and said "Take me home. Or, something similar. He, Miss

Sadie and you saved my life," he finished.

"Me, all I did was hold your hand and watch you," Hannah said.

"No, you saved my life by being there. How could I die with you watching?"

She kissed him and washed his face with a torrent of tears.

The next week, he was up and walking around slowly with a stick Arthur brought him. He wore the Bowie everywhere. It was a habit he would follow all of his days.

Israel Pope had learned a lesson he would remember the rest of his life.

Danger was everywhere. Never be caught unarmed. And carry enough gun for the worst scenario. He had enough money to buy a large caliber Northwest Trade Musket or maybe even a Hawkin rifle when he got to St. Louis.

St. Louis was the starting point for about everything having to do with westward travel. He just had to make it there alive with only his knife and wits.

******

By the end of April, Israel thought he was physically ready for the trek to St. Louis and a river boat north.

He told Hannah, who was apprehensive.

"Remember, you have support here, especially

Arthur and my sister. Through barter for meat, you should have more than enough food to hold you over. I will leave Pa's long rifle for your protection. You have the big skinning knife I was carrying when we met.

We will split the money. It's more than I made on the Shenandoah trip.

What I had planned to leave, but cannot now, is Amos. I am strong enough to work, but walking over three hundred miles would not only take too much out of me, it would make me late for when I think the parties will be leaving."

"I will be alright. I am just worrying about you. What if every bear out west is the size of the one you killed. And, wild Indians on the warpath?"

"Honey, I should be in good company most all of the time," he said, naively, but believing his words.

"And, I will be counting every minute until I get home with money and presents for my beautiful wife," he added.

"When will you leave?"

"Arthur's winter wheat is ready to harvest. I will stay and help him get it in. I aim to shame Pa into helping. He's going to get a share since half is on our field. It was the original deal, even though he didn't pay a damn cent for the field, the cabin or anything.

Once Arthur gets the wheat to the miller, he will have enough to get a plow and some more tools. He's been doing pretty well with Mr. Cross and the chimney business. He's a good man and a good provider. Maude did well. All you got was a rolling stone."

"I got my hero and the love of my life. I love everything about you. If you weren't an adventurer, you would not be the man fate threw me in with. I just wish I could go with you."

"I wish you could, too, Hannah. I will be looking for beautiful land we can claim. Then you will go with me. Hopefully, Arthur and Maude, too. He needs good growing land and equipment. And, some mountains on the horizon."

"How long do you think you will be a fur trapper?" she asked.

"Probably not more than a couple of years. I want to stay home with my beautiful wife and our children."

"What will you do then?" she asked.

"Good question. I'm working on the answer. Maybe a small ranch. I hate farming but might like raising and selling cattle or horses."

"Do you know how?" she asked.

"Not right now. But, I am a hard worker and fast learner. I didn't know how to handle a gundalow, or take out an attacker, or kill a bear. I can learn how to ranch. I'm sure of it."

"No worries here. Just checking. I'm with you through thick or thin."

"Hannah, you didn't answer about Amos. Will you be okay without the mule?"

"I'll just stick the skinner in my belt and the long rifle over my shoulder and walk through town. I am Mrs. Bear Fighter. Mrs. Bear Fighter does not need a mule."

"Seriously, I'm sure between Arthur and your Pa each having mules, I have access if I need one. But, it's not like I will ride up to Lexington alone. If there was a trip up there, I'm thinking I'd ride in the bed of the wagon with your sister. Wouldn't surprise me to see Arthur getting some sort of wagon soon, anyway. I'm sure borrowing something from your father is not his favorite thing. He doesn't seem to respect him much," she said.

"Smart man, our Arthur," Israel replied.

"We have fun, don't we Israel?" she asked, smiling.

"We sure do, wife. We sure do!" he responded.

The three men got the wheat in and taken to the mill in Jacob's wagon. Arthur gave Jacob the agreed-upon share and asked if he could borrow the wagon to go to Lexington the next day to look at farm implements.

Israel rode with him. It was his first real jaunt away from the village since the bear attack. He found the bouncing wagon took more out of him than he would have guessed.

Arthur found a plow and a few more things he needed.

They looked at a general merchandise with some guns in the back. Israel found a serviceable flintlock

Indian Trade musket somebody had brought back from the West. It was of less value in Kentucky than Colorado, the Dakotas, or Wyoming. Definitely less expensive than it would be at one of the annual trapper rendezvous. He bought it and got the merchant to throw in some powder and balls. The powder included two brass flasks. One was for priming with finer powder, the other to throw full charges into the barrel. The latter held a full pound of 2F black powder.

"This one is to get me to St. Louis. After, who knows," Israel said.

"It was so cheap. I might keep it as an extra. Can you imagine being in the middle of dangerous country and breaking your only gun?" he asked Arthur.

They stopped at a field along the way home and tried it out. They both decreed the smooth bore was "accurate enough" up to fifty or seventy-five yards. Rainbow trajectory set in after seventy-five yards and the groups grew to eight or ten inches in diameter. But, like a generic fowler, it had the capability of being loaded with shot for birds and small game as well as with buckshot for deer or social purposes. It may well have been the most versatile gun and popular gun carried during the entire history of the fur trade.

"A full load of powder and a sixty-two caliber or twenty bore ball might have stopped the bear before Bowie time," Israel noted.

"Would have been nice. You scared the living hell

out of me, brother!"

"Scared it out of me, too. I have never been afraid of anything before. This bear. Arthur, it was so big and so mad. I don't know why I didn't die right there."

"'Cause you are too mean to die!" Arthur snapped. Israel knew it was not because his friend was mad, but because the incident scared him over possibly losing his friend.

"On another subject," Israel began. "How firm are you and Maude about staying in Boonesboro forever?"

"I reckon where we ended up is no better than where we started from," Arthur said.

"My thoughts exactly! I will be seeing some pretty prime land starting once I get off the steam boat. Not sure where it will be yet. But, I think I will see the great prairies, mountains, maybe even deserts. I may find a better place. Maybe land on a little river with tillable soil and evergreen woods on one side and a field on the other. May have mountains showing in the distance."

"The lawyer fella in town said with the improvements might help to sell our places to new folks coming through and wanting to settle," Arthur said.

"I had better get him to stand by on selling my part of the property. No way in hell I can get Pa to do an adult job of selling it. He'd just walk out and leave it for the next freeloader walking by. How about this?

We go see him when we get back and I will give him two powers. One to allow you to decide to sell my property if you are still here. Two will be if we are both gone, to sell it if Pa vacates."

"I think it'd work. Your folks would only vacate together, so it wouldn't kick your mother out...." Arthur agreed.

"We won't tell Pa. I hate to say it, but I don't completely trust him. It's not a matter of honesty, but a matter of lack of judgement," Israel said. His friend nodded agreement.

They went back by the lawyer's office. He drew up a simple agreement gratis. He knew he would get his fee handling the sales and closings. The lawyer was pretty good about reading people. He read these two young men as up and comers. They would be heading West sooner than later. Based on the improvements, he might buy the properties himself.

"What do you have plans to plant, Arthur?" Israel asked.

"Corn, beans, and squash for sure. Maybe potatoes and onions, too."

"Starting off the the Indians' Three Sisters, huh?" Israel said referring to the name for corn, beans, and squash.

"I didn't know they were. But, they are sure good staples to have and there's a market for each. I'd like to have a couple of hogs. But, I have this feeling you are going to find some really prime land out West. The hogs would be hard to move a thousand miles on a trail," Arthur said.

"Not if they were salt-cured, Tidewater Virginia style, in the back of a wagon! We won't be going quite yet. But, I'll be looking for land for you and me as much as for beaver pelts."

"I wish I could go with you, but…."

"Nobody in the whole world I'd rather have riding beside me. But, your contribution here is so crucial to both of our successes, Arthur."

They stopped at Arthur's place first and unloaded the new implements. The next stop was to drop the wagon at Jacob's. Arthur unharnessed his mule and left the wagon. He rode the mule bareback to his waiting wife. Israel rode Amos to his.

Later in the evening, Hannah looked up from his shoulder and asked, "Got a date for leaving yet, Mountain Man?"

"Next week if it works for you, honey."

"Works alright. The sooner you go, the sooner you will be back with your handsome self and all the beaver money."

"Arthur and I were talking on the way back. I'll be looking for a prime place for us to live. Both families. So, don't get too attached to Boonesboro."

"I have one attraction to Boonesboro, and I'm lying on his shoulder. Find me a moderate climate with a river out front and a view of mountains in the distance. Maybe woods behind."

"I understand there are rivers out there which have hot springs in them. You can sit in them and warm up with snow falling," Israel said.

"Well, add one of those into my picture of our little slice of heaven. I can just see you now, walking out there like a jaybird and hunkering down in the hot water to relax," she said.

"Think you'd dare join me?" he asked.

"Join you? More like I'd flutter past you like your own little jaybird and find a place to sit myself down!"

He smiled and she could see him visualizing the sight. Good time for a long kiss, she thought. She acted upon her impulse.

"Looks like we are going to have another night with lots of laughing and little sleep, my husband," she said.

******

The following Monday, Israel said his goodbyes and aimed Amos towards St. Louis. The trip was three hundred sixty miles as the bird flies. He reckoned on making it in five days.

Israel did not push the mule hard. He had camping gear including some small iron cook pans, an axe, food and powder and shot. The mule was strong, but the man wanted him to last a long time. It took him several days more time than he anticipated. Israel rode into St. Louis on the following Tuesday.

He reckoned he would book Amos and himself on a steam-powered riverboat heading upriver. He found quickly he reckoned wrong. Riverboats did not want horses, mules or other livestock aboard. They had to travel downstream by boats like the Shenandoah gundalows, but larger. Once the river became more navigable, steamboats took over for the trip to the Gulf of Mexico.

The northbound boats like he needed were known as Mississippi broadhorns.

A recent innovation was some of these flat bottom scows being equipped with steam engines and paddle wheels so more weight from freight and livestock could be taken upstream also. It appeared he was destined to one of those, or riding.

Israel and Amos watched one come in and moor in front of them. Once the boat was tied up and unloaded, he asked the price for a man and his mule. The quoted amount was acceptable to Pope.

He looked around.

"Where in tarnation am I going to sleep. I sure don't want to waste two bits on a hotel room with four guys sleeping in two beds!" he thought to himself. He saw several grizzled looking men who looked like they were or are mountain men.

"Fellows, any recommendation on where to sleep in St. Louis without getting a hotel room?" he asked.

"A bunch of us trappers think like you do. We like to sleep outdoors. The wind carries the snoring and other bodily noises off better outside. We got us an encampment just downriver. About a half mile. Come on down, son, if you've a mind," one said. Israel nodded and grinned. "See you there in a while."

"Man! Real mountain men. A couple had those new Hawkin rifles, but most had trade muskets like mine. Several even had Bedford County long rifles," he thought.

Israel decided to save his camp food. He spent what a room would have cost on travel food at a restaurant. Real bread, ham, cheese, honey and more. He mounted Amos and headed downriver before dark.

The camp was quiet. No drinking or yelling. Yet, at least.

"Hello, the camp! Alright to ride in and put my bedroll down?" he called.

"Are you a rip roaring sonofagun? Faster than lightning? A man who fights bears barehanded? If so, come on in!"

"I'm not sure of the first two, but I can show you the scars on the last one!" he said loudly.

"Talk is cheap, boy! Show us proof," came a chorus of replies. Israel tied Amos to a tree, using a long rope and walked over.

He sat his trade gun on a log and pulled off his shirt.

"Walk up to the fire, Bear Fighter."

He did and men crowded around and peered at his scars.

"You ain't the kid from around Boonesboro what took on a big bear with a knife are ya?" one asked.

"I am from Boonesboro all right. It wasn't just a knife. It was a genuine Bowie knife. This claw hanging from my neck on a beaded rawhide was one of my bear's."

They crowded closer to view the claw, which looked more like one from a large grizzly.

"I heard about it from up river. They said you climbed on your mule and rode an hour, bleeding all the way," one man volunteered.

"I didn't know anybody but those around Boonesboro knew," Israel said.

"Was in all the papers, boy. Lots of folks was talking about it. Fella had a religious-sounding name."

"Like Israel Pope?" Israel asked.

"Yes, exactly!" a couple of men joined in.

"Pope's my name. My pa is called Jacob Pope. We are from Virginia originally."

"Well, Bear Fighter, unsaddle your mule and spread out your bedroll. If ya got anything to throw into the mix for dinner, feel free."

Israel contributed a bit of ham, bread and cheese.

He needed to save something to eat on the boat.

During dinner, Israel kept his mouth shut and learned a lot from these men. Most were experienced beaver trappers and Indian fighters. He knew there was some exaggeration in the stories but reckoned all were based on some truth.

"Is everyone taking a broadhorn upriver?" he finally asked.

"Yep, it's about the only choice for a man with a horse or mule. Or, a family with a cow or ox. The steamboats don't want livestock. Just people," an old man named Jed Hunt said. Israel had listened to the conversation as men ate and drank coffee around the fire. Everyone seemed to respect the old man. He seemed too old to be heading into the wilderness. He was stiff and had a hard time sitting cross-legged around the fire, getting up and getting his balance. Israel liked him instantly, but worried about him surviving in the wilderness. Especially in the mountain winters he had heard to be so fierce.

As things settled down and some crawled into their bedrolls, Israel sidled up to Hunt.

"Mr. Hunt, what do you plan to do? Join an expedition or be an independent?"

"I have a good name, sonny. But, you might have noticed I'm ten years older than Methuselah. I doubt Sublette and the American Fur Company, or ones of his ilk would hire me. What are your plans? Do you know much about trapping?"

"Nossir. Not a whit. I'm a good hunter. It is obvious I have not learned to smell bear yet, but I plan to work on it," Israel said. Jed chuckled.

"Do you have money for traps and supplies? Seems you are armed sufficiently. You will need a winter coat and snowshoes. Winter moccasins with fur lining, too."

"I have some money. I admit I'm kinda playing it by ear."

"Want to throw in with me? I have the experience and the traps. I can teach you. I am at the end of my trail. I don't want to die in the city. I want to die in the Wind River Range of Western Wyoming. If I teach you, would you pick a nice overlook to bury me, say some words, and put a cross over my grave?" he asked.

"Mr. Hunt, I'd do it anyway, whether we were pards or not. I'd be honored to trail along with you and learn from you."

"Well, it's a done deal then," he said. "I will make sure some of the respected fellows here know what we've agreed to and know my traps, rifle, mule and all are yours when I don't make it back. Don't want anybody to think you murdered me for my gear."

"Mr. Hunt, I will do everything possible to make sure you do make it back."

"Son, call me Jed. And, I know how I feel. I won't make it back. And, I'd really rather spend eternity looking over a valley or stand of tall trees, or babbling stream. Not a damn city like this here one."

"Alright Jed, what can I throw into this partnership, other than what you already suggested?"

"If you have a couple of bucks for a ticket on the broadhorn, it sure would help."

"Sure. Since you have traps, we can use my trap money for your ticket and the things you say I need like snowshoes and a heavy jacket and all. Other than the ticket, where do we get the rest of what we need?"

"There will be a trading post where we get off. And, others on the trail to the Wind River country. Maybe we can get some fresh meat along the way to trade and you can save some coin," the old trapper said.

Israel checked on Amos. He had plenty of browse. Israel also changed from tying to hobbling him, so he had access to more to eat.

He climbed into his bedroll pretty contented. He already missed his pretty spitfire of a wife, but meeting Jed was a good piece of luck.

While it would be sad to bury a new friend, he stood to learn and gain a lot from the old mountain man.

The next morning, about a third of the encampment boarded the same powered broadhorn. With two ear piercing toots of the steam whistle, it pulled away from the dock.

Israel Pope, soon to be a mountain man, was on his way.

"Beats all hell out of riding up to the trapping grounds, Israel," Jed said.

Israel nodded, watching with fascination as they chugged past the shoreline. The gundalow running a rapid was more exciting but letting someone else handle her and enjoying the ride was even better. He wished Hannah could see this.

There was a catwalk around the building which took up much of the hundred foot scow. A steam engine and a fuel pile rode behind the structure. The captain operated the boat from a shack on the top front of the building. The stern part of the structure was partitioned off for livestock. After the livestock was a cargo room. The remaining fifty feet was for people. Up to twenty people at a time could climb a ladder and sit on the roof. Israel sat up there for a while, then went back under the shelter to talk with Jed.

"Where do you plan on getting off this boat, Jed?" Israel asked.

"I figure around the village called Ft. Armstrong. It's one of the last stops. We will head to Des Moines, a little place at the confluence of the Raccoon and Des Moines Rivers. Many of the fellas will branch off to follow the Missouri River. It's the dividing line between trapping country and civilization.

You and I will go to Omaha. We'll pick up the Platte River and follow her damn near to the Wind

River country," Jed said.

"Is there much civilization along the way?" Israel asked.

"Not so much. The towns I mentioned are mostly trading posts and villages. There's a trail we can follow. There are some small trading posts here and there. We should get the main items we are lacking at Omaha. Could be small pickings after Omaha."

"How far is the Wind River Range from here?" Israel asked.

"A ways. Probably a month. We can stop at likely places and trap beavers. I figure we will get to the Windy around mid-to late summer. If we don't….or more likely, you don't, make it back by fall, you will have to winter where you are. So, try not to find yourself on the plains where wood and game are scarce. You'd be better to be in the woods. Even if you have to winter in the Windy."

"What you are calling the Windy is the Wind River Range, right?"

"It is. If you got enough money left, I'm thinking we should get another mule and a sawbuck pack saddle. I don't know about you, but walking doesn't sound good. Which is why I have a riding mule and a pack mule. You should also.

We will shortly have to have winter gear. And, get more food in case you have to spend the winter out there."

"Jed, I am okay at tracking small game. Even deer. Will you teach me how to cut sign on men, whether Indians or whites?" Israel asked.

"I will teach you all of those things and more. I never had no son nor grandson to show skills to. You are going to be him. It's the only way you will survive once I pass. Another thing which is real important. When we pass landmarks, we will stop and you will memorize what they look like from the coming back side. It will show you the right way back. You don't want to accidentally walk into land where you will be killed.

I hope to make it to Wyoming country. If you had to escape, it would be tempting to go south to Utah or Colorado than the reverse of the way we came in. But, don't do it because the next place you will hit going east is Kansas. It has Indian activity you will want to avoid if possible. In or out, the route I will show you is the safest."

Within a week, most of the trappers branched off to follow the Missouri River. Within two weeks, Israel and Jed were traveling alone. The lessons commenced.

"Let's stop and you get down. Ain't no need for me to climb down for this lesson.

Look at the deer track and tell me about it," Jed said.

"It's big, so probably a buck. It's deep and well-defined. I think it was made in soft wet dirt. It rained where we were a couple nights ago. Probably here, too. There are bits of leaves and dust in it. They blew in after the track set. The tracks are widely spaced and spaced to tell me the deer was running from something. But, I don't see wolf or bear or panther tracks chasing him. I reckon it was something to his side spooking him," Israel said.

"You did well, Israel. I read it almost the same way. But, it's big because it's a buck elk. Something you probably have not encountered yet. Hopefully, we will find some dangerous game or maybe man tracks to study soon."

The next day, two trails intersected, and some moccasin prints appeared going in their direction.

"Now. Look at these. Moccasins. Probably three sets. Going in our direction. When do you think they came off the trail coming in from the south and took this trail? What kind of Indians?" Jeb asked.

"First, how can you tell they are Indians. We are both wearing moccasins."

"Walk beside them a few feet. Then, look at your tracks beside theirs and tell me if they are the same."

Israel did. He studied his tracks and the others.

"The others are pointed a bit inwards. Kinda pigeon-toed," he noted.

"Indians tend to walk toes pointed in. More comfortable way to walk in soft sole moccasins. Some trappers do too. But, most would be riding, not walking. What else?" Jeb asked.

"They are walking fast, but not running."

"How do you know they are?"

"Because of the distance between the footprints. Also, running would have deeper toe indentations, I believe." The old man nodded.

"Your top knot might depend on the next question. How far ahead of us are they?"

"I'm not sure, Jeb. Not much debris has blown into the prints. They have not dried as hard as the deer prints yesterday. I can't narrow it down any closer than six hours to two days," Israel admitted.

"Neither can I from the tracks. So, we have to look for other signs. Walk four or five feet off the left. I will ride the same off the right. We will see if we see anything which would help us."

Jed stopped his mule after two hours.

"What do you see?" Israel asked.

"One of them took a dump here. Come check it."

Israel had been leading Amos. He dropped the mule's reins and walked over and squatted down.

He sniffed it and lightly stuck a finger in it, immediately wiping it on a leaf.

"It's not warm but is still soft. Do you think a few hours ago?" Israel asked.

"I 'speck so. Much longer and it would have dried out. Riding, we will catch them before dark. I'd say maybe make an early camp and let them get ahead. Tomorrow, we will keep track of their sign. Hopefully, they will turn off on another game trail. They seem to be going somewhere specific because of the way they are walking," Jeb said.

"I vote we make the camp half a mile off the trail just to be careful," Israel suggested. Jeb agreed.

They rode their mules through the trees, keeping a sharp lookout. There was a fairly flat space between a group of spruce trees.

They dismounted and hobbled the mules near some grass.

"Make a habit of walking a full circle around your camp before you start a fire or get your bedroll out. Depending on the threat and terrain, maybe half a mile, maybe too hundred yards. Each situation is different. With Indians in the area, I would make it wide. Always take your long gun, ammunition, knife and tomahawk with you. Everywhere, boy."

Israel took the trade musket and walked a half mile circle around their intended camp. He always wore his Bowie but did not own a tomahawk. Yet. He did not see anything and returned to camp.

"Since we know there are Indians in the area, I think we should not make a fire. If we didn't know, we'd still dig a fire pit with a hole off to the side and a tunnel connecting it to the main pit. Air being sucked in the hole and through the tunnel will burn the fire more efficiently and cause less smoke. The hole will hide a lot of the light from the flames. We have a small shovel on my mule. You should get a smaller spade to keep in your saddlebag at the next trading post. And, a tomahawk. Good for cleaning branches. And, killing," Jed added.

After thirty years of ranging throughout the wilderness West, Jed had an uncanny sense of direction and tried to impart it on Israel. Israel was a fast learner. He would have to be to make it back to his wife alone. It saddened him to see his friend become slower and stiffer and eat less each day. Israel worried whether he would make it all the way to the Wind River Range.

He determined if Jed made it close, he would build a travois and deliver him to his promised land.

The two mountain men stopped for the night by a fast-moving stream. Jed reckoned they must be in the Laramie Mountains. They had crossed miles of grassland. The plains were interesting to Israel, but he knew he did not want to bring Hannah to a land relatively without trees.

"Sonny, I'm slowing down fast now. We are in Wyoming Territory. Probably about three hundred miles from the Wind River country. While you were setting up camp, I walked along the stream. There's plenty of beaver sign.

I figure this might be a good place and time to teach

you how to be a beaver trapper. Let's have some of the fresh venison and some fry bread and start fresh in the morning."

"Sounds like a good plan, Jed. I am hungry as a three tooth bear. You want the venison cooked in the pan or roasted over the fire on a spit?"

"Pan's good enough for me. Faster, too."

The night was warm enough to use an open front camp. They awoke, as always, at dawn and walked silently to the stream after coffee.

"Beaver are like an army engineer. They build pretty fancy dams and hideouts. They can dive under the water and swim though a hole into their houses. Predators cannot make it through the hole.

They are pretty territorial and keep to regular patterns, which makes it easier for us.

Here's how you cut sign on whether beavers are working an area. First, look for tracks like these," Jed pointed out tracks in the soft dirt by the stream.

"Look for where they gnawed down a tree to make their dam or hideaway. This here is what a beaver gnaw looks like."

"The easiest way to decide it's beaver country, without the things I just said, is to look for their dams. You can spot them pretty easily just looking up and downstream," Jed said.

The stream had all of the components of beaver activity Jed taught.

"The best thing to attract a beaver to your trap is beaver castor. It's an oil made from the glands of a beaver. We can make it from the first beaver we catch, but most trading posts out this way sell it. So, I'd say we concentrate on getting some pelts to trade now.

They also love poplar. We can find a poplar tree pretty easy here and use some twigs and add some mushrooms.

Israel, it is real important to remember beavers don't eat meat. So, never use meat in a trap."

They found both mushrooms and a poplar tree. Jed had Israel gather a bunch of twigs and baited a line of traps in positions in the water Jed chose.

"When you are heading back to your family after the winter, collect a bunch of spring poplar buds and simmer them a few hours in oil. Strain it through cheesecloth or muslin into a jar. That'll be poplar oil you can put on sticks to sweeten them for beavers.

You can also mix it with a bit with melted beeswax to make a medicinal salve. The Indians use it for wounds, burns, and skin rashes. It's a good thing to carry a little screw top metal jar on your treks," Jed said.

After the traps were set, Jed had Israel do another armed loop around the camp to make sure the Indians had not doubled back.

When he returned, the verbal woodcraft lessons

continued.

"You sure are a good teacher, Jed. It's like you have done this before," Israel said.

"Ha! Well, you caught me. I was a school teacher back in Fincastle, Virginia before I headed out here to become a trapper."

"How did you learn?" Israel asked.

"I joined a Hudson Bay expedition, then one of Ashley's. Both had experienced trappers to show the majority of us fellows the ropes. Most of us were farmers and such just looking for adventure and wealth. We had a lot of the first and not so much of the second. The companies made the money. We trappers made enough to pay for a helluva week at June rendezvous and go home broke."

"Think I will pass on rendezvous."

"Naw, you should go. Lots of goods worth looking at and it's history in the making. Just avoid the wild women and alcohol and buy what you need and can get at a good price.

We already missed this year's rendezvous. They are in June to sell the winter's trapping. The 1835 one will be held in June at Malachite's Big Hole on the Green River.

Assuming you winter in the Windy, you should go to the rendezvous on the way home. Sell your furs, buy a gee-gaw for your wife and make your bones as a real, bonified mountain man," Jed said.

Israel realized the scheduling of the rendezvous, his best opportunity to sell pelts, would cause him to be away for a full year. He did not know much about the rendezvous' and especially when they occurred. At this point, there was no way to get a letter to Hannah. Something hit him hard. He did not even know if she could read. Of course his family or Arthur could read a letter to her, but how little he knew about her struck home all at once.

The two stayed where they were, trapping, for several weeks. Jed said a passel of pelts would be worth something at the next trading post. It would be where they would buy their last supplies for winter, except for heavy coats and moccasin boots. Jed changed his mind on those. "Let's get them from a Kiowa tribe I know just past the trading post," he said. "The quality will be better and the price, too."

They split a full load of beaver pelts, with the preponderance carried on Jed's cargo mule.

Two days later, the mountain men made it to a trading post which was on Horse Creek, where it flowed out of the Green River. A month previous, the rendezvous had been held there. Signs of fire pits and some trash remained. It would be the site of the 1835 rendezvous also.

They tied the three mules outside of the post and walked in. Jed was warmly greeted by the owner. He introduced Israel as the "next generation of mountain man. The smarter variety."

"We are looking for lead, powder, sides of bacon, a bear skin for Israel, a couple of bottles of beaver castor, and a bunch of Green River skinning knives to trade," Jed said.

"You are in luck. I had a wagon train of items come in for the rendezvous. Wouldn't you know it? It got held up by a flooded river and missed the big meet. I can sell most of what you want at half price. If you have a few pelts, I can take them off your hands. I had a couple wagons go out several weeks ago and one left only half full."

"We got a load of pelts from down the way. Israel will be back in the spring with a bunch and trade 'em to you at the rendezvous."

"Jed, you said Israel will be back. How about you, old friend?" the trading post owner asked.

"Mal, I am sinking fast. It is unlikely I will see autumn. Israel has promised to take me to the Wind River Range. I want to spend eternity looking over them mountains."

"I'm sorry to hear such talk from one of the original mountain men. Jed, when were you born?" he asked.

"1755," Jed said.

"So, you are pushing eighty real hard?"

"Real damn hard, Mal. I might even trip over it next month. My advanced age must be a frustration to the two or three braves who may have tried to kill me over the years. Those who are still alive, I mean!"

"You came to the rendezvous before last, but did not have pelts to trade," Mal prompted.

"True. I had been scouting and leading a string of pilgrims to Oregon for the last couple of years. I figure young Pope here will do the same after a season or two chasing pelts. Fashion is a persnickety thing. One day, beaver hats will be old news and our industry will die. But, I figure," Jed said, looking Israel in the eye, "being a scout for the army, for surveyors, or for wagon trains, will be a job for a good mountain man for another twenty years."

"Wal, then I got another twenty years of trading. This is pretty country and I reckon settlers will flock here one day."

The two mountain men bought food, a tomahawk, and twenty-five Green River knives made by the Russell factory in Greenfield, Massachusetts. These skinning knives were prized by Indians and trappers alike due to their good carbon steel blades. They were famous for holding a sharp edge. Israel determined he would keep three as skinners and backups to his Bowie.

Their beaver pelts remaining covered the cost of several bottles of beaver castor oil, some poplar oil, a tomahawk, and a supply of powder and lead. Israel had a small lead pot and molds for round balls. After a day's work was done, he could melt the lead over a hot campfire and cast sixty-two caliber balls. He would also carefully grind his 2F black powder into finer powder to put in his lock to ignite a charge when the flintlock sparked.

The two pushed off for the Wind River Range they viewed on the horizon.

CHAPTER 3

The mountains on yesterday's horizon proved to be a two-day ride.

"Do you have a spot in mind for us to build a camp, Jed?"

"Yep. I have a log open fronted cabin on a rise. There's a stream a hundred yards below. Water is pure and cold and there's beaver in it. A half mile downstream, it ends in a lake. Lots of beavers there and fish, too," Jed said.

"I have been reading Thomas's Old Farmer's Almanac," Jed continued. "It says we are due for a cold winter with a lot of snow. I'm thinking we set our traps in the morning and work on adding a front to the cabin. Mebbe even a fireplace. I didn't put one in because I did not know how. I could not afford to smoke myself out into a blizzard. Or, worse yet, burn the damn thing down and be stranded with nothing in the wilderness no matter the weather."

"A Boonesboro chimney builder helped with my cabin at home," Israel said. "He showed me how to do it. My friend, Arthur, apprenticed to him and will take over his business. We might be able to build a good drafting chimney in your cabin after all, Jed."

"A chimney would be mighty welcome, come snow. You can't even go out to the privy without snowshoes. Which reminds me. We'll stop at a tribe of Kiowa friends on the way. We need to get you a coat and some snow shoes."

"How about for you?" Israel asked, fearing the answer.

"I won't be needing them. Once I get home to the Windy and finish learning you everything I have to teach, I will be ready Israel."

"You sure you want to rush this dying thing my friend?" Israel asked.

"I have some lead balls in my carcass and a real painful arrowhead I couldn't dig out.

They pain me more every day. Along with the normal stiffness and pains what come with being eighty."

"Oh! Happy birthday, Jed! I got you a little something."

He handed Jed a paper sack with some hard candy.

Jed peeked inside and Israel saw a big smile appear. And, maybe a hint of a tear.

"Boy, nobody has given me a birthday present for

nigh on to seventy years. You just don't know how much I appreciate this."

"Jed, my Pa and I don't view life and responsibility the same. You have been like the pa to me I always wished he'd be. I appreciate you and what you've done. I appreciate the time you take teaching me. I know in the next year I will go through some things and say to myself 'damn, I'd be dead now if Jed hadn't taught me what to do in this situation.'"

"I like passing my experience on to a deserving person. Want a piece of candy?"

"Nossir. Every piece is for you to enjoy."

They rode on toward the Kiowa village. Both happy. Each lost in his thoughts.

They reached the village midday.

Some braves rode up to check them out and, passing scrutiny, lead them in. Several recognized Jed as a friend. They were taken to the chief.

"Lone Bear, this is Israel, my friend," Jed said.

The man, perhaps twenty years younger than Jed, nodded solemnly.

Israel did the same.

"Israel is known as Bear Fighter among the mountain men. Israel, show Lone Bear your claw and your chest."

He did so. The chief reached out and took the pendant claw in his fingers and examined it closely.

"How did you kill this bear, young one," the chief

asked in accented, but understandable English.

"I shot him badly as he attacked. Then, in the fight, I stabbed him in the chest, then the throat."

Israel pointed to each place for emphasis as he spoke.

"The claw is of a very large bear. You do not look big enough or strong enough to fight such a bear with your hands and a knife."

"I had no choice. Either kill him or die," Israel said.

"What knife did you use?"

"This Bowie knife," he said drawing the knife and handing it butt first to the chief.

"I like this knife. It is a good blade," Lone Bear said.

"I am sure Bear Fighter would give you the knife as a token of his friendship," Jed said.

Israel, though not wanting to part with the Bowie, knew it was necessary. He withdrew the sheath from his belt and handed it to the chief with a small bow from the waist.

He saw a big smile grow on the chief's face as he turned the blade and the sheath over and over.

"I will give my new friend a gift, Jed. What would be a good gift for him?"

"He came to trade for a winter coat and a pair of snowshoes, Lone Bear."

"Yes. Those would be appropriate gifts for such a knife!" he nodded and someone Israel reckoned was his wife scurried off.

She returned shortly with an appropriate coat. It was bear hide with the hair inside and some beadwork outside. It fit his long, lean frame well.

"Thank you chief. I will wear this with great pride, knowing it was a gift from you."

The chief motioned them to sit around the small fire. Israel sat cross-legged like the chief. Jed sat as well as he could. It was clear he was not comfortable.

A young Kiowa girl brought them water in a large gourd. They passed it around, each taking a drink.

"This is White Feather, my granddaughter. She has fifteen seasons. One day, she will be a Story Teller who tells our history to future generations," Lone Bear said as the girl gave an impish grin to Israel, still wearing his new winter coat in the late summer. He hastened to take it off, fold it and lay it on the ground beside him.

"What is your plan for this time?" Lone Bear asked Jed.

"Israel and I will go and trap beaver at my old cabin. He plans to make it more habitable. My time has come, my friend. I will not be with Israel when he stops on the way to rendezvous and his home in Kentucky."

"It is the way of things, Jed," Lone Bear said, nodding.

"I have had a good run, my friend. Good friends and honorable enemies. I have never been too hungry or hurt more than I could stand. I have stood before the mountains and streams and seen the sunrises and sunsets. What more could a man ask?"

"Nothing," his friend, Lone Bear, said quietly.

As they rode toward the Windy, Israel asked, "Will you teach me to speak Indian?"

"Better I teach you a bit of sign language. There's a difference between the dialects of the plains Indians and those from the mountains and further south towards Santa Fe."

"We can get into the instruction as soon as we air out the shelter and decide what we are going to do about making it weatherproof and warm," Israel said.

The camp was situated as beautifully as Jed had promised. It overlooked a fast moving stream, had mountains to the back and both sides and a long valley in front. The valley stretched all the way to the Kiowa village they had just left almost a day ago.

"Israel, we didn't get you any winter boots."

"I thought about those. Luckily, I have some tall leather boots I brought from Virginia. They will have to do, I reckon."

"You will need to grease them up with lard or something. If you could kill a bear, it would be passable meat and provide good grease for everything you need to lubricate."

"Are there many bears up this way?" Israel asked.

"Some black bears and a few grizzly's. If you go

bear hunting, take my Hawken and leave me the fusil."
Jed always referred to the Northwest Trade Musket
as a fusil, the old name. He pronounced it "few-zee."

"You will need a fast moving ball driven real deep
to kill a big bear. I think you already know from previous experience," Jed grinned.

"I sure do. And, I don't want to take on another bear
with a Green River knife, now my Bowie is gone."

"Aw, you'll get another one. Your Bowie earned a
friendship money can't buy, boy. I'm surprised Lone
Bear didn't throw in his granddaughter with the coat
and snow shoes he liked you so much."

"My wife is about the same age as White Feather. All
I need is two young females. I have to admit though,
White Feather's beauty takes your breath away."

"Wal, ya just never know," his friend mused.

They did not have to air out the open front cabin or
shelter. Israel poked around and made sure no snakes
or rats had built homes in it or were in the ceiling.
He grew up around snakes and generally hated them.

They camped in the shelter for the night. Early the
next morning, they got the beaver traps out. To save
the supply of poplar twigs, Jed showed him how to use
leafy twigs of any tree and put a drop of beaver castor
on them to entice the animals. Israel laid a trapline
around dawn and they walked back to the cabin.

"My feeling is we should erect a fireplace outside the
existing structure to save a lot of log cutting. We need

a saw and don't have anything but one axe. I will build a fireplace and raise a chimney. Then, we can build around it, add a side wall, then a front with a door. The windows can be on the front, facing the sun."

He drew a design in the dirt, using a stick.

"I'm thinking we can skip a window covering up here. We can make small log shutters for night and cold weather. And, take them down to let cool air in during the summer or just air the place out."

"You ought to take a Kiowa wife. They provide and own the home. She will put up a teepee and you will be done. Cool in the summer, warm in the winter," Jed said.

"I have a wife."

"She ain't here," Jed responded.

"Seems to me to be a sure way of guaranteeing getting scalped in your sleep, one wife or another," Israel said.

Jed laughed but did not pursue the conversation further for now.

"Jed, what's your real name? Jedediah?"

"Naw, Jed is just a nickname. My real name is John."

"I promise my first son's name will be John, then. John Hunt Pope."

"Calling him after me would be real fine, son. Real fine."

******

Israel brought in a number of hides over the next few weeks. He expanded his trapline to the border of the lake their stream ran into. Before adding to the house, he built a curing shed on the back of the open face shelter. He also built a shed for the three mules and a small corral. He already knew the mules would be fine outside with an occasional layer of snow on their backs. They did need a shelter to go in and some winter forage. He watched what they ate and tried to replicate supplies of it for the shed.

Jed taught him how to make the beaver pelts more valuable by tanning them. He killed a deer and hung it for the meat. The deer's brain and water were a tanning solution. After, the fleshed out hides were washed and rolled and stretched until they dried soft. The stretching process was far more exhausting than any other aspect of the trapping process.

Jed assured Israel properly tanned pelts would fetch a worthwhile premium at the rendezvous or wherever the pelts were sold or traded.

After the first week of stretching hides, Israel could hardly flex his hands. He was not a perfectionist. He did, however have pride in his work and wanted to make his efforts financially as worthwhile as possible.

Jed stopped going down to the stream or going anywhere much farther than the makeshift privy. Israel feared his friend's oft-predicted end was near.

Israel lugged stone after stone from the stream.

Not having a bucket, he built a travois and loaded it by hand with clay from the stream. They had one bucket, but it was for hauling drinking water. Clay stuck to the bottom was not feasible.

Jed watched with interest as the young, now full-fledged mountain man built a fireplace, then a chimney. It took a week because he had to build a ladder to stand on for the top of the chimney.

Israel felled trees whose diameter matched the logs in the shed and had one of the pack mules drag them back to the site. A logging chain was added to the shopping list which already included a shovel and another bucket. A few days later, he added nails to the list.

He cleaned the branches off, larger ones with his axe, smaller with the tomahawk.

Israel notched the logs and began laying them. He decided to rewet the clay and chink the logs once he had built the new parts of the cabin.

Two weeks later, they had a weather tight cabin. He built a chair for Jed to use sitting out, looking over his favorite view.

Israel tried to spend as much time as possible with his old friend. There was still so much to learn. He knew time was running out.

"What do you think of your new cabin, Jed?"

"Best damn cabin I ever had. If you quit trapping, you could build cabins for a living. I suspect you could not stay in one place long enough to have such a job though. You'd want to see over the next horizon, wouldn't you?"

"I fear you are right. It worries me about being married. How can I provide a stable home for a wife and children?"

"Some do. There's a young fella named Kit Carson. He's maybe ten years older than you. He has a family. Dan Boone had one. It's said his daughter Jemima was really his brother Ned's child. Ned and Daniel's wife thought Daniel was dead after a long absence and took up with each other. I figger having a family can be done. Of course, it takes the right woman. And, maybe a brother who ain't too impatient."

"Jed, did you ever have a wife?" Israel asked.

"Long ago. I'm sure she's dead by now. Couldn't put up with my wanderlust. Just up and left while I was on my first walkaround. Never knew where she went."

"Did you have children?"

"Not so's I know about. I guess I could have along the way."

"Where was your first walkabout?"

"Kentucky with Boone. Hell, I was around half a century old when I was on the Corps of Discovery."

"You were with Lewis and Clark?" Israel asked incredulously.

"I was about your age when we went to Kentucky.

I helped build the fort where your cabin is. Put a lot of wear on my moccasins before the trip from Harper's Ferry to the Pacific with Will Clark and Meriwether Lewis. The Corps of Discovery was sure a humdinger of a trip!

We even tried out air powered rifles. They were accurate and would drop a deer like nobody's business. Never figured out why they didn't become real popular."

"Did you know Sacagawea?" Israel asked.

"She was a fine woman. She'd have been a mountain man's perfect wife. She was married to a Frenchie at the time."

"Whatever happened to her, Jed?"

"It's a real mystery, boy. We all thought she died young. Then, a rumor started circulating she left her husband. I think his name was Charbonneau or some such.

The rumor has her returning to Indian life. She is supposed to be an old lady living right here in the Wind River Range!"

"No! Amazing," Israel said, wanting to meet her and pick her brain about her travels.

Jed did not talk about Sacagawea further, despite Israel's interest. The younger man thought he knew more but chose, or had promised, to preserve her privacy.

Jed was invigorated by the remembrances and

talked while they ate dinner and he dozed off. Most of his stories were about the Corps of Discovery, or Lewis and Clark Expedition.

Israel absorbed more history than he could imagine. John Hunt had virtually explored with Boone, knew every famous mountain man, and had walked or ridden America and seen places before any other white man.

The next morning, Israel fixed strong coffee, bacon and fry bread for breakfast. Jed had a good appetite and they talked more about the old days.

He helped Jed out to his chair and the old mountain man sat there enjoying the warmth of the sun.

Late in the morning, he poured two cups of coffee and took one to Jed, who was dozing in the sun.

"Want a warm up on your coffee, Jed?" he asked. There was no answer. He was not snoring, as he usually did sleeping.

Israel tapped him. Nothing. He felt his heart. Nothing there either. Apparently the time had come.

They had selected a spot overlooking the stream and the valley.

Israel got Jed's spade and began to dig a grave. He took his time, in case Jed was just deeply asleep or unconscious. He knew why people had wakes for the dead. In case they woke up.

He dug the rectangular hole deeply. Israel did not want predators to get to his friend.

Israel went to the cabin and lifted his friend in his arms and walked back to the grave. He was surprised how light in weight this big man had gotten in the months they had known one another.

He put Jed's feet in the hole and eased his shoulders and head down.

It did not take long to fill the grave and tamp down the dirt with his moccasins.

Israel turned and faced the sun.

"Lord, I'm sending you my friend. His name is John Hunt. He was a good man and a pioneer. I hope you will take good care of him. He deserves it. Amen."

The Bear Fighter broke down convulsing with sobs. He would miss his friend and think of him always. Israel was alone now. Winter was coming on. This time, the wind and snow would be the next bear he had to fight.

He would fight and he would win. Israel Pope was not a quitter. He was a man who would fight almost to the death, and then some.

******

The next day, Israel split a log and made longer and shorter planks. He tied them together with rawhide in the shape of a cross. When he got nails later, he would nail the cross piece on. He had a wrought iron rod as part of his grill and cooking kit. He built a fire and let it burn down to coals.

He stuck the rod in the coals until it was red hot. Using the rod to write letters on the arm of the cross, he wrote "John Hunt 1755-1836". He pushed the cross into the soft dirt at the head of the grave.

"God bless you, my friend. I hope this is your best journey yet."

Israel walked back to the cabin feeling very lost and alone. Solitude and self-sufficiency character-ized the life of a mountain man. He would get used to it. Very quickly.

He sorted Jed's belongings. He knew the Hawkin was loaded, so he left it in the corner where Jed kept it. None of the clothes fit him, so he rolled them up and put them out of sight. He added Jed's Farmer's Almanac to his own Bible and Selected Plays of Shakespeare on the bookshelf he constructed the day after his friend's death.

Each day, Israel checked the trapline and collected beavers. By late fall, he had a marketable load and would have to use both of Jed's, now his, mules to take them to rendezvous. He rode Amos around the area and familiarized himself before winter set in with a vengeance. It was important to find game trails and also places he could defend if attacked by hostiles of any nature. He also wanted to find a bear for grease, meat and to supplement his blankets at night. He carried Jed's Hawkin rifle on those jaunts. Israel remembered his late friend's advice about needing its power for bear hunting.

He missed his Bowie knife and intended to replace it as soon as he could. It was the perfect close-in fighting weapon, when his ten or twelve pound long gun was empty or the enemy was too close.

The skies grew gray and the wind picked up. Winter was surely coming. He reckoned he had time to make a trip down to the Kiowa village.

He wanted to tell Lone Bear their old friend was gone. He also took Jed's clothes, washed in the stream and hung to dry by the wind. He knew someone in the tribe could get some use out of them and reckoned it would be a sign of good faith on his part.

Lone Bear greeted him solemnly. Maybe he was always solemn. It was more likely, Israel thought, he saw the single rider coming and knew Jed was gone.

Jed had allotted himself a piece of birthday candy each day. There was half a sack left. He took it to the tribe and gave it to the chief and his granddaughter. The girl took great delight in it. He found she spoke English almost as well as he did.

When Israel mounted Amos to leave for the cabin, he knew he would not see or talk with another human for six months or better.

He rode to a hilltop and paused Amos, turning in his saddle, he raised his arm and waved at the Kiowas in the distance. He could see Lone Bear and White

Feather return his wave.

Israel Pope knew he had lost one friend, but now had at least two in the Wind River Range.

He rode on and checked his traplines before dark. Five more beavers to skin and begin to tan. Tomorrow, he would check the traps along the lake shore. Tonight, he would read by candle light and sleep warmly. He feared warm sleeping may become more difficult with each passing day. Israel loved the sound of the wind whistling around the cabin at night.

The three mules had grown heavier coats. He let them browse where they wanted to save the feed he put away for winter. He appreciated their strength and toughness.

As he thought of strength, a vision of his friend Arthur came to mind. Meeting him was surely a blessing. Fate put people in his path. It surely had Hannah when he heard her screams in Hell Town at Front Royal.

Israel hoped she was alright. Getting married and then left for a year was a lot to ask of a sixteen year old. She would be about seventeen by the time he returned. They had spoken at length about the absence before he left. He told her it could be a year, because of the trapping season, the inability to leave during winter and the sheer distances involved. He thought she understood. Time would tell.

He donned the new Indian winter coat and went

out to talk with the mules.

"Hiya. You all doing okay? You two miss old Jed? I sure do. Amos, how are you? Are you warm enough? Finding sufficient browse to keep your belly full? It's real important in this cold weather. I won't be riding you much when the snow comes in deep. We might go out some to look for a deer. Fresh meat is as important to me as fresh browse is for you.

Y'all know what I forgot in my planning? Gloves! My hands are going to freeze. Now, unlike Ma, I am not good at sewing. I figure I can get two decent mittens made out of one beaver pelt though. Sounds like a project for tonight, huh?" The mules seemed to like the conversation. Only Amos made the odd noise, but he knew the contact helped mules and man.

He went to the tanning shed and picked a pelt. Using a charcoal stick, he made the outline for one mitten. He cut it out with a Green River knife and duplicated it three more times. Tonight, he would sew the four pieces with the luxuriant fur outside. Once finished, he would turn them inside out and have a fine pair of mittens. He would make a slit on the inside of each mitten for his trigger finger. He could fire Jed's Hawken rifle or his fusil with either hand while wearing the mittens.

"I've been smoking the hides outside to keep them soft. It looks like I will be catching beaver into the winter. It will be snowing a lot of the time I need to smoke hides. Maybe I could build a smoking kiln inside the tanning shed. It would extend my season," Israel thought aloud.

He sat and contemplated how to do it, then set out to build the kiln with left over rocks from the chimney. Boonesboro chimney builder Gideon Cross taught Arthur and him to always collect and save more stones than necessary for repairs and additions. He had automatically done it when adding a chimney to the cabin. A week later, Israel was smoking hides inside after tanning and stretching them. What pleased him the most was the smoke did not permeate into the main cabin.

Having built a smoker, he realized it had other uses. He had collected a number of mushrooms. He would smoke those for winter use. He also decided to both smoke and salt fish caught in the stream and lake. He fished during his trips to check his beaver traps and collected a number of fish to smoke. He decided to put salt on them also, not really knowing anything about smoking or salting fish.

By mid-winter, he was snowed in. Snow blew with heavy winds. He put on his snow shoes, heavy coat and mittens and checked the traps every day or two. His catch dwindled as the beavers stayed in their lodges.

Israel finished the plays of Shakespeare and read the Bible cover to cover. The only thing he had left was the Farmer's Almanac Jed had left. He finished it by the end of what he reckoned must be February. He kept a board cut out of a log with hash marks to record days, so he was within three or four days of knowing the actual date. It was important so he would not miss rendezvous.

"I should do well this year. Lots of pelts and my tanning has gotten good. I need to ride Amos and use both of Jed's mules for transporting bundles of pelts. I sure hope I can get coin instead of barter goods for my pelts," he thought.

He needed to take money back to Hannah to survive while he trapped the next season. Israel began forming an idea. He had no clue how she would respond to it. He wanted her to come out to the Windy with him while he trapped. He knew Arthur and his sister had commitments and probably could not get away. He decided to work on his pitch to her about becoming a mountain girl.

Late in the day towards the middle of March, he heard the mules raising a ruckus.

Israel grabbed the Hawkin and checked its lock. He put on his coat and possibles bag and ran out the door to the noise. It was coming from down by the stream. There were already patches of green there and the mules had been foraging there of a couple days.

He immediately saw what the problem was. A medium grizzly was just up from hibernation and saw the mules as a viable dinner. As the bear ran towards Amos, the mule turned and gave him a hard kick with both hind legs. The bear squealed and backed off. The three mules circled and developed defensive postures.

From fifty yards, Israel took careful aim and shot the bear behind the shoulder. It should have been a kill shot.

The bear did not get the message and turned to face his new adversary.

Israel did not measure his powder. He poured in a copious quantity and rammed a patched ball home. He spilled priming powder as he rushed to prime the lock.

By the time the lock was cocked and the rifle was up to his shoulder, the charging bear was barely ten feet distant.

Israel pulled the light set front trigger and the big rifle boomed. He stepped to the side and held the rifle like a club by the barrel and fore stock. He could not see the bear in the cloud of smoke.

Within seconds, he saw a dead bear almost at his feet.

"Sure beats my last bear encounter!" he said aloud and thanked the good Lord for him still being alive and unscathed. Especially without his Bowie knife.

Israel checked the mules, now munching away again. None of the three had any injuries he could see.

He walked back to the cabin and got a rope and the

sawbuck pack saddle. He returned and put the saddle on Jed's pack mule. He tied the bear around the hind feet and guided the mule dragging him back to the cabin. Keeping the hind feet tied, he threw the loose end of the rope over a stout tree limb.

He tied the end on the sawbuck saddle and moved the mule so the bear was hung upside down.

Israel bled him then gutted him. He left the rest of the butchering and skinning for morning. He would have to be alert for wolves after his prize bear tonight. He had the mule pull the bear higher and tied him off to the tree trunk. The meat was now out of predator reach.

Israel would slice strips of bear meat for jerky and bits to preserve for pemmican as soon as berries were available. He would butcher steaks and loins and salt them down for later use. The job would take all day tomorrow.

He took stock of his meat supplies. Israel reckoned he had more than he needed. The snow was down to around a foot deep.

He loaded a lot of bear meat and the untanned skin on the sawbuck saddle the next day and started off for the Kiowa village. Israel knew they had a lot of people to feed and relatively few hunters. He walked ahead of the bear and gift laden pack mule. Between the mule walking through snow and him wearing snow shoes, the trip took much longer than normal and it took him most of the day to get there.

His gifts to his friends were greatly appreciated. He gave the bearskin to Lone Bear. Israel knew his wife was a master tanner. He suspected White Feather, Lone Bear's favorite person in the world, would end up with it.

He also brought coffee beans, a great treasure to the Kiowas. They had coffee and pemmican for dinner and smoked a pipe, passed around the fire from chief to guest to elders.

It was a ceremony to commemorate a friend bearing gifts. Israel realized how much he had missed human contact over the winter months.

Lone Bear got him to recount the story of his first bear attack and show the scar and the claw he wore around his neck. Then, the story of this bear. Lone Bear shared what he called Israel's Indian name with his elders.

"Bear Fighter. It is so. Proven by his scars and his gift to his Kiowa friends," the chief said.

As the men began to leave for their own teepees, Lone Bear motioned towards a space near his own bedroll.

"It is too late and too cold to ride back to the mountain, Bear Fighter. Stay here where it is warm and you will be surrounded by friends."

"I would be honored, Lone Bear," he said, worrying only about the tall pretty granddaughter who had been smiling at him ever since he arrived. She was Hannah's age, and seemed far more mature. He had thought about her many times during his winter solitude, "I have more wife than I can really handle right now. I sure don't need a raven-haired flirt. It is so," he quoted his friend silently. He was almost relieved when she adjourned to her own teepee for the night. Almost.

Israel made it back to his cabin the next day and resumed his routine. White Feather let no stoicism show. She was visibly saddened with him leaving. It was still cold, but he could feel an improvement in the weather. He planned to head to rendezvous around the first of June, now a month off.

He added more tanned pelts to the shed.

"I may have to use all three mules to take pelts and walk, leading them the whole two day's to rendez-vous," he said aloud.

Israel pulled in all the traps and considered his trapping season over. He realized he had made a mistake and trapped too late into the year. He trapped during breeding season, which would likely impact his harvest of pelts during the coming season.

"Jed, where are you when I need your advice, old friend?" he asked rhetorically.

He had some decisions to make before leaving. Israel knew he could not take both the Hawken and the trade musket or fusil. There were other things he needed to leave behind also. He decided to carry the Hawken rifle to rendezvous and on to Boonesboro.

He had to make a cache for the items to be left. He went into the woods behind the cabin and dug what reminded him of a grave. He lined it with clay, followed by small logs. Israel then built a rack above the ground and put his cached objects on it. The fusil was covered with bear grease and rolled in a deer skin. He draped an oiled skin over the rack and filled the hole with dirt. He carefully covered the surface with leaves and twigs. When he had finished, nobody would be able to tell anything was below. He scraped a maple tree with his Green River knife. It could have been a deer antler scraping.

When the time came, he saddled the mules and loaded the pelts on Jed's two. There were pelts left over and he knew he would have to walk, leading all three. Israel placed the remaining pelts on Amos and tied them down with his blankets and camping gear. He carried the Hawken in a sling over his shoulder.

"Sorry, boy. I know you aren't a pack mule. But, you have to do this for me once."

He could swear the mule looked at him with reproach, then turned his gaze away from the man.

Israel stopped at the Kiowa village. There was activity and he asked what was going on.

"We are going to rendezvous," Lone Bear said. "We have items to trade. The women have been busy all winter tanning hides and making fringed leggings, coats and moccasins like you are wearing. We will trade these things for tobacco, wool blankets, and muskets with powder.

You should delay a day and go with us. It will be a nice one day walk, Bear Fighter."

"I will do it, my friend."

The next morning a contingent of about ten tribal members left. They walked, except for Lone Bear. The other horses pulled travois with their camping gear and trade goods on them.

The members of the tribe were as excited to see the rendezvous as was the young mountain man.

******

The small procession could hear banjo and fiddle music and smell food stewing over fires well before arriving. Israel realized his sense of smell had heightened living in the wilderness. He had learned to be more aware and the air seemed more pure. Towns had so many people, animals, mills and food cooking it all seemed to blend together.

In the wilderness, everything seemed more distinct.

Jed had told him he would "go Indian" before he knew it. The old mountain man emphasized it would be a good thing when he did.

"You get Lone Bear to teach you about Indian beliefs and their religion. I promise you will like it and take to it," Jed suggested.

Israel led the three mules beside Lone Bear's horse and mentioned it. Lone Bear spent the whole ride telling him about Indian beliefs about nature and creation and stewardship of the land. As always, the old mountain man had been right. And, strangely, Israel thought, little of what he heard conflicted with his Christian beliefs developed from his nighttime Bible reading.

The Kiowas set up several teepees and made fire circles a half mile outside the perimeter of the noisy gathering.

Israel left his furs with them and walked into the rendezvous.

He was wearing his original wide brim hat, a fringed buckskin war shirt, matching leggings, a breechclout, and moccasins. He had a tomahawk and Green River knife in his belt and possible bag over his shoulder. Israel carried the early model flintlock Hawkin Brothers rifle.

Except for his still sparse beard, he looked like a fully seasoned mountain man.

The trading post owner was busy and Israel politely waited his turn. The man did not recognize him immediately.

"You are the young man with Jed Hunt. Did Jed make it?" he asked.

"Nossir. He passed in late fall. I buried him right where he wanted. He was a fine man. If I have a son, he will be John Hunt Pope."

"John? Wasn't his real name Jedediah?" the man asked.

"He told me everybody always thought so, but it was John."

"How was your trapping season, Pope?"

"I have nothing to compare it to. I have three mules loaded with pelts waiting with my Kiowa friends just outside your encampment here," Israel said.

"So, you came with Lone Bear? He is a good man."

"He is. I need your advice on selling my pelts. I will pick up trade materials on the way back through in the fall. I need to sell for gold or silver coins to take home to my wife in Kentucky."

"You are early, so gold or silver will not be a problem. I will write down a fair price on a scrap of paper for you. Don't take a penny less. Let the buyer mention his price first. It may be higher than this. You should not hesitate to bargain. How is your tanning work?"

Israel led him out to inspect the pelts.

"Judging by what I see here, your tanning is pretty good. I think you have a knack for it.

Take all your pelts around and let them see how well they are tanned and cleaned. It will help the price they pay you. Will you be coming back in the fall?"

"I will. Maybe late summer. Perhaps I will bring my wife," Israel said.

"Can she stand being shut in during the winter blizzards up on the Windy?" the owner asked.

"I will describe it to her and ask. I don't really know," Israel said.

"Fatherly advice Jed would give you? Avoid the card games, drinking booths and whoring tents. You will get poor from the first and sick from the other two. I mean it, son. Sell your pelts, walk through and experience this thing we call rendezvous, say goodbye to Lone Bear and head to Kentucky to your wife. I will see you on the way back through. Before leaving, stop in to see me. You can buy whatever you might need for the trip, like powder, lead, pemmican and jerky and the like."

"I will take your advice. It is much like what my Pa told me about Hell Town on the Shenandoah when a couple of us took a gundalow up. I followed his advice and will yours."

They heard yelling and a general commotion in the middle of the trade tent area. Israel saw a man the owner identified as the sheriff running towards the noise.

"We better check on what's going on," the trading post owner said.

The trader at a pelt tent was yelling. They arrived just as the sheriff did.

"I've been robbed of all my purchase money! It was

two men. They looked like gamblers, not mountain men or Indians." He pointed in their direction of travel.

"How long ago?" the sheriff asked.

"Just now. They are headed in the direction of the Indian camp!"

"It will take a few minutes to round up a posse," the sheriff said.

******

Israel peered in their direction. He saw small puffs of dust. They must have hidden mounts at the edge of the rendezvous.

"Sheriff, we don't need a posse. You and I can get them if we leave now," he said.

"Alright, young man. Raise your right hand." Israel did.

"You are deputized. You got a horse?"

"I have a mule at the Kiowa camp. We have to go there anyway."

Israel ran and the sheriff trotted his horse alongside.

"Lone Bear, did you see two whites ride past here a few minutes ago?" Israel asked as he mounted Amos.

"Yes. They were riding like squirrels with their tails on fire," his friend said. His beautiful granddaughter stood, eyes firmly fixed on Israel. He smiled at her. He could not help smiling every time he saw her.

Israel and the sheriff took off in pursuit.

Amos not only kept up with the sheriff's old horse but began to pull ahead.

They introduced one another on the run over to the camp.

"Sheriff Lamb, I see them ahead."

"We are chasing escaping felons. When you get a clear shot, take it."

Israel never shot a man before but had no qualms.

When they got within a hundred yards, he raised the Hawken and cocked it. He took aim and pressed the trigger. The rear robber fell from his horse. He hit the ground hard and bounced several times. If the ball did not kill him, the fall would have, Israel thought.

Without missing a hoofbeat, they rode as Israel reloaded in his saddle.

The shot just sped the other man along with more alacrity.

As they passed the one Israel shot, they saw his eyes wide open in the sun.

"Humph. Guess he's dead," the sheriff said without slowing down.

Israel's next shot was from two hundred yards. It knocked the hat from the rider's head. Apparently, it scared him so badly he fell off his horse. He scrambled up as the horse rode on. He was staggering around, holding what appeared to be a broken right arm.

"Fine shooting, Pope. You want to stay on as a deputy?"

"No, I have a wife in Kentucky to get back to. But, thanks anyhow."

Israel rode off to collect the two loose horses. One had the money on it. The sheriff stayed to question the injured suspect.

Israel found the first man's horse near his body. He strained and got the corpse on the saddle and tied his midriff to the saddle horn and his feet together with a rope running under the horse's belly. Sheriff Lamb had the man with the broken arm mounted when Israel got back.

"Lifting this man gives new meaning to the term 'dead weight,'" Israel told the sheriff.

"What will happen to the prisoner?" he asked.

"We don't have a prison nearby. I'll probably let him go, broken arm and all. Vigilantes might track him down and hang him. I doubt they will be able to leave the whiskey and loose women at the rendezvous long enough to fool with him though.

I sure would not want you on my trail, Pope," the sheriff said as he hung the money bag on his saddle horn and slapped the surviving man's horse. The horse took off in the direction the men had been escaping. "Better an uncomfortable ride than a noose," Israel thought.

They rode past the Kiowa camp on the way back to the rendezvous.

Lone Bear nodded and his granddaughter smiled.

******

Israel walked the pelt tents, looking for the best price. He found it at the tent of the man whose thousand dollars he recovered.

Just as he was told, he was able to beat the price the trading post owner gave him on the scrap of paper and to be paid in gold and silver coins.

Israel felt rich. He had a multiple of what he expected to earn. He also had his year's earnings all at one time. Feeling grateful, he went shopping.

He bought moccasins and a beaded Indian dress for Hannah, his ma, and Maude. He got an upscale Green River knife for Arthur and for his pa. He purchased moccasin boots for himself and a wool trade blanket and two pounds of tobacco for Lone Bear. He bought necklaces for Lone Bear's wife and White Feather.

Israel walked back to the Kiowa encampment. Lone Bear was pleased with his gifts, as were his wife and granddaughter.

"I will head back to Kentucky today for the summer. I will be back when the leaves begin to turn colors and the wind gets cooler. Perhaps my wife, Hannah, will come. I don't know, my friend."

Lone Bear nodded his acknowledgement. Israel learned early in their friendship the chief used nods, more than wasting words, to communicate. It was a trait he began to emulate himself.

As he turned to mount Amos, White Feather grabbed him in a tight hug. She buried her face in his buckskin shirt. He did not know what to do, so he returned it.

"Come back alone. I will be waiting," she whispered so only he could hear.

He smiled at her and said "I don't know what the awaits me in Kentucky, so I cannot give you a real answer now."

Israel turned Amos eastward and rode, leading Jed's mule Henry, towards where he would get a Mississippi broadhorn down to St. Louis. The front of his buckskins where White Feather's face had been was wet. He left the pack mule in Lone Bear's care until his return.

He put spending coins in his money pouch and secreted the rest in several places in his gear. If he was robbed, he wanted to protect as much as possible.

The road to the Mississippi was clear and recognizable from the trip out. He met experienced mountain men, beginners and pilgrims all along the way.

He found a big gundalow heading downstream to St. Louis. He did not have to pay the higher tariff for a steam-powered one. He got Amos and Henry settled in the stock corral and found a place up front where he could watch the river on three sides.

The Mississippi, with snow melt at its headwaters, flowed fast. The trip with the current was faster than going against it had been, even with steam.

St. Louis came into view much sooner than he expected. He saddled Amos and tied his gear on.

There were two last purchases he wanted to make. It took him an hour of visiting stores to find the one he wanted.

One was a replacement Bowie knife. He had heard the famous knife fighter went to Tejas in the Mexican territory to settle. The blades had evolved over the past few years.

This one had a blade over eleven inches. It had a deeply clipped point with the top quarter sharpened almost as sharp as the bottom. The rest of the top had a soft brass strip to catch the blade of an adversary's knife in a fight.

Israel's hand would be protected by a double iron guard, called a quillon. The handle was walnut and in the shape of a coffin. It came with a well-finished leather belt sheath. Israel immediately put some of his bear grease on it to soften and protect it.

His second shopping plan was for some new books and found three. He bought several books by Sir Walter Scott, Frankenstein, and a book of poetry by Edgar Allan Poe.

Israel was not sure which purchases excited him the most. The knife was needed, but the books were wanted. Either way, he was pleased with both types of purchases.

After a year without one, it was comforting to have a Bowie on his belt.

He made it back to Boonesboro by mid-June.

As he rode down the Boonesboro Road from Lexington, he did not get a feeling of home. The Wind River Range was home. He hoped Hannah would join him there.

There was a horse tied to a tree at his cabin. Israel noted it was tied where it could be seen from his parent's cabin, but not from Arthur's.

He dropped the reins on Amos and listened. He did not like the sounds of pleasure coming from within the cabin. Leaving the Hawkin leaning against a tree, he pulled the big Bowie and kicked the door in.

The view he saw was the one he wanted the least to see. Some young fellow in bed on top of his wife.

The man turned, shocked and scared but in a defensive manner.

The look on Hannah's face was stark terror.

The man, who appeared to be about Israel's age, rolled and grabbed a skinning knife off the table beside the bed. He sprang up wearing just his shirt.

The two moved at each other and circled as Hannah screamed.

Israel feinted with the Bowie and the man jumped back, tripping on the bed and hitting the floor.

He got up and stabbed at Israel, wounding him slightly. Israel avoided the killing jab and slashed down, off balance. The man swung his hand down and their wrists hit, knocking Israel's blade further down.

The razor sharp Bowie blade almost emasculated the man who had cuckolded him. Blood gushed from the wound and the man screamed in a sound reminding Israel of a Wind River mountain lion late at night. Hannah had not stopped screaming.

The man sat back against the bed, rocking back and forth holding his wound and moaning.

A shadow darkened the door and Israel spun around, ready to kill.

He lowered he knife when he saw it was Arthur with his shotgun.

"What the hell, my brother?" Arthur said, adding "I saw him roll outta bed with Hannah and grab his knife. We need to get the sheriff and I will tell him what I witnessed."

"I agree, Arthur. We have to do it. If it was up to me, I'd bury them both deep in the woods and clean up the blood," Israel said, staring at his wife.

"No, Israel, I think Tom here will suffer the rest of his life from his wound and the embarrassment."

"How about me? You bring in the sheriff and what will I look like?" Hannah screamed.

"It's a little late for you to worry about your reputation, don't you think?" Israel asked her through clinched teeth. His tone made her blood run cold.

"If your pa is sober, we will send him for the sheriff.

If not, I'll go," Arthur said.

"Sober? He does not imbibe."

"He started drinking when your ma died a few months ago, Israel. I'm sorry."

What he thought would be a happy day ended up quite the opposite. A pregnant Maude appeared and ran to him, crying.

"Maude, please check on Pa and see if we can trust his worthless ass to fetch the law," Israel said softly.

Hannah still sat in the bed naked, the top half of her body in full view.

"Cover yourself, damn it!" Israel ordered.

No wonder his parents had not interfered with Hannah's extramarital activities, Israel thought. Ma was dead and Pa was drunk. Where the horse was tied, Arthur could not see it.

"I planned on staying here for the summer. I will leave tomorrow and go back to the Wind River Range. I will think about whether to allow you to go with me or stay and face the shame with your friend here. I don't much care either way right now."

He turned his back to her as Maude returned.

"Pa is passed out. I reckon Arthur, who says he saw most of it will have to make a report to the sheriff," she said.

Arthur agreed and took Amos to save time.

"Stay here and doctor up your boyfriend, Hannah. I don't want to see you until I leave tomorrow. Anybody who approaches my camp in the woods tonight dies on the spot," Israel said coldly.

He walked out the door with his sister.

"Not the welcome you expected," she observed.

"No. Maude, when and how did Ma die?"

"I think she kind of gave up with Pa's worthlessness, Israel. We all knew it. She was loyal and suffered in silence for years. She told me towards the end she was glad you and I took after her pa and not our own. She caught a cough and didn't fight the sickness. She's buried in the churchyard."

"When are you due, Maude?" he asked his sister.

"I'm not real sure. Probably around November or so."

"I know you and Arthur are happy. I sure am happy about you expecting. I cannot think of better parents anywhere on this earth."

"We are happy. He talks about us coming out to live near you. Neither of us ever really liked how crowded Kentucky was by the time Pa dragged us here," she said.

"It's sure beautiful country. The sky goes on forever, the streams are cold and pure. The only problem is when winter hits, you are inside for a few months. I went out to work the traplines, or to get meat from the shed, or go to the privy. Otherwise, I read by candle light."

"I don't see being cabin bound so horrible. If a

wanderlust like you can do it, Arthur and I can, too."

"Maude, I am going to give Hannah one chance and one chance only. If she goes with me and can learn how to be a trustworthy wife, so be it. If she stays, I will see a judge in Lexington and get the marriage broken. With Arthur's testimony along with my own, it would be a simple trial."

"Israel, you are 'way more fair than I would be. I'd leave her ass here to stew in the juices she caused. Maybe she will stay with Tom, the miller's son. I sure don't think they will be having any children. Your Bowie seems to have grown since you left. How did such a thing happen?"

"New one. I gave the old one to a friend who is chief of the Kiowa tribe near me. He and John Hunt are the wisest men I ever knew."

"Who's John Hunt?" she asked.

"A well-educated mountain man who took me under wing. He taught me how to trap, track and generally stay alive. I buried him up on the mountain. He lived a full life until eighty."

Israel was coming down from the stress caused by any life threatening fight. He had no thoughts of regret about the result of the fight. Nor would he if he had killed this Tom person.

"How do you feel about slicing up Tom?" Maude asked.

"It was him or me. I didn't mean to cut him how I

did. I meant to slash his gut. His hand knocked mine down and he suffered for it. I really meant to kill him in self-defense."

"So, you weren't aiming there for retribution?" Maude asked.

"Nope. Not at all."

"You're not blaming him?"

"No more than her. It takes two pigs to wrestle in the mud. She's as much at fault as he is."

"If she leaves with you in the morning, are you planning on killing and quietly burying her along the way?"

"Probably not," he said, looking his sister in the eye.

"You are different as a mountain man. Different from my big brother. What happened, Israel?"

"I guess I grew up. I saw the survival of the toughest in the Wind River country. I learned from Jed and from Chief Lone Bear. My Indian name is Bear Fighter. I learned from him, too," he said, fingering the claw around his neck. Maude understood him. Probably better than anyone else.

"You look pretty happy, Maude."

"How could I not be. I have a wonderful husband, a wonderful brother and little Israel or Mary growing for delivery in late fall," she said.

"Who's Mary?" he asked.

"Arthur's mother."

"Oh. Is she still alive?"

"Yes, back in Virginia. Have you and Arthur talked about the mountains where you live?"

"No, Maude. It's been a bit busy since I arrived. Tonight, though," he said.

They heard hoofbeats.

"Must be Arthur and the sheriff. I guess we'd better greet them. I don't want to appear to be a fugitive from the law," Israel said.

"Well, boy. You've gone all mountain man since I saw you a year ago," the sheriff greeted Israel.

"It's my calling, sheriff. I'll be going back tomorrow. This was not the reception I expected," Israel said.

"Arthur told me what he saw. Why don't you give me your side of the story?"

Israel told him and showed him the puncture wound. Israel's story and Arthur's were exactly the same. The sheriff went in to question Tom. Hannah had gotten the midwife, Sadie Peters, who was tending Tom.

His story was essentially the same. Adding "I wish I had let him kill me. I parried and hit his wrist with mine and knocked the big knife down to my unprotected region."

The sheriff took Hannah by the arm and led her roughly out to the yard where Israel, his sister and brother-in-law waited.

"I have heard the stories and all agree. Adultery is a crime in Kentucky. Most judges designate a number of lashes in public for the participants. As a frontier sheriff, I have some leeway in selective enforcement of the law based on circumstance. We don't have judges and courthouses around every tree.

It is my feeling, Tom Alston has received a life sentence of embarrassment. Unless you, Israel, demand his arrest, I figure on letting him go.

Now, Mistress Pope. I understand you have choice to make. Either stay here as a tainted woman or go out West with your legal husband. Am I correct?" he said staring at Hannah.

"You are, sir."

"What is your choice?" he asked.

"I will leave tomorrow and go to the Wind River Range to live with my husband," she responded.

"You go West, young woman and I will forget your name. You ever come back into my jurisdiction, I will arrest you for adultery. Do you understand me?" he asked.

"I do, Sheriff. I surely do."

He mounted a fine Kentucky horse and rode off without another word.

Israel turned to his friend and his sister.

"Might we have one last family dinner tonight, before Hannah and I head out in the morning?" Israel asked.

"If you think it the best thing under the circumstances, sure we can," Arthur said.

"I bought some things for everybody. We won't know when we'll get together again, so why not risk dinner?" Israel said.

"We have plenty of fresh vegetables, but not much meat," Arthur said.

"I brought some smoked trout from the mountains, Arthur, as well as bear jerky," Israel said.

"Hannah and I can add fry bread to the menu," Maude said. Hannah had yet to talk, wondering where all this was going. Maude took her sister-in-law aside and suggested she go down to the stream and wash Tom's blood and other fluids off before dinner. Israel heard and handed her a folded buckskin dress and moccasins to put on. She was shocked he would give her a gift after today's fight. He did not explain. He just returned to conversing with Arthur.

Hannah returned to help fix dinner. She had braided her hair and put the Indian dress and moccasins on. She could have passed for an Indian, except for her light eyes.

They settled to eat. Israel missed the fresh vegetables in his solitary life.

"The area around the trading post where the rendezvous is held is ranchland or, perhaps, farmland. People are settling there. A builder of chimneys and even cabins would stay busy when he was not farming," he told Arthur.

Israel was complete and frank about living along

the Green River. He spoke candidly of the long hard winters, stuck in one's cabin for months.

"Is there much Indian activity?" Maude asked.

"The nearby Kiowa are good people and my best friends in the region. I reckon you could get a raiding party through one day. Maybe Sioux, Arapaho, or Cheyenne. Has not happened yet, to my knowledge."

"Tell me about the Kiowas," Hannah asked, speaking for the first time.

"They are tall, handsome people. The chief's granddaughter is a year younger than you, but is already almost as tall as I am. He is a wise man and gives me good advice. We have discussed Indian religion and I want to learn more from him. They live in teepees which are warmer and more stable in the winds than my cabin. They do not waste anything and revere the earth like a religion," Israel responded.

"How do the teepee's stay warm in the winter?" Arthur asked.

"They have a fire ring in the center. The skins of which they are made are wind and waterproof. The smoke from the fire is drawn up through the opening in the top. Interestingly, it is the women who own the teepees," Israel said.

"Well, who owns the land?" Hannah asked.

"The Great Spirit, or God."

"How do they sleep?" Maude asked.

"In pallets of bearskin or other skins on the ground.

The teepees are dry and warm inside. In the summer, they open the flaps at the top more and open the door. The flaps seem to me to catch the breeze."

"Do they have a perfect life?" Hannah asked.

"No, nobody really does. They get hungry sometimes when game is scarce, or cold if they have not put away enough wood, I guess. But, they seem to me to be a happy people who plan for the future and accept what comes. I'd say their outlook on life is better than most of us will ever have."

Israel had brought presents. His father had sobered enough to join them for dinner and did not speak. He merely nodded at his prodigal son.

"You see Hannah's gift of dress and moccasins. Maude I got you and Ma the same. Ma's was a little larger. You might need hers for now and yours for after the baby." He gave the dresses and moccasins to her.

"Arthur and Pa, I got each of you a good Green River knife and beaded sheath. And, brought you some coin. We work on shares here."

He gave two bags of gold and silver coins to the men. The bags appeared similar, but Arthur's was much heavier. Today, he had made Arthur's heavier yet so his father would not pour money he did not earn down his throat.

He talked at length about the Wind River Range and the good farmland and ranch land along the Green River and its tributaries. He said he hoped

Arthur would follow him out with his family when he returned in less than a year. Arthur nodded almost imperceptibly, but Israel caught it.

Quite unlike the plans he had riding into Boonesboro, Israel made a camp in the woods. He built a small fire pit, though it was warm out. He used the fire to brew a pot of coffee and sat drinking it under sparkling stars.

He heard a twig snap and moved back from the fire, his Hawken rifle at the ready.

"Don't kill me, Israel. It's Hannah. I am scared and want to be next to you."

"Come to the fire."

When he saw it was her, he uncocked the rifle and put it down.

She went straight to his bedroll, took off the buckskin dress and got in.

Israel slowly sipped his coffee from the pewter mug. He focused on the cicadas and the night birds. He listened to the wind move through the trees. Finally, tired and ready to sleep, he crawled into the bedroll. His wife nestled in by him and cried softly.

He put his arm around her and presently she fell asleep.

Israel Pope, mountain man, laid awake for hours staring at the stars…. Wondering what he was going to do.

CHAPTER 4

They left early the next morning. Hannah rode astride Henry like a man. Or, as White Feather would have ridden. They made good time to St. Louis and found a northbound steam broadhorn.

They talked when necessary. If Hannah was thinking about her lover, it did not show. She was quiet most of the way. They opened a sack and shared a lunch of cornpone, cold bacon left over from breakfast before boarding, and water.

They had chosen a location near the bow, but out of the way of the boatman handling the long bow sweep oar.

"Are we going to talk about this, or remain silent for the duration of our years?" Hannah asked.

"What would you like to talk about?"

"My actions. I was wrong and I'm sorry. I was lonely and I made a mistake. Weren't you lonely while you were cooped up in the cabin for months?" she asked.

"Yes."

"And, what did you do about it?"

"I thought about you, Hannah."

She did not have a response for his answer.

After a while, she spoke again.

"Will you ever forgive me?" she asked.

"I already have. You made a mistake. You apologized. You chose me over this Tom, or you wouldn't be on this boat now."

"Will we be happy and live a long, happy marriage?"

"I am not a fortune teller. I don't see why not though," he said.

"Do we have a long way to go?"

"Are you asking about relationship or travel?"

"Travel. I have had enough of relationship talk."

"Yes, it's a long ways from here. We will travel upriver to a place called Ft. Armstrong. We'll get off and ride to Des Moines, then on to Omaha. Omaha will be the last big trading post. From there, we will head west to the Wind River Range. Depending on stops, it will take three weeks from here. A lot of it will be crossing prairie."

"Will you love me again by then?" she asked.

"Love is a steady thing. It doesn't disappear and reappear like blowing out and relighting a candle. Stop worrying about it and let nature take its course, Hannah."

She moved over closer to him and went to sleep. She was a pretty young woman in a buckskin Indian dress, immodest for the time. It showed a scandalous amount of ankle and calf. The other passengers noticed her. They also noticed a very serious young mountain man husband with a big Hawken rifle and one of the largest Bowie knives yet seen on the upper Mississippi River. Most kept their glances to themselves. The few who didn't got a warning glare in return.

Whether from travel or the emotions of the past few days, Hannah slept until dark.

Israel put a wool trade blanket around them. It was off-white with red and blue stripes. The wool kept the damp night winds from chilling them. It was nice after a long winter, to have a soft woman with her head on his shoulder and her warmth to keep him comfortable as he kept watch.

They picked up their bags and set them on the dock at Ft. Armstrong. Hannah, with a Green River knife in her belt, guarded their belongings. She had no idea how much gold and coin was hidden in them. Israel retrieved the two mules and their saddles from the stock pen at the stern of the broadhorn and brought them to the side to offload. It took several weeks to pass through Des Moines and reach Omaha.

"This is the last serious shopping we will hit. Is there anything you need or want?" Israel asked.

"I could use some linen for female reasons. Maybe a winter coat and boots for the cold weather you have been warning me about."

"All reasonable. We also need to get staples like coffee, flour, corn meal, some sides of bacon, salt, gun powder and lead. A real shovel, saw, another bucket, and a logging chain would help a lot."

"Can we afford all those things?" she asked.

"Yes, but we will have to shop carefully and save some money for later."

They purchased all the items on their list as well as gifts for Lone Bear and his wife and granddaughter.

Israel also found a fifty-four caliber horse pistol. It took a heavy charge and had a leather scabbard which hung on the saddle horn. It used the same caliber balls as the Hawken. Unlike the long guns, it had the newer percussion lock. Israel knew it would not be shot as much as the rifle and the trade musket, so a can of one hundred percussion caps would last for a long time.

Israel hung it on Henry's saddle horn for Hannah. Along the way, he loaded it and had her fire and re-load several times. He had never shot a percussion pistol before. He found it amazingly accurate and powerful. It could knock down a horse, a deer and possibly a small bear. There should be no doubt about its short range effect on two-legged varmints, Israel told his wife.

Israel pointed out the Wind River Range looming

on the horizon. They were still a long ways from the mountains, but the day was bright and clear. By the middle of the day, they arrived at the trading post where the rendezvous was held most years.

They stopped and bought last minute fresh vegetables and a side of salt cured ham. Israel also got a wedge to use splitting logs for the fireplace.

He peered into the distance and did not see the Kiowa village.

"Where are my Kiowa friends?" he asked.

"They moved closer to the mountains. Closer to you also. They are on this side of the lake you trap on. I am guessing the camp is five or six miles from your cabin."

"Excellent. Lone Bear and his family are good friends. I'm glad they will be closer neighbors," Israel said, hiding his concern about the flirtatious White Feather and the questionable Hannah living too close for comfort. He knew he had to stop at the village on the way back and deliver his gifts. It was the right thing to do, no matter how awkward it was.

They rode on and circled the lake to arrive at the village. Several warriors rode out to escort them in.

"Bear Fighter, you have brought your squaw to meet us," was Lone Bear's greeting. With some trepidation, Israel stole a glance at White Feather. She was smiling warmly. "Thank, God!" he thought. After her parting message, he was worried she would run off in tears or come at Hannah with a skinning knife.

"I have. This is Hannah. She, of course, needs a good Indian name, Lone Bear."

"We must think on the matter. A name is a serious thing. Young woman, do you know what your mother was thinking, or maybe heard as you were being born?"

Hannah was baffled but thought for a moment.

"She told me the house next to us was on fire while I was being born. They could not move her because I was already visible in birth," she ventured.

"If she was Indian, she would have named you something like Born with Fire," Lone Bear said.

Hannah shocked Israel with her next words.

"She was half Mattaponi Indian. My name is Hannah Fire Winder. The 'Fire' is short for 'Girl Who Was Born With Fire,'" she said.

Lone Bear smiled.

"Fire is a good name. I will call you Fire. Tell me about the Mattaponi tribe."

"The Mattaponi Tribe is an old tribe. They live near a river of the same name in the eastern part of Virginia. My mother is descended from the great chief Powhatan and his daughter, Pocahontas."

"Damn!" Israel thought, "I have two Indian women, one pretty and one beautiful. This is going to be uncomfortable."

White Feather was still smiling.

"What is she scheming?" Israel wondered. Finally, she spoke.

"You are my friend's wife and my Indian sister. I will visit you. Perhaps I can show you Indian ways and you can teach me white ways?" she said to Hannah.

"I would like it if you visited. I feared I would be lonely with only Israel."

Israel saw a faint cloud pass over both Lone Bear's and White Feather's faces at her suggestion their friend would not be sufficient company for her. Both remained stoic and Hannah missed the message.

"Girl Who Was Born With Fire and I have brought some small gifts for you," Israel said, hoping to change the subject. He reached into the packs on the sawbuck saddle and withdrew three Hudson's Bay blankets, tobacco, some pewter mugs, and a sack of candy. He remembered how much his friends had appreciated the remainder of Jed's birthday candy.

The men smoked and talked. White Feather and Hannah wandered off somewhere, leaving Israel very uncomfortable. What if only White Feather returned?

He took a puff and passed the pipe to the warrior next to him.

Hannah returned intact and still smiling.

They had another hour's riding and left well before dark.

"What a beautiful view!" Hannah exclaimed as the cabin appeared on the side of a hill.

Israel checked it for vermin and used his flint and steel to spark a fire. It did not appear anyone had used it during his fairly brief absence. He viewed his bed. It was larger than Jed's simply because Israel was a much taller man. Perhaps he and Hannah could both fit in it. Otherwise, he would have to get his axe and new saw out.

He shouldered the mattress sack and took it outside while Hannah was unpacking their gear. Using a Green River knife to avoid sticky sap on his Bowie, Israel collected fresh spruce boughs to fill the mattress for comfort and aroma.

Hannah brought the items she unpacked into the cabin.

"So, our bed is ready. We should use it. I have been thinking about it."

"Aren't you hungry," he asked.

"No, White Feather and I picked and ate berries as we walked through the woods. I like her. She really is striking to look at. I thought I would be jealous, but I'm not."

Israel took the last comment without responding.

He finished placing longer storage life items in the root cellar he dug months ago. When he returned to the cabin, he saw Hannah sitting up in bed, her bare shoulders showing. She motioned him to her. Stomach growling from no dinner, he joined her for the rest of the evening.

The next morning, she looked up from his shoulder and asked, "would you rather have had White Feather here last night?"

Israel looked at her for a long time before answering.

"Where do you get this stuff? You are ruining any chance we might have of a normal marriage with stupid questions, Hannah. It's not like if you don't like an answer you can walk down the street and hop on a steam train home. Even if you could, where is home? How about grow the hell up and take what we've got and make the best of it?"

Israel had no idea what she was thinking. She just nestled back into his shoulder and went back to sleep. "Is she alright in the head?" he asked himself silently. He thought about it as she snored quietly.

"Yes. She's not crazy. She thinks too much. These irritating questions are a personality thing, not a brain thing," he decided based on gut reaction. He also decided these provocative questions were really irritating. And, the Indian heritage? Her dark hair and eyes were appropriate for it. But, was she just making up what she thought people wanted to hear? Could he ever trust her and whatever came from between her lips?"

Israel saw a glow in the sky as the sun began to introduce itself to a new day. He got up and put a pot of coffee on the fireplace swing iron. Stirring up the coals and adding some more small wood, he went out and checked around the house. He saw the four mules grazing by the creek.

He went back in and saw Hannah with two mugs of steaming coffee. She still had not dressed, but it did not bother him. She was really pretty, after all. Not beautiful. Beautiful described the other one. He wished right now, White Feather was not so beautiful.

"Good morning. Ready for a wilderness day?" he asked.

She took a big slurp of coffee and mumbled "Sure."

"What do you think of putting in a vegetable garden? I bought some seeds a few months ago. We have beans and squash. There's a good place out on the side of the cabin."

"How about I take it on as my project?" she asked.

"An excellent idea, Hannah. I'd be real proud of you."

She smiled and padded outside, still semi-dressed, to survey the garden plot.

"Good thing we don't have neighbors who drop in," Israel thought. "Maybe she's part flirt and part just natural. Whatever she is, she's sure a fascinating and perplexing person to try to figure out."

By lunch, she had a ten by twenty plot laid out and the soil loosened for planting.

"Do you know how deep and how far apart each type of seed should be?" she asked.

"Where's Arthur when you need him? I don't have any idea at all. I wonder if your new sister, White Feather, knows? Indian women do the planting and the men hunt for meat, generally," he said.

"She said she might ride over today. I will ask her."

"I wager she will know. Probably, she will show you and help you," Israel said.

"You can either wait for me to go down to the stream and take a bath or make our lunch yourself," she said. "I am covered with dirt."

"Go ahead down there. I will make something for us. Watch out for rattlers along the way. I've only seen one since moving here, but ya gotta be careful."

"I will," she said, dropping her coverup. She began walking towards the stream two hundred yards distant.

Israel went in and took stock of food he could prepare for lunch. He sliced some ham with a Green River knife dedicated to cooking use. He also sliced bread they picked up at the trading post.

He heard laughter and grabbed the Trade Musket on the way out of the door.

From outside, he realized it was female laughter. He looked and saw Hannah and White Feather cavorting in the stream, throwing water on each other and giggling.

He walked down. White Feather was standing in two feet of water waving at him.

"Come on in and get cleaned up," Hannah yelled. White Feather smiled invitingly.

"Not now. I will finish making your lunches. Come up when you are through."

He walked back, thinking White Feather was even more beautiful than he had dreamed. And, Hannah inviting him? What should he make of it? Was it a test?"

Israel decided to think about anything else. Ham sandwiches were a poor substitute, but were all he could summon to think about.

Ten minutes later, the two walked in. White Feather had put her buckskin dress on and was carrying her moccasins. Hannah did not have anything at the stream to put on, so she picked up a dress in the cabin and slipped into it.

"Nice bath?" he asked both.

"We had fun. It was very refreshing," White Feather answered. Hannah just gave him an angelic grin.

They had the sandwiches and cider for lunch. The two girls, which term Israel now changed to women, talked about the garden and how to plant it. They finished and went to the garden and sacks of marked seeds sitting waiting to be sown.

Israel knew he had over-trapped the stream and lake the past season. Another stream fed the lake from further away. He would ride over and check it as a possible trapping site for a couple months off.

"I'm going to look at a more distant stream for trapping as it gets cooler. I will see you ladies in a few hours."

"See you then," both said simultaneously and giggled.

He saddled Amos and took the Hawken, leaving the horse pistol and musket for Hannah.

Israel focused on the matter at hand and tried not to think of his current and potential woman problems. The two becoming friends was the last thing he would have expected. He had not made any overtures to White Feather but knew she had him in her sights. Hannah was unstable at best. He made himself plan his trapping. How far would he have to go beyond the new stream to get a steady flow of beavers in his traps? Would his several times a week trap checking become overnight trips? Would he have to bring Hannah?

He would ask Lone Bear if there were any hostiles in the area. His friend would know. He sent out small parties of warriors to patrol the area daily.

Israel worried about Northern Cheyenne's and Sioux particularly. Jed told him they had lived in the area earlier and came back periodically. He feared they were not welcoming of whites or the Kiowas.

As he approached the stream feeding the lake from the opposite side of what he thought of as his stream, he saw a nice-sized buck.

Israel slipped off Amos and found a good rest for the long shot. He knew the Hawken could drop the deer from the one hundred fifty yards.

He pressed the set trigger, took aim and touched the hair trigger. The big gun recoiled and the deer disappeared in a cloud of gray-white smoke. Israel rolled to the side and saw the buck leap, run ten feet and drop. Fresh meat!

He mounted Amos and rode over to the deer. A half hour later, the deer was bled and gutted. He left it hanging as he scouted along the stream. He saw beaver sign aplenty. It was an easy ride from the cabin. He would wait until the pups grew up a couple months more and try to target the fully-grown beavers if he could.

Israel took the deer carcass down from the limb and slung it over Amos's back, behind the saddle. The mule was good natured and took it in stride.

By the time he got back, the garden was planted and the two women were sitting on the stoop and chatting. He reckoned his next house project was to use the new wedge and split some boards for a wood floor under the porch overhang Jed called the "stoop."

Then, maybe a couple of chairs. Maybe three at the way things seemed to be going.

"White Feather, I cut a haunch off the buck for us. Why don't you take a mule when you head back later and carry the rest of the deer to Lone Bear?"

"It is very kind. You are a good friend to my grand-father and the Kiowas. I will do it. Riding back will also allow Fire and me to visit longer than if I was walking."

"I consider your tribe my closest friends, except for my sister's husband Arthur who is many miles away. You are welcome here any time," he said, noting his wife's apparent agreement.

Two hours before dusk, he got Jed's riding mule out.

"I prefer bareback, please," White Feather said. She hugged Hannah and Israel. She hopped on and Israel put the deer in front of her and she held him on. Without a saddle, there was no good way to tie him. She rode several hundred yards and turned to wave.

"I really like her," Hannah said.

"She is a good person," Israel acknowledged.

"She likes you a lot."

"It's because I am almost like one of the tribe. Now, you will be also. She seems to like you a lot, too."

"She does. This is the first time since I was a little girl, I had two important people in my life who cared about me," she said, giving Israel some hint as to her issues.

"I want to ride out for a few days and look for more beaver signs. Do you want to come with me? It may be too dangerous to stay here alone."

"I will come. Do you think White Feather can come with us?" she asked.

"It's up to her. I don't know what responsibilities she has at the tribe. You can certainly ask her. Her parents were killed in a raid years ago, so Chief Lone Bear and his wife raised her. She is the apple of his eye, for sure," Israel said.

"You wouldn't be mad if she came?"

"Hannah, you should have figured out by now, little makes me mad. I take most things in stride. Attack a loved one, and I am ready to kill. Otherwise, I am pretty even tempered."

"How about Tom? He did not attack me."

"If you remember, he attacked me, though. Shouldn't it count if I am attacked?" he asked.

She looked like she had to ruminate over his question. Sometimes, he thought, she was fairly smart. Other times, he hoped any children they had would inherit his brain and not hers. He reckoned she was cunning, but not quick on logical things. At least, she did not seem to be mean.

It was not raining much for the time of year, so Hannah had to go to the stream with the bucket and bring back water for the garden. After a few weeks, he could see sprouts popping up.

White Feather came for visits frequently. Lone Bear approved her accompanying them on a search for beaver sign.

They left early in the morning on three mules. White Feather had renamed Jed's Henry as "One Who

Plods Along," but he seemed happiest when she was riding and talking with him.

Lone Bear suggested heading southwest into the Wind River Mountains and check the Big Sandy River for sign.

Hannah stopped and threw up several times during the morning portion of the ride.

"Must have been something you ate," Israel said, adding "But, I ate the same thing."

White Feather laughed.

"It is something in you, sister, but it's not breakfast causing you to get rid of it. It will take care of itself in nine months or so," she told Hannah.

At the mention of nine months, Israel perked up and listened.

"What do you mean, White Feather?" Hannah asked. Unseen, Israel rolled his eyes.

"I mean you have a little Israel growing inside you, silly sister."

Hannah's eyes got as large as pewter mugs as she comprehended and thought about her condition.

"What will I do?" she asked.

"You will do what any other mother does. You will watch your belly get bigger, the baby will come out, you will nurse it and he will grow. One day, you will be old and he will take care of you."

Israel tried to read Hannah's thoughts, but could not even come close.

"White Feather, should I take her back to where a midwife can deliver the baby?"

"Of course not. The Kiowa women have been successfully having healthy babies since the beginning of time. Towards time for her, just bring her to the village. We will look after her and teach her what to do with a little one. Just like her mother would teach her."

"What would we do without our Kiowa friends?" Israel asked aloud.

She looked at him and he caught a faint wink Hannah did not see. He just smiled.

Hannah threw up again. This time, Israel was pretty sure it was nerves, not pregnancy, causing it.

"Fire, try to drink some water from your gourd," White Feather suggested.

"I'm not thirsty," she responded.

"Do it for me. It is important, Fire."

Hannah took a swig from the gourd hanging from her saddle horn.

******

They did not reach far into the Wind Rivers until almost dark. Israel found a protected site and took care of the mules while White Feather built a fire.

The women made bacon and coffee and warmed beans previously cooked and transported in a clay pot. Israel circled the area to check for threats, then walked back.

"The air is colder up here in the mountains," Israel noted as he stretched out the bedrolls. He walked off into the trees to relieve himself. When he came back, he saw his bedroll had been moved to the middle position. He wondered which one moved it, or whether it was a joint operation.

He placed the Hawken in close reach, along with the Bowie and Hannah's horse pistol.

In the dark, he heard White Feather slip out of her buckskin dress and into her blankets. Hannah did the same on the other side.

Israel soon had a dark-haired head on each shoulder. He stared up and the sky, its millions of stars sparkling back at him. Odd how the mountain skies were so clear, he thought. Warm, happy and a little uncomfortable, he continued to stare at the sky.

Just before dawn, he fell asleep. He still had a head on each shoulder.

Israel awakened to the smell of coffee and bacon.

"What better way to wake up?" he said.

"Did you sleep well, Bear Fighter?" White Feather asked.

"I was comfortable but stayed awake thinking."

"What did you think about?" she asked, Hannah obviously monitoring the conversation.

"How lucky I am," he responded. It was true. Further, the listener could put whatever meaning on it she wished. He was learning. Slowly, but learning.

After eating, he left them in camp and rode Amos along the Big Sandy. The snow melt had subsided and it was low. The banks were showing and extended out to beyond where deeper water had been several months ago.

Israel saw some beaver dams and other signs of beavers along the edge. He would come back here with all of his traps in a month.

In the meantime, he would build an open face cabin, not unlike Jed's had been before they added to it.

During the season, it would be easier to stay here than to ride back and forth.

Perhaps Hannah would stay with the Kiowas. He had no idea how fragile she might be during pregnancy. It was totally out of his sphere of knowledge.

He read some of Edgar Allan Poe's poetry to his two women. He had begun to think of them as such, though only treating one as a wife. He wanted to read Shakespeare to them but feared the Elizabethan English may be confusing to both, albeit for different reasons.

Perhaps it was the meter or maybe his deep resonant voice, but both enjoyed the recitation and asked for him to always read to them after dinner.

"I want to do this for our son or daughter also," he said, "to have them used to reading. It is the way to broaden one's mind, even when school is not possible."

They were back in several days. They had picked wild berries along the way and had plenty to make pemmican and to share with the tribe.

The garden was dry, but watering brought it back to where it should be. They would dry the vegetables they did not eat fresh. At the time, it was the only preservation he knew how to do.

He rode back out alone, taking the new logging chain and axe on the pack mule. He also committed one of the treated canvas tarps for a roof underlayer for the shelter. It took him four days to build it. He was pleased with the shelter and knew the tarp under the split and overlapped boards would help keep rain and melting snow from dripping on his face at night. Israel gathered stones from the river and built a fire ring with a connecting smaller air draw hole and a stone tunnel to draw air into the fire pit itself. Before he left, he laid in a supply of firewood and erected a roof over it.

The cooler weather set in quickly and he had a decision to make. Should he take Hannah on the ride? It would mean a three-month long stay trapping before the serious snow began. Would White Feather come and stay with her at the cabin? Or, better, could she go to the Kiowa village and stay there?

The three spoke about it on White Feather's next

visit. She suggested Hannah stay with her. She had her own teepee and would welcome the company.

Without saying, Israel would take more food than his pregnant wife could ever eat in his absence. He did not want to strain his friends' stock of winter provisions.

He packed her and the food and took her to the village. Lone Bear, knowing how close she was to his granddaughter, treated her as another granddaughter. Her quarter Indian heritage, true or not, helped cement the bond.

Israel hugged his wife and his admirer, solemnly nodded to his friend and rode off.

He stopped at the house and packed everything he thought he needed on his pack mule. He had a full season's worth of beaver castor, his traps had been oiled with bear grease. He took the Hawken and the musket.

Upon arrival, he unloaded both mules then proceeded to build a bed, table and a chair. He put five large nails in the inside wall for hanging his long guns and his winter coat. Smaller nails accommodated his snowshoes and hat. Nails were a luxury deep in the wilderness. Otherwise, it was to bore a hole without proper tools and fashion a peg.

Israel Pope was now ready for some serious trapping.

The next day, he set off. With the beaver castor

in his possibles bag, he strung the full set of traps on the sawbuck saddle and mounted Amos. He led the pack mule to the narrows of the Big Sandy where he saw signs.

They walked for a mile, dropping traps at intervals which showed the most beaver signs.

Once he was out of traps, he returned to the start and began baiting and placing them. It took him all day to lay a mile of set and baited trapline. Now, it came down to checking them every day and bringing the beavers back to skin and tan.

During the day, Israel hunted small game and shot a couple of deer. The meat supplemented the beans he kept simmering on the fire with bacon in the pot. He fixed fry bread to go with it. Every day as he returned from collecting the beavers he caught, Israel retrieved the jug of cider cooling in the river and took it back to the shelter to have with dinner.

The first snow hit after two months. It was a big one. He had to use snowshoes to go to the river and to collect his catch and return. He left Amos at the shelter.

The first night after the snow, he regretted not putting a front wall on the shelter. The next day, he delayed the trip to the river in order to build a taller reflector on the fire pit. He needed to bank his fire for the night and deflect as much heat as possible into the sleeping area. For the first time, he regretted sleeping alone. He had become spoiled.

It was bitterly cold out. He still had his homemade mittens. Taking the sharp Green River knife, he cut off an eight inch wide strip from a wool blanket and made a scarf.

The next time he went to the river to check his traps, he tied his hat on and wrapped the scarf around his neck and tied it securely. It increased his warmth considerably. At least until he could supplement it with a knitted wool toque or stocking cap.

Israel's beaver take from the new location was good. He had excellent experience getting to the rendezvous early and being among the first to sell prime pelts last year.

He planned to do the same thing in early June, now a month off.

For some reason, Israel felt an ominous fear. He did not know what it was or why he felt it. He had to wrap up this season and head back. Even before rendezvous.

He loaded the pack mule two weeks later. He could only carry half his take.

Israel would drop the first load at the cabin and return for the second before going to the village to pick up Hannah. The trip to the trapping camp and his own cabin would take three days each way.

He made both trips and cached both loads. It was a good year's income for anyone who decided to steal it. A large tree had fallen a hundred yards from the cabin. It left a large hole which he lined with a tarp. He put in both loads and covered it with fallen, dead branches. Somebody would have to be deliberately looking for it to find this cache.

It was not beyond the realm of possibility. However, he thought it was beyond the realm of probability.

The farther east he rode, the warmer it became. It was as if he rode out of winter and into springtime. The warmth of the sun felt good on his face. He bet Amos liked it too.

He rode down the slope to the Kiowa camp.

Lone Bear met him without his normal happy greeting. Something was wrong.

"What is it my friend?" were the first words out of Israel's mouth.

"Girl Who Was Born With Fire is gone, Bear Fighter," He said.

Expecting she had run off or something, Israel asked where.

The chief moved his hands upward towards the sky.

"She passed this life delivering your son. We gave her a proper Kiowa ceremony. She was put in the ground. We burned her possessions. The horse pistol was saved, since it was yours. You should burn your cabin to complete the process.

You have a fine son. He is with White Feather. One of the women nurses him. You need a wife to help with this son, Bear Fighter."

"I think you know the wife I always loved is right here," Israel said.

"It is so. You should go to her with my blessing. She is headstrong enough to not require it, but you have it, my friend."

"Thank you, Lone Bear. I will be a loyal and good husband." The chief nodded and Israel walked to White Feather's teepee.

"I am back and heard the news, White Feather."

"My friend and your wife will be missed. Perhaps more by me. I believe you rescued her and she had no place to go. She told me you did the right thing by her. The honorable thing."

"I believe I did what was right to do."

"What will you do now?"

"I would like to marry you and have us raise my son together, if you will take me?"

"I was ready to take you when I first laid eyes on you. Of course I will. I have already started raising little Night Hawk anyway. A hawk was calling its mate loudly while he was being born. It was a sign for a name."

"I would like to see Night Hawk. He will also be John Hunt Pope."

"Who was he? You are Israel Pope"

"John Hunt was my friend Jed. I promised him I would name my first son after him."

"He is being fed. He is almost old enough to have

soft food. Follow me," she said.

They walked across the village to another teepee.

"This is Woman Who Walks in the Sun. And, this is your son."

The wet nurse burped the baby and handed him to Israel. He had never held a baby in his life.

The tiny person looked up at him with the same blue eyes he had. The baby seemed to recognize him, then threw up on his buckskin shirt. Both women laughed.

"Welcome to fatherhood," White Feather said.

The baby seemed to laugh when the women did.

"He's like a miniature person," Israel said.

"Of course. He will be tall like you. He is already taller than some older babies here. He is perfectly formed."

The baby took another look at his father and promptly went to sleep.

"Let's go back to my teepee and put him down. He has a bed next to mine. To ours. Did my grandfather tell you our belief is you should burn the cabin? We can move my teepee up there and be just as comfortable. Maybe more."

"He told me. I fear burning it may catch the forest afire. What if we just deserted it?"

"It may serve the purpose, but we need to talk with the council of elders. They will know.

"There is a good spot for the teepee nearer to the

stream. I would have built the cabin there, but Jed already had built the bones of it before I ever got there," Israel said.

"What is the usual gift to the wife's family for allowing her marriage?" he asked.

"A horse. Since I am the virgin granddaughter of a chief and not terribly ugly, it would normally be a fine horse," White Feather answered.

"Not terribly ugly? You are the most beautiful woman alive!" Israel said, meaning every word.

"Do you think so?" she asked in surprise.

"I sure do. There is no doubt in my mind."

"Then, I guess you need to go horse buying at the rendezvous. I think the mule Fire had would not be enough."

"Can we wait a few weeks until rendezvous?"

"It is the way. We will have to wait for the ceremony."

"Let's find out about abandoning the cabin instead of burning the whole forest down," Israel suggested.

They went to Lone Bear and Israel told him his concern.

"I was taught by a very wise chief to be a steward of the land and its animals. The cabin is near dense forest. If we burn it, it is likely to start an unnecessary forest fire. Trees and animals will suffer for many seasons. Will you ask the council of elders if it would suffice to just abandon the cabin and live somewhere else?"

"I will ask. Your question is thoughtful. A Kiowa would ask such a question. After you marry into the tribe, you should consider becoming a Kiowa."

"I will my friend," Israel promised, knowing he had been given a large compliment.

Israel followed White Feather back to her teepee and sat and watched his tiny son sleep and make small noises. He found it fascinating. It was like a little him. He gently lifted the baby into his arms and it cooed but did not awaken.

He sat cross-legged holding the baby for hours, White Feather lovingly watching both. He was sad Hannah had died in pain. And, guilty he was not there to hold her hand. There was nothing he could do about it. She had her best friend with her and Israel knew the Indian midwives were every bit as good as Sadie Peters back in Boonesboro. It was life. People came and went. He hoped Hannah found peace wherever she was. Though she looked part Indian, he suspected she was an opportunist. It was not the first time he heard her say something she thought her audience wished to hear.

Later, Lone Bear came to the teepee. They were still sitting, Israel holding the sleeping baby proudly.

"The council has talked about your concern. They agree, it is not worth the possibility of a fire. They have said you should not sleep another night in the cabin. Move your things out and burn all of Fire's

things in a fire away from the woods. It is a ceremony. If you wish, a wise man will come and conduct
it with you."

"I would appreciate him guiding me, Lone Bear.
Would you like to hold Night Hawk?" Israel asked.

The chief took the baby and held him. He studied
the small face, its eyes closed, its lips in a smile.

"He is a good baby. He will grow tall and be a
hunter like his father."

The baby made a small noise and the chief smiled.

"See, he agrees with the wise old chief," he said.

"I want him to look to you like a grandfather. Is it
alright with you, Lone Bear?"

"Yes. I will treat him as a grandfather would." He
handed the baby to his granddaughter and got up.

"Remember, do not ever sleep in the cabin." He left.

"I did not want to interrupt, but 'great' grandfather
would be more appropriate," Israel said.

"No, grandfather is just fine, Israel. I will call you
by either Israel or Bear Fighter for now. I am searching my heart for an appropriate short name. You will
know when I have found it."

"What if it is not appealing to me?"

She smiled. "If the spirits choose it, who are you to
question either it or your wife?"

"When we go to the rendezvous, I will stay at the
camp with Night Hawk. To be an Indian woman at
rendezvous is not safe. You go, sell your pelts, find

a horse to trade for me, and return to the Kiowa camp. We may be able to marry there, if a wise man accompanies us."

"Nobody would bother you if I was there," Israel said.

"You are Bear Fighter. But, you have one shot in your rifle and one in the pistol Fire carried on her mule. Then, it is down to knife and tomahawk. You would probably kill five or six before you fall and I am their victim. Who would raise little Night Hawk? Besides, why would I want to go and see drunken white men dancing with one another and acting like fools?"

"Good points. On second thought, I agree."

He dragged himself away from the woman he could now admit to loving and the baby of whom he was so proud.

Following the Kiowa custom, he camped outside the cabin. He piled Hannah's clothes and her small number of possessions in the fireplace.

When White Feather guided the wise man to the cabin the next morning, it was obvious Israel had slept outside. He offered them coffee. The wise man did not speak fluent English, so White Feather translated.

Israel already had a fire built in the fireplace. Once the wise man began to chant, White Feather instructed Israel to feed each possession of her late friend's into the flames. He then spoke to Israel in Kiowa.

"He says to remove anything of yours, then seal the cabin to keep the spirits inside. Never come in or sleep inside again."

Israel poured the man more coffee and gave him one of several nice smoking pipes and some of the tobacco he had bought for barter. He removed his few last things, like the swing arm for the fireplace.

Not having a hammer, Israel took the top of his tomahawk and nailed the door and window shutters shut. The wise man seemed pleased. He looked at White Feather, who said something Israel did not understand. The man rode off, leaving the two alone.

He sat in a chair he built. Hannah thought it uncomfortable and never used it. White Feather came and sat in his lap and put her head on his shoulder. They sat there until almost dark, not talking. Each was lost in his and her own thoughts.

They rode the two mules down to the spot Israel suggested for the teepee. She liked it, facing the setting sun, then turning to the other three directions. She paused at each. Finally, she turned to him and said "It is good." Her grandfather's granddaughter.

They rode to the village and arrived just before darkness fell. Both were in a rush to see little John. He was with the wet nurse, still happy and smiling.

The baby particularly beamed when White Feather took him. He had not known any other mother. To him, she was and always would be his mother. It was clear to Israel she felt the same about the baby.

He rode back to the new campsite in the dark. He led the mule the two women used back. He saw the pack mule feeding in the meadow. He would need all three at rendezvous.

Israel set up a trail camp. He would improve upon it after he recovered his pelts and went to rendezvous. The weather was perfect for sleeping under the stars.

The next morning, he transferred his pelts to the three mules and walked them back to the Indian village.

"You have had a good year, my friend," Lone Bear greeted him, looking at the laden mules.

"I was blessed with a good place and a great deal of luck," Israel responded.

"I just hope the prices are high this year. What we get is based on two things. One is supply. The other seems to be demand for beaver hats back east and across the ocean. The last worries me. One day styles will change and my lifestyle will go away."

"Then, you can move around living like a Kiowa, Bear Fighter. It is not such a bad life. We do not fight other tribes as much anymore. The fighting will increase as white man takes territory. Other tribes who have moved on will come back to recover their old land. We are in for violent times. It will be red against red and red and white against each other. I am too old to fight. My warriors have not fought for years. We may move deep into the Winds. It is where the white man finds it too hard to live. It may be peaceful there."

"I will go with you, Lone Bear. You can count on it."

"I know, Bear Fighter," the chief said.

******

Israel asked White Feather to help him write a list of things the Kiowas needed or would like. She did and chose items he would never have thought to include.

The tribe moved close to the trading post as they had each year of rendezvous.

Israel walked in, leading all three mules. He came early again and offered well- tanned pelts. He got top dollar and was paid in gold and silver coins instead of trade credit. He used the coins to buy what he needed and what the Kiowas needed.

A trader had bought a number of salt-cured hams from eastern Virginia. Israel bought three for his family and five for the Kiowas. He bought them needed blankets and tools. This year, they returned with several large wheels of cheese. Flour, cornmeal, salt, sugar, cider, dried beans, bacon, coffee and some hard candy almost finished his purchases.

The last two were a handsome horse and a necklace. The horse was a fine one from Kentucky. It was a dark stallion, raised on bluegrass. Everything about him said speed.

They married in a Kiowa ceremony following the rendezvous.

Israel traded blood with Lone Bear and in a ceremony following the wedding, became a Kiowa. The act carried a great deal of pride and meaning to him. No matter where he went or what he did, he would always be a Kiowa at heart.

They moved White Feather's teepee to the site near the stream. Israel was surprised how quickly it came down and easily it was transported to the site. The long lodge poles were just dragged behind the mules, the skins of the teepee atop them.

Little John no longer needed the wet nurse and was happy with the new colors and smells of the woodland and the babble of the stream.

Israel determined not to trap the stream for another several years, to let the beaver population renew. He would not repeat his over trapping mistake of the first year.

By late fall, White Feather and some women from the village constructed a new, smaller teepee. Israel and White Feather would take it to the mountains and erect it beside the shelter for fall and winter trapping. They would use the shelter as a tanning and storage shed while living in the teepee.

The season passed more efficiently than the previous two. Israel trapped and cleaned and White

Feather tanned and softened the pelts.

Israel's profits grew with the following rendez-vous as did his reputation as a good trapper. So far, unlike many others, he had avoided contact with hostile Indians. He stayed in his mountain area, well away from trails.

"I am here to trap, not to fight. If they come to me, I will fight for all I'm worth. But, they will have started it," he told Lone Bear during a visit.

"I am told things are stirring up among the tribes," his friend said. "They are feeling angry because of the large number of whites moving in on Indian country. There will be attacks. Being a white Kiowa will not protect you. Where you live in the winter may protect you and your family. I worry about here and where you are in the warm seasons.

I believe we have one more season of peace. Then, hostiles will attack whites and Indians both. The council of elders met on this. We have decided to move the village and this band of Kiowas further off the trails. How would you like neighbors up in the Wind?" he asked.

"I would like it. Almost all my family would be together then."

By early fall, the move was complete. The warriors hunted hard to bring in meat to cure for the coming winter. Jed's Almanac said it promised to be a bitter one.

Israel helped with the hunting.

One morning, Lone Bear joined him. Lone Bear had his own trade musket, loaded with a single large lead ball.

Israel shot a large elk. It would provide much-needed meat. They hung, bled and gutted it and hauled the rope higher so predators would not get it before they returned from their hunt.

Lone Bear's dog alerted on something and almost went crazy on the scent. They followed on foot, silently padding in their moccasins.

The dog had treed a medium bear. Lone Bear shot it out of the tree. It hit the ground with a thump, shook itself and came at them growling.

Israel did not have time to shoulder his Hawken. He fired from the hip and hit the charging bear.

The fifty-four caliber ball was not enough to stop the charge. The bear knocked Lone Bear over and came at Israel.

Israel butt-stroked the bear with his Hawken and dropped the heavy rifle in favor of the almost twelve-inch blade of his Bowie. Instead of waiting, he charged the bear, growling as ferociously as the animal had.

Israel drove the blade into the back of the bear's neck. It went in up to the hilt by the handle. The bear collapsed. Israel backed away, picked up his rifle and began to load it.

The extra shot was unnecessary. The bear died

where he fell. Standing on the bear's shoulders, he used two hands and slowly withdrew the blade. It took every ounce of strength he could summon.

Lone Bear voiced a loud and long war cry of victory. Israel joined him as the forest reverberated with the primordial cry.

The old man clasped both hands on the young one's shoulders.

"You are well named, Bear Fighter, and truly a Kiowa."

"It was you who dropped him out of the tree. I just took some fight out of him," Israel reminded the chief.

"I have seen a bear charge a man. But, not a man charge a bear. This feat will spread among the prairie tribes like wildfire. And, the legend will live with the stories told by the Kiowas."

Israel nodded almost piously as he took the rope from around his shoulders and tied the bear's hind legs together.

It took both large men to hoist the bear up to a height for Israel to begin on him with the Green River skinning knife. To him, the Bowie was a weapon only. A tool not to be used for work but saved for killing.

There were thirty Kiowas in the village. The bear and elk provided meat, grease, skins, bones for fishhooks, claws for necklaces, and more. Virtually nothing went to waste. By using it fully, the Kiowas honored the animal in its death.

Israel believed this creed to the very depths of his heart.

"It is so," he said to himself, and smiled.

The winter was rough. Israel's pelt catch was behind the previous several years, but not disastrously so.

Young John was growing fast. He stayed with Israel and White Feather most of the time but enjoyed scrambling around behind the man he called "grandfather," as much as possible. He was growing up Indian.

Israel did not consider it a bad thing. He also wanted him to be exposed to the white ways. There was only one way he could get such exposure.

CHAPTER 5

Israel and Arthur had communicated by letters between the trading post where Israel shopped and Boonesboro. Israel knew his friend was anxious to move on. He spoke more and more about an intermittent move to Omaha, a place Israel knew well. The trip to the Pacific coast was a commitment which was final in nature. Arthur and Maude had agreed, they wanted a few years partway before moving across the whole country.

Though the letters took several months to be delivered, he finally got a letter saying Arthur and Maude had finally decided to move. They set a date to start towards Omaha.

They set the move to Omaha to occur mere weeks after rendezvous.

Israel knew he needed to sell pelts at what was very likely to be the last mountain man rendezvous.

As each year, the 1840 rendezvous was scheduled for June.

Israel was there. The whole temperament of the event had changed. It was less than a money and whiskey flowing celebration than a sad acknowledgement of the end of an era.

Fashions changed, as Israel had foretold. Silk had prevailed in fashion over beaver. Worse yet, the beavers had been trapped almost to extinction. Lack of planning and greed would have killed the industry even if style had not contributed to its death at all.

He left White Feather and John behind for this trip. He wanted the boy to meet his aunt and uncle, but Israel knew the speed of his travel would make the trip grueling.

He left the rendezvous saddened at the passing of a tradition and way of life. Despite a good offering of pelts, the style change impacted prices negatively. Israel received half the money from the past year for a similar amount and quality of pelts. The industry the occupation of the beaver trappers were both over.

He rode Amos on familiar trails, camping late and rising early. Arthur had written what route he and Maude planned in case Israel missed them at Boonesboro.

Just in case, Israel planned to pick up the route northwest of where he expected them to be. He would ride towards them instead of riding to their old farm, missing them and having to trail them.

It worked. He met them three day's out of Boonesboro when he recognized the wagon and camp.

******

"Hello, the camp! Where's the coffee?"

An obviously tired Arthur climbed out of a bedroll under the wagon, followed by Maude who still appeared partly asleep.

"Well, you're a sight for sore eyes!" the big man exclaimed.

"More like tired eyes! Is that my sister, or just some sleepwalker who ambled into camp?" Israel asked.

She hugged him. "I've missed you so much, brother."

"And, I have too. There's never any excitement around except when you are there," Arthur said.

"Well, I am here with you all the way to your new Promised Land."

"Where are John and White Feather?" Maude asked.

"Both are in the Wind River Range. I will tell you more once I get this fire rebuilt and you bring coffee beans out," Israel said.

Once the fire was going and settled into proper coals, they put on bacon and coffee and frybread for breakfast.

"First, I don't notice Pa around. Did he stay in Boonesboro?" Israel asked.

"I'm afraid he took to the bottle after you ma died. He fell and hit his head some weeks ago. Maude went over to check on him, cause he usually came over for coffee. She found him on the floor and saw he had bled to death. We buried him in the church yard by your mother."

Israel took the story without saying anything.

"How about White Feather and the boy? You wrote us Hannah died," Maude asked.

"I found Hannah may have been part Virginia Indian. She was readily accepted into the Kiowa tribe who became my family. She was with child. While I was trapping in the high country, she went into labor early and did not make it. When I returned, I found John, who they named Night Hawk, was being mothered by the chief's granddaughter. She was Hannah's good friend.

I married her a few months later. She is beautiful as I will prove to you.

I knew I had to ride fast after selling pelts at the rendezvous to meet you in time to actually be of use. So, I left them at the village. I do have some likenesses to share."

He pulled White Feather's and his medicine bags out from under his buckskin shirt and removed two lockets.

"Here is White Feather and here are all of us," Israel said.

"Lord, Israel. She is beautiful. Probably the most beautiful woman I ever saw. And, the little boy looks like a certain tyke I played with as a child. Of course, he didn't have a beard then," Maude said.

"White Feather was a good friend to Hannah. I was gone and, like in the letter I sent you, she and Chief Lone Bear took care of her, got her buried and all. John has grown up Indian. He's quite a little person."

"You know when he's ready to go to school or learn white ways, we'll take him gladly," Arthur offered.

"I do. I was going to ask you to, but you beat me to it."

"Like I said in the letter about us going to Omaha, we are easing into this wilderness thing. We really want to settle once and for all on the Pacific Coast, like Oregon.

But, we need to build up a farm and sell it for some more grubstake first. The land near Omaha is cheap and good for farming, I hear. I have some money from the sale of the two properties in Kentucky. The lawyer who drew up the agreement between us bought it all himself to resell. We did not get prime value, but for a quick sale, we did fine. Your part is in a separate envelope," Arthur said.

"Why don't you just hold on to it?" If I don't get killed first, I will either get it or one of us will use it for raising John," Israel said.

"Killed first?" Maude asked.

"Where I ride is pretty violent country. The trapping was bad enough. Trapping is over. There will not be any more rendezvous. Most of the trappers are becoming scouts or wagon train leaders. Since the whole world seems to want to settle in Oregon, there's a lot of opportunity leading pilgrims there. But, it's across the Continental Divide, some changeable rivers, some deserts and through hostile Indian country. Riding up front makes you the first target," Israel said.

The trip to Omaha took them through Kentucky and Illinois to St. Louis. They crossed the Mississippi River and then Missouri to the Missouri River. They followed the river up to Omaha. The trails were distinct and well-traveled. There were trading posts along the way and the trip was not unduly arduous.

Arthur sought someone who dealt in land and was shown a small patch of farmland on the Elkhorn River. There was a ferry nearby and a general store.

Arthur studied the land and remarked about its possibilities to Israel. He bought it for cash and a day later had a deed in hand. They moved their camp to the best spot for a house.

The trees on his land were not tall enough to cut for cabin timbers. They felled some and a local man showed them how to make sod walls for part of the home.

Arthur was unhappy with the sod home aspect and said "I will have wood brought in from Omaha with what is left of the Kentucky money. The sod place will be sufficient for a few months," he said.

"Arthur, if you need to use any or all of my share of the sales from Boonesboro, go right ahead. I'm flush enough for now and you and Maude need a solid home here. Who knows how much it will snow?"

"That's real kind of you. I think we will have enough."

"Don't hesitate to use all you need. You are like my brother. What's mine is yours."

Before he left a week later, Arthur and Maude had a real house, although two walls were sod. Building it into a small rise helped construction and gave them some protection from the wind.

He rode out and got back to the Kiowa village in time for cool weather. It was good to be back, nonetheless.

Like many mountain men, he had become a guide for wagon trains going to Oregon or California.

Almost all of the earlier trips were to Oregon. California journeys did not really pick up until the end of the decade when gold was discovered.

Being a wagon train master was not as lucrative as the fur trade had been, but took far less work and equipment. Just a lot of riding. And, unfortunately, a lot of Indian warfare along the way.

Israel added an arrow scar in his right shoulder to go with the bear wounds. The wound made him shoot left-handed for three months.

Between wagon trains, he hired on as a scout for the army. He told them he would scout for exploration parties and surveying parties.

This was a time of great change in the West. Territories were being split into smaller territories. Some territories were applying for statehood. The need for defined lines was great and the army was well-suited to handle much of the task. Not discussed publicly, it gave them intelligence they needed for their next big initiative.

It was one Israel Pope was to ascertain quickly.

******

He led a party of army surveyors with a cavalry escort. They surveyed along the Snake River.

"Are you familiar with this country, Pope?" the captain in charge of Israel's latest survey party asked.

"Familiar, yes, Captain. Have I actually been here? No. As we ride along, I will tell you what I know. Then, I have to do my job and scout ahead for hostiles and both Indian and animal trails worth surveying. Early French trappers called the mountain range the Grand Tetons because the reminded them of large breasts, or le grand tetons. I guess some of their hikes took them away from the ladies too long. A mentor, Jed Hunt, was on the Corps of Discovery with a man named John Colter. It is said he first rode into the hole or basin the Snake runs through. Later, a trapper named Davy Jackson pulled beavers out of here in the 1820's. No white men have settled here as I know about. The various tribes will winter here or just hunt. The woods around this area are full of deer, elk and about everything good to eat in the land."

"Why is it called a hole?" the captain asked.

"Just because it is encircled by mountains and the valley is real low. I guess if you looked down at it from heaven, it would look like a hole.

I better ride ahead and check what is or is not in front of us. I'll also circle around and make sure we don't have any surprises lurking behind us, too," Israel said.

They surveyed the area later known first as Jackson's Hole. Then, it became Jackson Hole.

They followed the Snake River into Idaho with their survey. It had been part of Oregon Territory. When Oregon became a state, the area now known as Idaho became part of Washington Territory. The final name, Idaho, was a blend of the Shoshone words for "Gem of the Mountains." This frequent change of names made mapping almost impossible.

Israel led the party on an expedition through this vast territory which was still years away from any non-indigenous settlement. The only whites who had seen its beauty were a few trappers.

"This is the most beautiful country I have seen yet, especially the Salmon River country," he thought. But the absence of any trading posts made it too desolate even for a mountain man. Even one with an Indian wife. But, one day…." he thought.

******

Israel's experience with scouting had been a good one, so he watched for more opportunities.

Several months later, riding on his fame for leading the Grand Teton and west survey, Israel was hired to scout for a company of cavalry at Fort Caspar. The area around the fort changed the name from Caspar to Casper, Wyoming Territory.

There had been several Indian attacks and the army was not even aware of the tribe or tribes involved.

A reactive force was prepared to track down the attacking war party.

Israel signed on with another former mountain man. He knew the man, Honus Smith, and respected his woodcraft and tracking. Personally, he though Smith was a hard drinking blowhard. The third scout was an Indian. He was called Green Turtle and did not volunteer his tribe. Israel thought perhaps he was a Lakota.

"Pope, you are head scout. So, you other scouts follow his lead," Major Jamison Cassidy ordered. He led two patrols. Each patrol had a complement of thirty. One lieutenant, a sergeant, two corporals and the rest privates. Cassidy was convinced sixty men in blue could vanquish multiples of any other sixty men anywhere in a fight against the US Army.

Israel started getting bad feelings about the officer just after leaving the fort. He decided very quickly Cassidy was a pompous megalomaniac, though his thought process used the words "power crazy dumbass" instead.

The three scouts rode together half a mile ahead of the larger group.

"Green Turtle, can you tell anything about what tribe we are trailing?"

"Ogallala," he said, without further elaboration.

"Are they a branch of the Sioux?"

The other scout nodded affirmatively.

"Why don't we ride further ahead and try to cut some better sign. Honus, will you ride back to the major and tell him what we are doing? Then, circle the troop and check behind us. Make sure they haven't done the same thing."

Without a word, the other mountain man spun his horse and galloped off. It did not appear he was going to circle at all. He was going to ride past the formation and straight to the rear.

"If the damn fool gets an arrow through his head, there won't be much loss to the world. Cantankerous, crooked drunk!" Israel thought to himself. He was not too sure about Green Turtle but trusted him a bit more than Honus Smith.

The two scouts found sign of a large war party ahead. The braves numbered at least as many as the soldiers. The difference was the soldiers had single shot muzzle loading carbines. The Ogallala Sioux, if they were such, likely had a few muskets and a lot of bows and arrows. They had far greater firepower than the troopers. Using surround and ambush tactics, they could diminish the cavalry's strength in the first skirmish.

"Keep riding and try to find out where they are stopping." Israel turned and rode back to warn the major they were closing in.

By dusk, as the army men were setting up camp, Green Turtle still had not returned. Israel feared he had gone over to the other side, or at the least had deserted.

"No money lost there, these cheapskates don't pay us until after we return," Israel thought.

Green Turtle returned after dark. Israel was surprised he came back. It was a bet he would have lost.

The scouts and Israel met with the major, who was having a drink with his two lieutenants in his tent. It was obviously not his first drink of the night.

Israel saw a meal sitting untouched on a folding table by is cot.

"Major, Green Turtle just got back from watching the Indian camp. The war party stopped there. It is apparently home base. There are women and children and lots of teepees."

"Excellent! We will approach quietly tomorrow and then I will sound the charge. We will kill every one of them!"

"Sir, I did not sign on to guide you so you could kill women and children," Israel said quietly between clamped teeth.

"You will guide me where the hell I tell you, Pope. And, give me no mouth about it! Do you understand me?"

"Clearly," Israel said as he turned to leave.

"Who said you were dismissed, scout?" the drunk major screamed.

"I am not one of your soldiers. I am here of my own will. I have not been paid and owe you and the army nothing. I am leaving to find your orderly and borrow a piece of paper and a pen. I will use them to write you my immediate resignation."

"You can't desert me! I'll court martial you!"

"I am not a soldier. You cannot court martial me. And, I will ride back to the Indian Agent for Wyoming Territory and tell him what you plan. It will likely be you sitting at a court martial if you follow through on your comments, Major."

"Lieutenants. Take this man into custody. I'm tempted to hang him for dereliction of duty right here and now."

Israel knew he was on thin ice. In the field this major had all the power to do whatever he wanted. He could convene a court martial, hang him and answer for it later. Later would be much too late for Israel. He hated to back down, but he had a family. He wanted to return to them.

The two junior officers hesitated. They knew their senior officer was sliding down a slippery slope. And, they saw Israel's hand move ever so slightly closer to the handle of his Bowie knife. A good man with a Bowie could wreak havoc in the confines of a small tent. They heard the tales of Pope killing two bears and who knows how many men with the very blade his hand was nearing.

"Major, perhaps we should address this after the action tomorrow. We need every gun we have, based on the report," the oldest of the lieutenants said.

"Damn it," the major started, but he was interrupted by the other officer who said "Perkins is right, sir. We need his gun. He's not going anywhere. He's known all over the Territory. There's nowhere he could go without being recognized."

Israel did not sleep well once he got in his bedroll. He spoke with the two junior officers later but did give the lieutenants his resignation. They asked him to stay voluntarily.

The next morning, he tried again to dissuade the major. Even cold sober, he was defensive and said how every Indian needed to die. Israel was surprised Green Turtle did not cleft his skull with his tomahawk. The Indian scout glared at the major but said nothing.

The attack, had it been on an equal enemy, was executed tactically well.

Unfortunately, their target, war party, had left before dawn. Only the women, children and old people remained.

Israel watched in horror, unable to stop the slaughter. He tried to save a toddler but was too late as the major himself rode in swinging a saber.

The soldiers were filled with a blood lust Israel had never seen. They were cheered on by their psychopathic major. The two lieutenants and the sergeants were at a complete loss to impact what was happening. Their faces were as horror-stricken as Israel's.

Towards the end, he saw the major chase a young Indian woman into a teepee. He heard screams. It was the final straw for Israel Pope.

In the melee, he slid off Amos and went through the closed flaps on the teepee's opening.

He saw the major, trousers around his ankles, atop the struggling woman.

Israel threw his left arm around the major's neck and pushed his right hand against his head. He stepped back pulling the soldier off the woman. He saw her. She was not a woman. She was a mere girl.

Israel, still protected by the closed teepee door, turned the major around and head-butted him. He went down.

Israel spied a tomahawk and grabbed it. The girl shrunk back. He slashed the blade downward on the rear wall. It left a four foot opening.

He put his finger to his lips to signify silence and motioned for her to go out the door. He thought fast, then fired his rifle up through the ventilation opening at the top of the teepee.

Israel turned and faced the door. Nobody could see in.

He slammed the blade of the tomahawk down on the major's forehead. It sunk in almost to the wooden handle. This man would never rape another innocent.

Israel left the major. His uniform trousers indicated what he had been doing.

He stepped out of the door. The killing had stopped.

He yelled out "Lieutenant Perkins! Here. Quickly!"

The lieutenant rushed in and saw his senior officer dead.

"What happened?"

"As near as I could tell, the major was raping a young child. A young brave we did not know about heard the screams as I did. He slashed the wall and killed the major. He dragged the poor child through the hole. I fired at him. I may have winged him. But, he is long gone now," Israel lied with a straight face.

The lieutenant called the older lieutenant in. They stared at the dead, undressed major.

"Mr. Pope tried to stop it, but a brave intervened and saved the girl. He killed this piece of garbage and escaped. Pope thinks he winged him."

"How do we write this up? It's not a good testimonial about the army."

"The truth is the only thing which will pass muster with a review board," Israel volunteered.

"Mr. Pope is right. We'll get him to write out what he saw and present it with our report. As far as I am concerned, this man was a renegade officer. He ordered us to kill women and children." Both turned and left Israel standing with the dead man. He saw the corner of a piece of paper in the army jacket on the floor. He pulled it out. It was his resignation from last night. He folded it and put it in his shirt.

Israel kicked the dead major in the side and walked out to the scene of a wanton bloodbath.

The two officers decided prudence dictated the company vacate the scene. As they rode away, Israel saw the little girl. Her look at him was unreadable. He did not blame her at all.

Israel's story corroborated the ones in the two

lieutenants' sworn affidavits.

When they got back, he offered to his testimony about the massacre to the base colonel. He was told in no uncertain terms, the action was in keeping with the army's mission to subdue the plains Indians. Israel was sickened. For the first time ever, he was not proud of his government.

Israel wrote a new letter of resignation and presented it to the colonel. He was sent to the paymaster and collected what he considered blood money. He would give every cent to his Kiowa friends. He was out of the army scouting business for good.

******

John was now nine. Israel told him it was time for him to meet his aunt and uncle and learn white man's ways. Once he did, he could choose whichever life he wanted. But, to be fair, he had to be familiar with both.

Before he left, he returned to the shelter up in the Winds. He cached his several years of net earnings in the ground and blazed a mark on a spruce tree with his tomahawk. He measured the number of steps back to his old shelter and wrote them down in ink. His letter was to Arthur and Maude. It said "Do not open unless I am dead." Inside, he gave instructions to the cache and advised upon his death they should take the full amount of gold and silver and use it for John's upkeep and anything they needed. He gave them full authority to act as his agent. He would give it to them when he saw them near the farm, he had helped them get to in Omaha.

The trip was about nine days by mule. White Feather was with child after nine years of marriage. She chose, with a great deal of sadness, to not make the trip.

Israel and John set off in the morning at daylight. Both hated to leave White Feather behind. She was the only mother the boy had ever known.

She was not due for several months, so the issue was more emotional than practical. A photographer had visited the trading post, and Israel had her sit for a daguerreotype. He had another made with the three of them. Both were put in lockets. He kept the first to always wear under his fringed buckskin war shirt. Both put the lockets in soft deerskin medicine bags tied around their necks with a leather thong.

It was these he had shown Arthur and Maude years ago in his visit to Omaha.

"Son, for our time in white man country, call me Pa and I will call you John. There are people there who are narrow minded. They are uninformed and think Indians are savage. Some of them have had relatives killed by Indians. No matter who you are at heart, you should be a white man there. Do you understand?"

"Not really, Pa. Are these people stupid?" the boy asked.

"Some probably are. There are stupid people of every color. Most are uninformed. You have my fair hair and blue eyes. Your birth mother claimed to be part Indian. Our beautiful White Feather is more your mother. It was her eyes you first looked into as a tiny baby. No one could love you more. Except me, of course. And, I love you just as much."

"What will it be like there?" he asked.

"In cities, every day is like rendezvous is to us. Lots of people and noise and scurrying about. Your uncle Arthur and aunt have a farm, so it will be quieter, but still closer to people than you are used to. You will learn how to grow things and tend to animals. It will be hard work. Just remember, life is hard. Once you expect things to be hard and face up to it, life gets easier. Things worth having take work. As Grandfather would wisely say 'it is so.'"

"He's a very wise man, isn't he Pa?"

"Lone Bear is one of the wisest men I ever met. I have been privileged to be his friend, son."

"What will my aunt and uncle be like?" the boy asked.

"Arthur was my dearest friend. I hope he always will be. He is a giant of a man. Bigger than me. Stronger than an ox."

"What's an ox?"

"Think of a buffalo who is gray and has short hair. And, it's a work animal, not a wild one."

"And, Aunt Maude?"

"Think of me as a girl." The boy giggled.

"What's so funny?"

"Does she have a yellow beard?" he asked.

"Not last time I saw her. She might now," he joked with his son.

"Really?"

"No."

"Is she nice?

"She's my little sister. I think she's pretty nice. But, I have not seen her for going on eight or nine years.

"So. She might have changed," John said.

"It's possible. I have. You have. Folks change a bit over time depending on what happens in their lives. But, if you start out good, you usually end up good."

"You will have a little brother or sister soon enough. White Feather and I will bring him or her to see you in Nebraska. Or you can come home and see the baby."

"I can teach him stuff you and Grandfather taught me. Like cutting sign, smelling danger, lighting fires, building shelters and all."

"You sure can, John."

"Do my aunt and uncle live in a teepee?"

"I suspect they still live in a house made partially out of dirt sod. There weren't many trees, so we had to cut sod and build a house out of it until wood could be brought in."

"What's sod, Pa?"

"It's like bricks made out of dirt, and you stack them to make a wall."

"Is it alright if I don't talk for a while? My mouth is getting tired."

"Yes, son. You can rest your mouth if you need to."

They rode on quietly for the rest of the day and made camp around dusk. Israel reckoned they were at the Medicine Bow River from. The pace and number of days on the trail indicated it, as well as what Israel remembered of the geography.

He planned to follow the South Platte until it merged with the North Platte River. They would follow the resulting Platte River. It was not the shortest way but had the most trading posts on the route than cutting across the plains of Nebraska. John did not see his first buffalo on this trip, but he saw his first herd of a thousand buffalo stretched into the horizon.

Arthur and Maude were on the Elkhorn River about fifteen miles from where the Platte turned due south. He was along the Mormon Trail. There was a ferry near his farm.

They came upon a farm meeting Arthur's description from his memory years ago. It was almost supper time when he hailed.

A large, familiar figure came out of the house at the

hail. He was followed by Maude and three little ones, perhaps two, three and five years old.

"Looks like you got some cousins, son."

They rode in and dismounted. Israel got a big bear hug from Arthur and a more normal hug from his sister, who time and childbirth had treated well.

"This is your nephew, John Hunt Pope. He is also known as Night Hawk to the Kiowas. John, this is your aunt Maude and uncle Arthur. And, a passel of children whose names I don't yet know."

The three little ones stared big-eyed at the tall man in buckskins, long hair and a beard.

John seemed pretty normal to them. They would find out very shortly he was more Indian than anything else.

"Old Amos has stood the passage of time well, Israel. So have you. But, you really look like a mountain man!"

"I paid a lot of dues to wear this uniform, Arthur. Even fought another bear. Fought hostiles while leading a wagon train to Oregon and another to California. I even staked out some land there. You should see the soil. You'd love it and the weather," Israel said.

Maude was squatting down in front of John studying him.

"John, you look exactly like your pa looked when he was your age."

"And, Aunt Maude, you don't have a beard!"

She looked at Israel.

"What on earth have you been telling this boy?" she asked.

"I told him you looked kinda like me. The beard was his take on it."

Arthur was trying to keep a straight face during this by-play. He put his big hand on John's shoulder and said, "Son, you and I are gonna be great friends."

Maude introduced their children, who Arthur had not mentioned in his letters.

Two were girls. The older one, John's age, was a boy.

"I made a big pot of beef stew. There's plenty, so let's go in and eat," Maude said.

"What's beef, Pa?" John asked.

The Calloway children giggled.

"Remember those cows we saw on the prairie?"

"Like skinny buffalos with less hair?" he asked.

"Exactly! Beef is meat from them, like venison is from deer."

"John has never had beef?" Arthur asked.

"No. Only deer, bear and elk. This will be a new experience for him."

Arthur looked proudly at the little boy. He was a tall child and a replica of Arthur's best friend who was standing beside both. He looked forward to John's visit, whether it ended up being two months or ten years. Either would have been fine with him.

"The Wind River Range is magnificent, Arthur and

Maude," Israel said during dinner.

"Tell us about it in a little while," Maude asked. "

"I showed you the daguerreotypes of us as a family and of just her on the last visit. Though it has been almost nine years, she looks exactly the same." He removed two lockets from a doe skin medicine bag strung around his neck and passed one each to Arthur and Maude again.

"Oh, Israel, she is so beautiful! And look how happy she is holding little John!" Maude exclaimed. She and Arthur exchanged lockets.

"You have done well my friend. We even hear about you here. There is a story about the other bear fight. And, you leading wagon trains and scouting for the army."

"I have stopped scouting for the army. They just want to kill the Indians. They attack a village and kill men, women and little children. I will not help them do it! It sickens me. And, we call the Indians savages! It's us who are the savages, Arthur. The only people I'd trust John with are the Kiowas and the two people he is sitting between right now."

"Israel, things are stirring up here in so-called civilization. Some states are for the continuation of slavery, some are against it. There's fighting in Congress. Eventually, there will be fighting all over. I fear the whole country will be fighting against itself.

There are Indian troubles, too. We are alright here,

but there have been raids along the Kansas River area. It seems a hotspot. Militias have grown in Missouri and the Extermination Order ran the Mormons out of the area. It seems everybody hates everybody. I am ready to pack up and get on one of your wagon trains to Oregon," Arthur said.

"It's not a bad idea, Arthur. The country in the northwest is fine. Kind of wet, but the weather is otherwise good. You would love the soil, I believe. But, I bought land in Northern California. The weather is even better and the soil seems just as good. I recommend you look there before Oregon. I think you will wish to stay in California and not move north to Oregon, Arthur.

Do you think you can sell your farm here?" Israel asked.

"I do. And, I still have some money left, part of which is yours, from the sale of the places in Boonesboro. From what I read about Oregon, we have enough to buy land there, even if we don't sell the place here," Arthur said with Maude nodding supportively.

"Do you think the same will be true in California? With the sale of the bigger piece of land having two cabins on it, you have a good grubstake, too."

"I do believe property prices will be similar. It's just a matter of deciding on the weather. You'll be able to grow crops either place. It's a long, hard trip to the Pacific coast. But, you already have start. Most folks start from Independence. You are already several hundred miles closer."

"How long would it take to get there with ox or mule drawn prairie schooner?"

Israel figured for a moment.

"Something around three months more or less," he said. "My only hesitation on the time has to do with when we leave. If we get caught crossing the mountains in the winter, it will take a lot longer," he said.

"Do you have a wagon train leaving Independence we could join from here?" Arthur asked.

"Not until late spring. Maybe nine months. I'll write and tell you a good place to meet up with us, Arthur," Israel said. He could tell his sister was excited about moving to the coast. Too many years in populous Kentucky and on the plains had her yearning for green grass, trees, and maybe a few blue mountains.

"Pa, why should I stay here with Aunt Maude and Uncle Arthur? Why can't I go back with you to White Feather?" John asked later when they were alone. They camped on the property. The house was too small to accommodate guests.

"You are asking a good question, son. I could tell you about the white man's ways. But, it is far better you learn them by living them. Though raised as a Kiowa, you are white. It's the world you will have to spend most of your life in. Eventually, many Indians will adopt white man ways—good or bad.

You need to know them. Even if you decide to go back to Indian life. Life is about choices. To make a good choice, you need to know the options. Do you understand?"

"I do, Pa. I will just miss you and my mother, White Feather."

"We will miss you. But, we will visit often and take you home. Think of this like going away to school. School, by the way, is one of the reasons you are here. There are schools. We don't have any near where we live. Even on the trail to Oregon, you will have your aunt, uncle and me to teach you. Uncle Arthur is one of the smartest men I ever knew. He doesn't talk a lot, but when he does, it's worth listening to."

"Also, he knows several trades, including farming. These are things you may need to earn a living. The trapper days are gone. Some fella in England started picking silk hats over beaver ones. Since his wife is the queen, everybody else did too.

We trappers also over-trapped. We did not do what your grandfather Lone Bear taught me....to be a good steward of the land. Take only what you need and honor it by using all of it and wasting none."

"My grandpa is a great man," the little boy said.

"The greatest I ever knew, son," his father agreed.

They had a good two weeks and Israel hated to say goodbye. He really missed his beautiful, kind White Feather and wanted to get back to her. She had trapped with him and their only separations had been when he scouted for surveying parties or led wagon trains to California or Oregon. He still was bothered by the last scout. Bothered a lot by what savagery he saw by the hand of "civilized" man. Bothered not a whit about what he did to the major. The act had no witnesses. The review board about the raid and his death ended with the version of the story Israel invented. He would not spend a day looking over his shoulder for a man with a warrant and iron nippers.

With hugs all around, he mounted Amos and rode west. He left Jed's mule for the boy to have. He still had a pack mule. It could be used by White Feather when she needed transportation.

******

Something urged Israel on. He made the trip back to the Wind River Range several days faster than the trip back east had taken.

As he came over a rise and saw the village, he instantly knew something was wrong. He pulled the Hawken from its scabbard and urged Amos onward at a gallop.

Smoke was rising from where several teepees had burned. Indian men and women were performing a cleanup.

Israel rode straight to Lone Bear's teepee, which still stood. He leapt off his mount and ran in calling first.

Lone Bear was propped up. His wife was missing. He had a wound in his right shoulder.

"White Feather?" Israel asked, almost in panic for the first time in his life.

"Bear Fighter, both my wife and my granddaughter are gone. The two loves of my life. Killed yesterday by a war party of Northern Cheyenne's."

"Did she suffer?"

"No, she killed one with your horse pistol and was drawing her knife when their leader shot her with an arrow to the heart.

I threw my tomahawk and missed his heart. I wounded him as one of his warriors shot me and my dear Cool Rain. They heard fighting right outside the teepee and left to join it, figuring I would die. I know I will die. But, I had to wait for you, Bear Fighter. To tell you who to follow and kill. I need the few warriors I have left to protect the village. It will be only you. You are enough. I know you. They will all die. Fifteen of them. I want the scalps of each one. Then, I can die in peace, my son."

"May I see my White Feather?" Israel asked, tears streaming down his face.

"No. All the dead are in the ground. Their goods are burned. We came from the ground and must return to it. The trail behind these attackers is still fresh,

Bear Fighter."

"Think about the things I must know. I will go and prepare for the ride. I will return to you very shortly, then leave," Israel said.

Israel left the teepee. He found a warrior and asked a favor. Twenty minutes later, Israel returned to Lone Bear's teepee.

He had shaven his face totally clean. His long hair was in two braids. An eagle feather was in it. His bare torso, corded with muscle, and his face were covered with war paint applied by the warrior.

Moving slowly and leaning on a spear, Lone Bear limped out to see him off. He brought a bow and quiver full of arrows and an extra tomahawk.

The whole village had gathered.

"Take these, so something of mine can kill the men who killed all who I loved. And, take the horse you gave me for the wedding gift. He is fast and smart. You will need both. He is yours. I will never ride again. We will look after the mule you care so much about.

The leader is a man I recognized. He had no heart. He is a fighter named Wolf Who Walks in the Night. He is muscular and tall. He has a scar along the side of his face. And, now, a wound in his right shoulder to slow him down.

Bear Fighter, you must kill him. Tell him you are my son and the husband of my granddaughter he killed. He must know these things as he dies. If you have the chance to torture him, do so. Then, bring me his scalp. If I am already dead, hang it above the ground I am in."

"Lone Bear, you have been a father to me. Please live until I return. I want you to know I have fulfilled your request. I want you to have the pleasure of going to meet Cool Rain and White Feather smiling because you can tell them they have been avenged. I will kill and scalp every damn one of them or die trying."

"Wolf Who Walks in the Night often stays at the lake in the hole of the Tetons. His trail appears to head there. He will know the Kiowa victory cry we made when we killed the bear. It would be a good last thing for him to hear!" Israel nodded. He put his saddle and gear on P'ahy, Lone Bear's horse. He visited with Amos and told him he would be back. He really was not so sure but told the mule anyway.

He tossed his shirt over the saddle and mounted. With the stirring victory cry of the Kiowas, he reared P'ahy on two legs and rode off at a gallop.

The tracks of fourteen horses were readily apparent. Israel had been told by the warrior who applied his war paint one Cheyenne had fallen in the attack.

He knew the horse was Kentucky race bred and pushed him, carefully monitoring his lather and breathing. He wanted to catch up with the war party. He would circle them. Then, he would ride far enough ahead to pick his battleground. By the time the war party arrived, his ambush would be set up.

Israel had two long guns, a horse pistol and a bow and quiver of arrows. He was pretty good with a bow and throwing a tomahawk. He knew he could not take on a minimum of fourteen warriors with three shots and some arrows in a standoff. He would die before half of them did. He didn't care if he died. He just wanted to complete his quest and his word to Lone Bear.

Israel knew the only way to win was to pick them off one by one very carefully. Shoot and run guerilla tactics. Like Roger's Rangers and Francis Marion. These warriors could smell and hear an adversary before they saw him. They would not panic when attacked. They would respond to the attack with horrific efficiency.

He rode half a day and slowed the great horse. His name meant "moon" in Kiowa. He saw a faint dust trail ahead. They had left the great prairie land and were a day's ride from the Teton Range. He slowed even more. A war party would be watching every direction. Especially behind. He could not give them any indication he was back there.

Every stealth attack he made, whether by arrow, Bowie, or thrown tomahawk, had to kill his target. He could not afford having a wounded warrior stagger back into camp and raise an alarm.

The war party rode at a moderate pace. They were still heading into the Tetons. Israel thought Lone Bear was right. There was a lake in a "hole" or basin surrounded by mountains. White man would later call it Jackson's Hole. Eventually, the apostrophe and "s" would fade away. They were headed straight for it. The lake would be a good place to winter if their main tribe was on the other side of the Rockies, or maybe even in the Bitter Root Mountains. Perhaps the main tribe was even wintering there.

He planned to make his first kill tonight. Picking off braves hunting would be ideal for day. He would have to act by opportunity.

The dust cloud dissipated. He assumed they had stopped. He rode more slowly and when he got within a mile of where he last saw dust, he dismounted. He took the Trade Musket, loaded with buckshot and the bow and arrows. He always now had one tomahawk in his belt along with the Bowie and a skinning knife.

He padded silently to within a hundred yards of the camp they were preparing for the night. Israel watched several warriors build a fire. Another went for water, carrying several gourds.

Israel laid in the grass on a knoll and watched, unseen. Bugs were crawling. A black racer snake slid over his body and he fought not moving as the five-foot long snake hurried on. "Damn good thing it wasn't a rattler," he thought to himself and shivered at the thought. He took a sip of water from his gourd. "Not too much!" he told himself. He could urinate where he lay but feared the smell might carry a hundred yards to the nostrils of the acutely aware Indians nearby.

Late in the afternoon, he allowed himself a piece bison jerky. He had not actually killed a bison yet. The Kiowas made delicious bison jerky. They smoked it with fragrant wood and soaked it in the juice of fresh berries whenever possible. His saddle bags had copious quantities of it for the quest.

Three hours later, he allowed himself one more sip of water and another strip of jerky. The two hunters he saw leave hours ago returned with a small doe and began dressing it out for dinner.

As near as Israel could tell, the Cheyenne's did not have anyone in the woods now. He moved forward on his belly, an inch at a time. It took him a full hour to move within fifty yards of the camp. In another hour, he was twenty-five yards away.

He waited. The moon was intermittently covered and exposed by moving clouds.

Israel saw movement. One of the warriors had gotten up and walked towards him and stopped by a tree. He was relieving himself against the tree.

Israel silently drew an arrow and aimed. He aimed for the center of the chest but was a bit high. He put an arrow through the man's throat. Luckily for Israel, there was virtually no sound. The arrow cut his spinal cord and he died where he stood. His fall was to soft leaves and dirt. No noise there either.

Israel crouched and moved forward silently. He reached the man, whose eyes stared sightlessly at the moon. A cloud covered the moon and the woods became as dark as pitch.

Using a Green River skinning knife, he scalped the warrior. Israel had never scalped anyone before, so he reckoned he botched it. It did not matter. He had a scalp and one of the men who killed his wife was dead by his hand. Now, a lucky thirteen more had to die. He had plenty of time. The winter might even make his task easier. Tracks in the snow? Yes. But these Cheyenne's could track a man over rock walls, so why worry about snow?

Israel retrieved P'ahy and rode to a nearby box canyon. He emitted the haunting Kiowa victory cry. It reverberated off the walls and could have come from any direction.

Israel rode off and found a place to hide and get some sleep. He slept like a baby, the bloody scalp beside him. As long as he lived, time was on his side.

He did what the Cheyenne's would have least expected. He rode around them and got in front of them. They did what he expected. They sent riders behind them to look for their unseen aggressor. He saw them from a distance and rode further away to look for a place for an ambush.

He picked a shady place on the trail where visibility was poor and laid a thin line of black powder from five feet off the edge of the trail to the center. He took a large brass powder flask with almost a pound of powder in it and tamped the powder down as tightly as possible. Timing was going to be of the essence. He laid the Hawken, Trade musket with buckshot, and horse pistol just inside the shadows by the trail. The bow and arrows were beside the guns.

Just as the war party approached the line of powder, he sparked it with his flint and steel. The only thing caught was the attention of the front warrior. He held up his hand to signal "stop." They stopped surrounding the unseen powder flask. It was covered with dirt and looked like a bump in the trail.

Israel aimed under two horses and shot the flask with the heavy Hawken rifle.

It exploded and the concussion shrapnel from the flask knocked down two ponies and riders.

Before looking at whether they were dead, Israel grabbed the smoothbore and blasted buckshot at a rider. It killed him and wounded another. He dropped the Trade Musket and picked up the horse pistol and killed another. Five down in varying states. He turned and disappeared into the woods, leaving confusion on the trail. He loaded the musket as it was faster to load and again used buckshot. Several warriors followed and he shot one in the gut. He dropped the musket and sent a flurry of arrows in the direction of the others, who jumped behind trees.

A quick count gave him six of the original fourteen dead or wounded seriously, counting last night's kill. Eight warriors remained to be killed.

Enough for now. He made good his escape and rode east for no apparent reason other than the direction looked like it had some hills in which he might hide and reload.

Five miles away, he turned north again to intercept the original route of travel. He knew the Cheyenne's were scouring the woods looking for him near the recent attack. He sure wished there was a repeating firearm other than the inaccurate and not dependable pepperbox pistols. There were a few double barrel fowling pieces, but he did not have one. Nor did he believe one more shot would make a significant difference.

"I need the rest of my powder for shooting, so no more bombs," he said softly to himself and P'ahy. The horse snorted. Israel considered it a good sign.

Israel circled around to the locations of the fight the next day. Since he had the scalp from the first night, he sought and found the shallow graves of the five yesterday. Apparently, the wounded ones died. He scooped the loose dirt off the graves and scalped the five warriors.

He circled left this time and moved four or five miles further away before galloping ahead of his best estimate of travel direction for the remaining eight warriors.

Israel knew he was going to have to hit and run fast and far for the remainder of his quest. The Cheyenne's were on to him. The Kiowa yell and six bodies had not been a very subtle signal somebody was after them and killing them.

He slept. The next morning, he moved closer to their suspected direction of travel and climbed a tall lodgepole pine.

Fifty feet up, he had a broad view and was hidden by the boughs.

He saw them by mid-afternoon. They were sticking to an old buffalo trail. He followed parallel to them from almost a mile away.

He waited for them to camp and saw one warrior move to the rear and begin working his way towards him. They were guarding their backtrail.

Israel watched the warrior powerful with a pot belly and shoulders and arms which could crush a man. He got within five hundred yards of Israel and took a position sitting against a rock. He was facing Israel.

Israel could not see any other warrior flanking this one. He seemed their lone rear guard.

Israel turned to the right and began working his way around the man at a distance of several hundred yards. He was careful, deliberate and slow.

Just before dark, Israel put an arrow into the warrior's chest. He nocked a second arrow and sent it into the man's temple.

The warrior was dead. Israel moved him so his leg was visible behind the rock to anyone coming to spell him from the camp. He also positioned the warrior's musket to be visible but commandeered his powder horn.

After darkness had fallen, Israel waited an easy bow shot away. An hour later, he saw a furtive movement in the trees. It was the relief guard.

Israel cast his tomahawk at the man. It turned three revolutions as he planned and the blade sunk into the relief's forehead. He was down for the count.

Israel waited a while, then moved forward and re-placed his tomahawk with one of the dead men's. He scalped both and moved far away. He mounted P'ahy and walked the horse quietly away from the area.

Man and horse did not stop for an hour. He now had eight scalps. Six left to go, including the leader's.

The next day, he tracked the Cheyenne's through a series of cutbacks in the mountains. He wondered if the canyons would make it difficult to determine where a sound came emanated.

Israel decided to try it. He took a sniper position

behind a tree with a low crotch he could use to steady the Hawken on.

As the Cheyenne's rode by, watching in all directions, he shot the second man in line and he dropped off the horse. Israel could tell from the way he flopped when he hit and the crack of bones, he was dead.

He sped P'ahy off at speed. He heard several horses in hot pursuit but knew the Kentucky purebred could outrun any Indian pony ever born. Israel heard shots, but no sound of musket balls whistling by. The shots were well behind him.

The goal was Wolf Who Walks in the Night and four more. Israel knew he was operating on borrowed time. Had the leader dispatched half his warriors on the first or second day to run down Israel, he would likely be dead by now. Wolf Who Walks in the Night had made a tactical error. Israel hoped it would cost him dearly.

Israel climbed another tall tree and spotted the remaining five warriors riding on the same buffalo trail an hour later. They must have stopped to bury the second in line. They had a destination in mind and were not lollygagging around.

Israel doubled back, dug and him up. Sure enough, his neck was broken. It did not really matter, however, as a fifty-four caliber ball had pierced his heart.

Israel added a ninth scalp to his collection. Israel moved off the trail and rode on, paralleling it from a mile away.

Israel knew he had some decisions to make. The logical approach here on out would be to pick one off every day or so from as far away as possible and use the speed P'ahy offered to get away. But, they were nearing what he and Lone Bear considered their probable destination. What if they were returning to a winter encampment with lots of reinforcements? Continuing under those circumstances would be suicide.

He needed to end this thing as quickly as possible. He also wanted to ride away. To see his son. To give the scalps to his old friend, so he could die in peace.

Israel got ahead of the Cheyenne's once again and set up another ambush.

He set out all three guns and used them once again with great success, killing three and retreating as fast as P'ahy would gallop.

The speed and ferocity of the attack seemed to spook Wolf Who Walks in the Night and his remaining warrior. They rode off as fast as their ponies could carry them.

Israel knew both were warriors and neither were cowards. They were looking for a place to fight on their own terms.

Israel was determined to damn well not give it to them. He pressed his pursuit this time and they turned to fight.

The time had come to do or die. From horseback at full gallop, Israel aimed the Hawken and dropped the second warrior.

He pulled P'ahy to an abrupt halt and dismounted. He walked towards Wolf Who Walks in the Night. The warrior was still mounted. His musket still strapped on his shoulder, the warrior charged Israel with a long lance.

The image flashing across Israel's mind was a knight in a joust or maybe Don Quixote charging a windmill.

Israel stood his ground as the pony bore down upon him the deadly lance pointed at his middle.

At the last minute, he sidestepped and fired the buckshot-loaded Trade Musket point blank.

The blast killed the pony and wounded the rider, who rolled clear.

Wolf Who Walks in the Night recovered quickly and leapt to his feet. The lance was ten feet away, so he drew his tomahawk. He was so bloody from the shotgun blast, it was impossible to tell where the specific wounds were.

Israel pulled the twelve inch blade Bowie knife. It was going to be up close and personal. Just the way Israel wanted it.

In a surprise move, the wounded warrior threw his tomahawk and hit Israel deeply in the left shoulder.

The blade stuck in, the wooden shaft quivering.

Israel gasped at the pain but did not cry out. He would not give Wolf Who Walks in the Night the satisfaction of showing weakness. Instead, he smiled at him and motioned him forward to engage.

Without waiting, Israel charged with a Kiowa victory yell. The big Bowie was glinting in the sun. He covered the seven feet in a second and a half and slashed viscously.

The surprise move, disemboweled Wolf Who Walks in the Night. The brave warrior looked down at his guts falling out.

In a snarl, Israel said Lone Bear's and White Feather's name in Kiowa.

Then, he gave out the Kiowa victory cry. True to Lone Bear's wish, it was the last thing Wolf Who Walks in the Night ever heard. The next slash of the Bowie severed his head.

The tomahawk wound bled profusely when he removed the head of the tomahawk. Israel took the only cloth shirt he still owned from a saddlebag. He wrapped it tightly around the wound. He found a stick and used it in the knot to make it firm against the wound. He did not know what a tourniquet was and even if he did, this was not tight enough to be one. It was tight enough however, to stanch the flow of blood running down his arm and in the dust.

He knew he needed to get out of here. He quickly

picked up Wolf Who Walks in the Night's head and scalped him. Then, he scalped the second warrior. He took the three previous ones as he back-trailed on the way home.

Fourteen attackers rode away from the Kiowa camp. Israel Pope had fourteen scalps in a buckskin sack on P'ahy's saddle.

He began the long ride back home.

After half an hour, he began to get dizzy. He fell off the horse into grass beside the trail.

Israel laid there for an hour before regaining consciousness. He struggled to mount the horse. He made it on the third try and rode on.

He put black walnut salve on the wound when he camped. He cut off a sleeve from the shirt and made another bandage.

Living on water and jerky, he rode for six days. His head was beginning to clear from the dizziness. He knew he needed water and rest more than anything else.

He finally saw the Kiowa camp. It appeared to be almost back to normal. Except his beloved White Feather was not there. Would Lone Bear still be alive and waiting?

Israel rode up to Lone Bear's teepee. It would have been burned if he died.

Weakly, he called out for his friend.

The old man, a mere shadow of his former self,

struggled out and sat down on a log.

Israel dumped fourteen scalps at his feet.

"It is done. The last thing Wolf Who Walks in the Night ever heard was the Kiowa victory cry. He was holding his guts in his hands. I cut his head off, then scalped him. Our loved ones can sleep in peace. They have been avenged, Lone Bear."

"You killed all fourteen and lived to ride back to me?" the chief asked incredulously.

"I did, my friend. As I promised you." The man, who appeared twenty years older than days ago, put both hands on Israel's shoulders. Tears ran down the faces of both men.

"My son, you have done what I wish I could have done. My time here has passed. I can die in peace now. I will see my wife and granddaughter soon. We will speak of you and your deeds. It is so."

Israel could not speak. He looked at this man who had been like a father to him. Israel's vision was blurred by tears. Tears of good-bye to Lone Bear. Tears of heartbreak for White Feather. But, for his son, his world had ended. Now, he must raise the boy in the image of the man he beheld. And, the image of Jed Hunt. He did not consider his image to be worthy compared to those two.

Israel recovered from his wound. He had good care at the village and the application of medicines used for many years by the Kiowas.

Lone Bear died a week later and was buried immediately. He returned to the earth according to Kiowa beliefs.

Israel watched stoically as the chief's teepee was burned. With it, an important chapter in Israel Pope's life went up in smoke.

Soon, he would leave the camp, never to return. He would still be a Kiowa. All of his days.

CHAPTER 6

Israel decided the right thing to do was to return to Arthur's farm and tell John about White Feather. He would tell his son her death was avenged with extreme prejudice. He also needed to recover from his wound.

He stopped at the cache and packed the treasure had saved in years of trapping, scouting and leading pilgrims west. He put it in P'ahy's saddlebag.

He stopped at the first military base he knew about and asked to see the surgeon. His wound was cleaned and stitched up. Not totally trusting the surgeon with his dirty hands, Israel bought a small bottle of the best whiskey a nearby saloon had. He poured half of it on his shoulder and let it run down through the stitched wound. It burnt like hell's fires. He then smeared a prodigious quantity of black walnut salve on it. He put his buckskin shirt back on and rode across the plains toward the farm.

******

The meeting was hard on both him and John. The boy had known only White Feather as his mother. Israel held him and mountain man and child sobbed.

He spent the winter with his friend and sister.

Israel left for Independence in the spring. He found his lament about single shot firearms had been answered by a man named Colt. He knew of the 1830's Patterson with its folding trigger and the almost five pound Walker hand cannons. Most of those had gone to the government. Texas Rangers got the Patterson's and the army got all of the Walker Colts and most of the Dragoons, but not all.

He bought a pair of .44 Dragoons for saddle horn guns and a pair of sleek 1848 pocket .31 calibers with six-inch barrels for his belt. They were weak but fired fast.

1849 brought news of gold being discovered in California. Israel had been there and even bought ranch land near San Francisco Bay for future use. He liked the lay of the land in the north of California better, with its massive trees.

He met a wagon train to lead. The mix of pilgrims was divided between prospective gold miners, drummers who carried trade goods to sell to the miners and farmers wanting to settle in California.

Israel, in his buckskins and long blonde hair was

considered picturesque. With the two revolvers in his belt and the Bowie, it was obvious he was not one to oppose verbally or physically. His bear fighting experience was well known.

He warned the single miners and drummers.

"This wagon train is full of women and children. I will abide no drinking, cursing, gambling, or fighting which will offend or scare them. There will be no second chance. I will exact my guide fee at the start of the trip. You break these rules and you will be left on the trail wherever you commit your offense. There will be no refund of the fee and no rejoining the train. If it is in the middle of a desert or hostile Indian country, so be it.

If anyone cannot follow these rules, or knows he will chose to not follow them, find another wagon train now."

He looked the men he thought would be the most likely offenders in the eye. His voice was like cold steel and left no room for misinterpretation.

Several men grumbled and walked away. If they decided to just follow the train at a distance, he would hang back and leave their bodies by the trail.

He led the fifty wagon long train back near the farm and his family joined the procession to California instead of Oregon. When no one was around, he split the money with Arthur to lessen the odds of it being lost.

Israel gathered all the families for a talk. He sat atop P'ahy as he spoke.

"Folks, I have given the rules to some of our single travelers. A few decided they could not abide by the rules and left. Good riddance to them. If they try to be hangers-on, I will stop them. You cannot have it both ways.

Our trip to California is around sixteen hundred hard miles. We will cross plains, mountains and deserts. We will go through hostile Indian country. Everybody needs to have sufficient supplies, including lead and powder, to make the trip.

The war with Mexico has been over about a year, so you need not worry about getting to California and being drafted into the California Battalion to fight.

For those going to Oregon, my friend Christopher Carson will meet us at Fort Hall several weeks after we cross the Continental Divide and the Rocky Mountains at South Pass. Kit will lead you up the Snake River into Oregon. There will be no additional charge. I will pay him a portion of the fee you paid me. Forty-Niners and California pilgrims will continue with me to California. We will go past Coloma, where gold was discovered at Sutter's Mill. Our miners and gold rush tradesmen can separate from us there and head north to whatever gold fields and camps meet their wishes. I will lead the remainder of the wagon train pilgrims to new Sacramento

City. It will be a good place to head for whatever farming or ranching land you want.

Once we get started, we will have some practice on circling wagons for an attack and other security procedures. I would like to find a cadre of experienced hunters who can break off and bring in fresh meat. If you are a good hunter or a scout, I need to know about it.

Beside me is Arthur Calloway. He will be the deputy leader. In my absence, go to him for advice or leadership.

Any questions?"

Israel received a large number of questions, many of which showed how ill-prepared some of the waggoneers were. He answered them patiently and Arthur responded to a number of them.

His final job was to identify and mark the wagons of the only physician and mid-wife on the wagon train. He felt sure their services would be needed before reaching their final destination. Both were going straight through to California. The mid-wife was traveling with her family. The doctor had gold fever and was going to be digging and panning.

The wagon train left the next morning. Over the next weeks, they practiced their defensive drills and got used to camping out each night. The prairie schooners provided little shelter except for shade and rain protection under the bed of the wagons.

The interiors of the wagons were loaded with food, possessions and, too often, furniture.

The covered wagon drivers using horses or mules to pull became irritated at the slowness of those who had oxen teams.

Israel acted at peacemaker daily and arbitrator only too often. The long slow pull up the constant grades began to favor the slower, more powerful oxen. Teams had to be unharnessed from wagons to pull horse or mule drawn wagons up steep slopes and mud stretches. Wheels came off and wagons had to be jacked up and the wheel reaffixed to the greased hub.

Arthur caught up with Israel and John.

"Israel, are you hungry?" he asked.

"Why? Do you have something to eat?" Israel asked.

"Just water, jerky and some hardtack crackers like you. I was just thinking. Remember how hungry we were growing up?"

Israel nodded and added, "And on the trip up the Shenadoah. We were hungry then, too. At least until you caught those trout."

"I guess my point is the common man is hungry all the time. My stomach growls so much I have begun to talk back to it. You know. Like you always talked with Amos."

"Ha, Arthur. John will tell you I still talk with Amos daily even though the boy is riding him. I don't want him to get jealous of the horse," Israel said.

"You know what's different now, Israel?"

"I know a couple things. Which one do you have in mind?"

"Well, for the first time, I'm not dirt poor. I have been poor all my life. You have, too. We had to scrunch and save just to buy a sheet of paper or a handful of nails."

"It's true, Arthur. We have some money. Why are we still hungry though?"

"Beats the living hell out of me, Israel. I guess the good Lord wanted us to be a little hungry to remind us to be grateful for all we have."

"If we ever lose the money, Arthur, John and I can teach you the Indian way. Unless you want luxuries like hard candy, or to use a gun, you can live off the land completely. The Kiowas, who made me a member, live comfortably without a coin among them. White Feather taught me so many things about living off the bounty of the land. You and I know about the meat. She taught me about berries to make pemmican with the meat. You can eat virtually any segmented berries. Or capped berries, like blue berries. You can grind dandelion roots and make a coffee substitute. Use pine needles for tea. The list goes on."

"I hope the Indians all last through the coming times, Israel. It's going to be hard on all of us, but especially them."

"Me, too, Arthur. Them especially."

They crossed the Wind River Range in a week, ending at South Pass. The pass, though its plateau was high at over seven thousand feet above sea level, was flat and provided a ready transit for wagons. Captain Bonneville had surveyed it.

As promised, Kit Carson met them to take a third of the waggoneers to Oregon. He met with Israel and Arthur. Arthur maintained the tally book with the names, destinations, and fees paid for each traveler. He had kept the people going to the two places segregated in the book and gave the Oregon-bound section to Carson.

Israel had already confirmed the final count and names of the Oregon travelers and moved them into the front of the line of wagons. Arthur computed the agreed upon forty percent of fee for Carson. They paid the scout in gold and silver coins. He departed the next day with his Oregon wagon train.

He camped with Israel and John the night before departure. Arthur and his family joined them at the campfire.

"Israel, will you make a job of leading pilgrims, now the fur trade is long gone?" Carson asked.

"No, Kit. It has too much interaction with people for me. I leave such to other scouts like you who like people more than I. People, in general, complain and argue too much for my liking. I am sick of it already. Once I lead these folks to California, this will be my last expedition.

Arthur and his family want to settle in land I have described the land north of the big bay in San Francisco to them. It is good farmland. I have some ranch land further south. John and I might raise a few horses. My P'ahy is good Kentucky stock. I want to see what kind of line he would sire."

"Well," Kit Carson began, "we are among the last of the true mountain men. Others, like Hugh Glass, are long gone. We escaped the arrows and tomahawks and blizzards to reach more senior years than most. Joe Walker, who developed the trail you will take to California, still lives.

Still and all, I sure don't see you on a ranch. Sitting still most of the time," Carson said.

"I have my boy to raise. I see troubles coming back east. This whole slavery thing is going to explode. I don't want us to be there. I am hoping California is far enough away to keep us out of it."

"Israel, are you saying you believe in slavery?" Carson asked.

"No, not at all. I have just had enough of fighting. Let the two sides of the issue fight it out. I just hope it will not be a deadly and protracted fight, like I fear."

"I do also, my friend. Maybe it won't come to Santa Fe either."

"Maybe. Are you heading out at dawn?" Israel asked.

"Think I can get my group on the trail at dawn?" Carson asked smiling.

"Only if you pour powder under each of them and light it."

Carson stood and walked to his blankets.

"I better get some rest then." He rolled up in a blanket and was soon snoring loudly.

"Bet his wife doesn't miss his snoring," Maude observed quietly engendering laughter which was not particularly quiet.

******

John rode beside Israel each day. He rode Amos and had the Trade Musket in the saddle scabbard.

A week onto the California Trail, Israel and John were scouting ahead and saw a dust cloud in the distance. He reckoned it was five miles distant.

"John, ride Amos back to the wagon train. Tell them to get ready in case the dust cloud is a big war party. Whatever it is, it's coming this way. And, fast! Go like the wind, boy. There's no time to spare!"

John spun Amos around and galloped off. Israel rode P'ahy towards the cloud, Hawken out and ready.

Within a mile, he saw it was not a large war party. It was several hundred buffalos. They were not stampeding but making their way along towards the wagon train.

The last thing as Israel wanted as master was for them to stampede. They were large and extremely dangerous and destructive beasts. But, he knew there was little way he could turn them.

They would be a good and much-needed source of meat. He stopped the horse and set up behind some tall rocks.

As the buffalo, more properly bison, approached within a hundred fifty yards, he began firing and reloading. They turned with no great alacrity and moved to the left. It was clear they would not obstruct the path of the wagons.

He dropped seven of the beasts. There would be a good meal tonight. He mounted P'ahy and rode back to the train. He recruited ten men to be butchers and they left their wagons for their wives to steer.

By the time the wagon train reached the make-shift abattoir, there was a good supply of meat for every wagon.

He taught the ones who did not know how to salt it and to dry it and make buffalo jerky for the trail. A lot of the meat would be eaten tonight at a large cookout.

Their wagon train had crossed the Continental Divide. The Rocky Mountains were behind them. They still had two deserts and several smaller mountain ranges.

As long as they were able to reach California before snow in the Sierras, and avoid hostile war parties, they had the worst behind them.

Tonight would be a celebration. People who were not starving, but whose stomachs had not been comfortably full for several months would have full belly's tonight.

They were on a stretch with few trees. The children were sent out to do their usual pre-dinner task. They collected dried buffalo dung for fuel. What little wood was available supplemented the dung. The air was filled with the aroma of prime meat roasting.

People whose faces had almost set with the grimness of obstacles at every turn were smiling.

They ate their fill and many curled up to sleep near the bonfires.

******

The aroma of the roasting buffalo wafted across the prairie and brought something else.

There was a war party out there, unseen even to Israel who had a nose for such things.

They attacked at full gallop early in the evening. Men ran back to their wagons to get rifles, muskets and fowling pieces.

Men, women and children fell at the first onslaught.

Israel fired his Hawken, always by his side. Instead of reloading, he pulled both five-shot Colt's and kept shooting. Arthur fired his fowling piece, as did young John.

Israel did not think the weak .31 Colt's killed anybody. He knew they wounded a brave for at least one out of every two times he fired. He made it back to P'ahy's saddle and grabbed both big .44 Dragoon Colt's. They carried a powder charge equal to most rifles.

He aimed and fired them with great effect. As other men retrieved their guns, the shooting turned the tide of the attack. The horsemen withdrew.

Israel did not know if they were in the middle of a rout or just falling back to plan another attack.

The physician, mid-wife, Arthur and Maude began to check the casualties.

Israel had John reload and gave him one of the loaded smaller Colt's to guard his cousins.

He moved along the perimeter, also itemizing victims as to death or seriousness of wounds. There were very few dead and fifteen wounded. Half the wounded were critical and many of them would probably die with the relative scarcity of care and medicines.

Horse saddled and ten pilgrims who were former Mexican War soldiers accompanying, Israel rode towards the Indians.

He counted about twenty. None had guns. All had used bows and lances.

A heavily armed charge now might end this matter. He spoke with his men and all agreed.

They moved forward at full gallop, yelling war cries and holding their fire at Israel's command.

The Indians remounted and charged towards them. This was not sniping like the way Israel was used to fighting. It was warfare.

When the two groups of galloping steeds closed to twenty-five yards, Israel gave the command to fire.

His group was virtually hidden in a cloud of gray-white gunsmoke. Half the Indian braves fell, either because of being hit or because their ponies were.

Israel fired the two Dragoons as he closed on them, one in each hand. When both clicked empty, he stuck them in the saddle horn scabbards and drew his standard default. The massive Bowie. He had a tomahawk in his left hand.

Horses, ponies and mules ran into each other. Man and beast hit the powdery dust below them.

It turned to one-on-one hand to hand combat.

The fight lasted less than five minutes. All the Indians were down and three whites. Of the three, one was dead, one critically wounded and one had minor wounds.

But, the threat was mitigated.

Israel, though he did not consider counting himself among the casualties, had several long cuts.

He checked the Indians first. Two were still alive. He took care they would not rise to rejoin the fight.

The surviving Indian ponies had run off. Israel determined to let them go. He did not have confidence anyone in his wagon train could saddle break them.

The critically wounded man died very quickly. Two bodies were tied over saddles. Both had families. The night had turned from celebration to mourning.

Israel knew, and would say, it could have been far worse. They returned to the wagon train. Applause changed to howls of anguish as two women recognized their husbands laid over the backs of their horses. Other women went to console them.

Israel and Arthur would appoint drivers for them in the morning, if needed. Probably, the women would drive their own wagons and friendly families would look out for them.

Five-man patrolling sentries were designated for the rest of the night. Meat from the pit was distributed with the widows getting a disproportionate share.

Israel cleaned his guns and made sure John did also.

"Boy, I watched you. You did real well. I am proud of you. You fired at the attackers, then guarded your cousins. No full-grown man could have done better, son."

"Thank you, Pa. I just did the things you either taught or told me to do. You were the hero, charging the larger band of warriors. We could see the fighting in the distance. It looked like fists and knives to us."

"It was fists, knives and tomahawks. Up close and

real personal. The worse kind of fighting, where every adversary knows he is fighting for his very life."

As Israel was saying this, he was putting salve on his knife and tomahawk cuts. He would take some to the man who had sustained similar injuries.

"Pa, were you serious about not leading any more wagon trains?"

"I'm thinking about not doing it any more. The money is good and not as hard a work as trapping was. I just like solitude, son."

"Oh! Here's your Colt .31 back, Pa." John said.

"You better keep it, son. Make sure it's fully loaded, but with the firing pin on the hammer tucked into the safety slot between the chambers in the cylinder. If you drop it, the hammer is locked away from the percussion cap and the gun won't fire."

"Thank you. It's a fine gun."

"For a fine son," Israel said.

******

They arrived at Coloma. The village had sprung up overnight near Sutter's Mill where gold had been discovered.

All of the Fortyniners left the train there. The drummers would open shops, base out of there to call on mines northwards, or both.

Israel took the rest of the waggoneers to the Napa

Valley in the California District of Sonoma. Less than a year later, Napa County would be formed.

Arthur liked the area. However, he and Maude were tired of moving so much. She started off tired of moving from wrong place to wrong place with her late father.

"I'd like to see more of California. I like the climate and the soil I've seen so far. I think it would be a good place to ranch and farm. How about if we put off buying land up here and go down to Alameda where your land is and look there?" Arthur asked.

"It sounds like a good idea to me. Don't you think so, John?" Israel asked.

"I do!"

They went to the village of Oakland and had the lawyer through whom Israel had bought his ranchland lead them to it. The acreage was rolling hills with some trees and lots of grazing land. It was much more ranchland than farmland to Arthur.

"How about this?" Israel began. I will take some of my treasure and build a house with enough bedrooms. We can all live here for now and Arthur and I will ride around the Bay area and let him pick several spots to take Maude back to for her vote.

Maybe I will pick up some mares and breed P'ahy and start a small horse operation. Every now and then, I will scout for an army surveying party or lead one last wagon train from Independence to

Oregon or California. Or, maybe not. John can grow up a rancher. If when he gets older, he wants to do something else, he can."

"Sounds like a good plan to me," Arthur said. Maude nodded her approval.

They went into San Francisco and found a house builder. He would haul lumber and roofing materials to Alameda. He had some time and a large deposit guaranteed he would start within days.

Arthur and Israel exchanged coins. Arthur received his share of the wagon train money as number two and Israel received the money from the sale of his property in Boonesboro.

"Where ya going to put this, Israel? A bank in San Francisco?" Arthur asked.

"I don't trust banks, Arthur. I will have the lawyer draw up a document leaving my money to you and John. He should get his once he is twenty-one. If we both were to die, you would get it all. In the meantime, we will cache it here. You will know where it is."

"I don't really want to know, Israel. Cache it and draw up a map. Put the map in a sealed envelope to be opened only upon your death."

"Alright, but I trust you, Arthur, above just about anybody."

"I know, my old friend. But, it's just good business to do it the way I suggest."

"Consider it done."

They set up camp near where the house would be. There was a stream nearby and Arthur found it had fish in it. He, John and the small children all took delight fishing. Israel and Maude took equal delight eating the fish they caught as well as salt water species from seafood shops during their weekly trips to San Francisco.

On those trips, they chose enough furniture to meet their needs.

Arthur decided to put in winter wheat and some potatoes and onions. They still had salted buffalo and buffalo jerky. Arthur used some of the skills he learned from Mr. Cross in Kentucky to build an ice house.

By fall, they had a fairly large house by their personal standards. Israel and John shared a room, Arthur and Maude had a room and the children had one. There was a large room for living in and cooking in, a pantry and a privy out back.

They had the builder construct a stable and corral. The ranch was complete. They just needed more horses and some crops.

Maude was at the house with the children. John went with Arthur to look at property in Marin and Sonoma.

Israel decided to ride around his property and view portions he had not seen. He saddled P'ahy and trotted off.

It gave him time to think. He had been a really good trapper. Those days were gone. He was a good scout but limited because he refused to lead troops to slaughter Indian women and children. He was a good wagon master. But, he intrinsically did not enjoy groups of people.

"So, what am I," he asked himself. "A woodsman. A fighter. A survivor. A parent. How can I use these things to make a living, unlike my father who had no particular skills?

Maybe I am going about this wrong. Maybe I should ask what I am not. I am not a people person. I am not a farmer nor a shopkeeper. I probably, despite the money I just spent on this ranch, am not a rancher. I am not one who enjoys staying in one place. Or, sleeping under a roof. I am not a good husband apparently, because my wives all die."

He had a conundrum. He acknowledged he was a philosopher. But, he had no interest in writing a book about his philosophy. Any more than anyone would have an interest in reading it if he did.

"Maybe I am a lawman. I enjoy cutting sign and chasing someone down. But, then, I would hate being in an office between bringing in criminals."

In the end, he decided he had two possible job skills he could tolerate. He could be a highly selective scout where he knew and believed in the goal of the employer and trip. Or, he could be a bounty hunter.

He had the tracking skills, the intellect, and the deadly prowess to bring about anyone in. On the saddle or over it. He would give it some thought. Maybe share his mental meanderings with his family.

Feeling only a little bit satisfied, he rode back to the ranch. Soon, he was listening to his sister and had the little ones crawling all over him. They took great delight in pulling the fringe on his shirt. The youngest, a boy, enjoyed chewing on it.

Thank heavens he did not grow his beard back. They would be swinging on it. They tried for his blonde handlebar mustache but were unsuccessful. He shared the thought with Maude who thought the beard hanging visual was funnier than her brother did.

"The next thing they will try is your long hair."

"Shhh! Don't give them ideas." It was too late as a toddler latched on and swung, his little feet clear of the floor. Maude broke out into hysterics.

******

Israel based out of his Alameda ranch for the next ten years. He had money stashed and made sufficient income with his horse sales and bounty hunting to not have to dip into the cached money. He raised his son and helped Arthur and Maude move to Napa and establish a farm. A farmer nearby was from Greece. He said the land reminded him of his homeland. Arthur began studying Greek crops and growing methods. Maybe it was time to try something other than corn, wheat and root vegetables.

He continued to teach John tracking. In his mid-teens, he could cut sign almost as well as his famous father.

About twice a year, he led a group of pilgrims somewhere from the east to the west, took a job guiding a surveying party, or tracked a fugitive for the money. His scouting career was about to take a sabbatical from 1861-1865.

The country was almost ready to explode. Abraham Lincoln, whose family had lived for a while in Pope's area of Virginia, was rising in politics and would be President soon.

Shortly thereafter, the new Confederate States of America would attack Ft. Sumpter in Charleston, South Carolina and the country would be at war with itself.

When the war began, Israel stuck to his original pledge to stay neutral. John, joined the Union Army as a scout. He learned from reading and talking with people about the violence perpetrated by both sides of the slavery issue. He learned about slavery itself and was angered it could exist in what he always thought of as a free country.

"Pa, I have to do my bit to make sure my children don't grow up in a land which tolerates one man owning another."

Israel agreed with him but held true to his oath to never work for the government again. He did not trust them because of the Indian policy.

He would see it actually worsen after the war when mass genocide of plains Indian people was cloaked by the killing of their subsistence in the form of millions of bison.

To Israel, killing a buffalo or bison was purely a one-time thing to eat. He knew killing them to feed the workers building the transcontinental railroad was a ruse.

Despite the money he could have made, Israel Pope never was a commercial buffalo hunter and did not respect those who were.

John initially worked under a flamboyant scout named James B. Hickok from Illinois. The strawberry blonde scout wore buckskins. Hickok had long hair and a sweeping mustache not unlike Israel Pope's. Hickok introduced him to a younger boy who was a Union scout at fourteen years old. His name was William Cody. John distinguished himself as a scout and became almost indispensable to his company. When Hickok moved on, John became head scout at twenty-three. It was dangerous work. Scout during the war often meant spy.

Father and son wrote weekly throughout the war. John thought it interesting Hickok, one of the coldest, deadliest men he ever knew, corresponded weekly with his brother.

John quickly validated his father's quotes, such as "you cannot tell a book from its cover."

John had married in 1855 at age twenty-one. His wife very quickly bore him a son, John Junior. A daughter followed five years later. They lived at the ranch in Alameda until the boy was five and moved to Kansas to be near John's new army assignment.

Abolitionist and pro-slavery violence started in Kansas before the war and continued during it. Israel, ever the prolific reader, had cautioned John against taking his family from the relative safety of Northern California to Kansas.

Israel sorely missed the little boy and tiny girl. So many bad things were happening in Kansas. Of all the places John's work took him, Israel considered Kansas the most dangerous.

******

The war provided some incidental income for Israel. A number of Confederate partisans from Kansas and Missouri were declared felons instead of the patriots they considered themselves to be.

Many escaped further west. California, Nevada and Wyoming were frequent retreats for them. The government was generous in both the rewards and conditions of bringing them in.

Israel, now in his late forties, became friends with the new sheriff of Alameda County. His name was Harry N. Morse. After the war, he would become perhaps the most famous detective in America, if not the world. His competition was the man who ran Lincoln's unofficial secret service, Allan Pinkerton.

Morse knew Israel Pope's reputation as a man-tracker and fed him with a good supply of wanted dead or alive warrants.

Israel seldom wore buckskins any more, other than a fringed buckskin jacket which had pockets and buttoned up the front. His fame continued to grow through his bounty hunting work.

He carried iron nippers to handcuff his prisoners, but seldom had the opportunity to use them. Far too many fugitives feared the noose more than a bullet and made last ditch stands.

His Colt .36 caliber Navy revolvers or his Henry rifle usually resolved the arrests. He liked both much more than the predecessor firearms.

Israel rode into the Alameda Sheriff's Office in late 1865. His long hair and mustache were blonde streaked with gray. He wore a dark suit, and a dark canvas duster.

P'ahy was being saved for stud duty. He rode a new horse. It was a powerful paint colored black and white. This horse, Bear, named for him and his father-in-law, had tremendous endurance and was perfect for riding down fugitives.

Israel immediately saw a bleak look on his friend, Sheriff Harry Morse's, face.

"What's wrong, Harry. You look like you've seen a ghost."

"It's worse, Israel. Much worse. Sit down at my desk."

"Israel, I just received a telegram from the commanding officer of a military post in Kansas. He wanted me to locate you as soon as possible."

Israel felt bile rise up from his gut. It had to be about John.

"Israel, I am so sorry to tell you this, but a war party hit the ranch John was renting and he and his family were all killed. Well, all except one. The little boy was recovered alright by neighbors. They armed up and rode to the ranch when they heard the shots. A full company of cavalry from the fort rode after the Indians, maybe Crows, but lost them. John was their best scout, he says here," Morse shook the telegram and handed it to Israel.

Israel read it as if in a trance.

"I have to go there now, Harry. The fastest way. I have some Indians to kill. Every damn one who set foot on my boy's ranch. They are walking dead and don't know it yet."

Harry Morse believed him. He heard the stories

about the Bear Fighter taking on two bears and having them for dinner. About a similar war party he tracked down and killed one by one with single shot guns and the damn big Bowie.

He looked at a man who was forty-eight years old. A man who had walked and ridden across the country. In the worst weather. Often without meals. Reputedly one of the best trackers who ever lived. Yes, the war party should start singing their death chant now. He would not give a plug nickel for any of them.

"Take the train out of Oakland. Put your horse on the stock car. Change at Denver or Chicago, I don't know which for sure. A train will surely run through Kansas somewhere near the ranch. Get to the boy. He is what counts most here, Israel. Little John. I remember when you would bring him into town. He joined us for lunch once, remember?"

Israel nodded.

"I need to go back to the ranch long enough to get a grubstake. I have enough stuff for a long trail ride already on the horse."

"You may not need to go back to the ranch. The bank in Nevada just sent the reward for the last fella you brought in over the saddle. I identified him and certified the reward. I have five hundred dollars cash money in this envelope for you. Get on down to the train station and bring the boy back." He handed Israel the envelope.

The tall former mountain man stood and proffered his hand to his friend with a badge. The man who would one day bring in Black Bart, the stage robber. One of the longest sought outlaws in American history. They shook and Israel turned and walked out the door. He had to go back to the ranch anyway to saddle Amos and take him for the boy to ride back. He also packed his full reserve of guns and ammunition. Other than train food, his only other item was a book on Indian tribes of America. He would do some serious reading as the train steamed along.

He was on an east bound train several hours later. Armed and deadly. There would be hell to pay and he would exact it. And, bring the boy back and raise him. He pledged to himself he would never leave him alone in harm's way.

Three days later, he got off in Kansas and retrieved Bear and Amos. He tipped the baggage man in the stock car for saddling the big paint and dependable mule.

Israel inquired about where the army post was. He rode over, took out the telegram and showed it to the sergeant who challenged him. Lee might have surrendered, but the war was still raging in Kansas. The post was on high security. He was led straight to the base commander.

"Mr. Pope, I am Colonel Sharp. I am sorry for your loss. It's our loss, too. Your son was our lead scout. You know something? He always said you were better."

"First off, Colonel, where's my grandson?"

"He's with the Taylor family at the next ranch west of John's. They rode in with armed cowpunchers when they heard the shots. They buried you son, his wife, and the small girl. Took them to the church and buried them there. They figured you'd want them to." Israel nodded.

"When did this happen?"

"Five days ago. I mounted a double patrol of about sixty troopers. We rode as fast as we could. We followed them into the unassigned lands due south. Lands designated Indian Territory. My authority stopped at the line, which is actually kind of vague."

"Mine doesn't," Israel said.

"I thought it would be what you'd say."

"Only thing I will need after I see the boy is another Henry rifle. Know where I can buy one?"

"We only used them for special units in the war. Our leadership in Washington thinks soldiers would waste ammunition with repeaters, so we will have single shots until the damn cows come home. But, come with me."

They walked to the post armory.

"Sergeant, you still have any of those Henry's?"

"Yes, sir, Colonel. Over here."

"Pull out the best one."

The sergeant withdrew a brass mounted sixteen shot lever action repeater. It was the forerunner of the Winchester rifle.

The colonel levered the action and looked in the chamber.

"Sergeant! This rifle will not function properly. Immediately surplus it! I will sign the paperwork. Give me a hundred fifty cartridges. I will dispose of them also."

"But, Colonel…."

"Just do it, sergeant and do it right now!"

"Yes, sir!"

They walked out and he handed Israel the rifle and cartridges.

"Thank you, Colonel. I will put this to real good use."

"Lieutenant?"

"Yes, sir, Colonel."

"This is scout Pope's father. Please get a mount for yourself and escort him over to the Taylor ranch for me. He needs to retrieve his grandson."

"Yes, sir!"

No sooner than they came into sight of the Taylor ranch, Israel saw John come running out towards him.

"Grandpa!"

He caught the boy in two arms and lifted him up on the horse. He held his grandson to his chest as the boy sobbed.

"They killed little sissie. She was hidden in the ice house with me. She heard the shooting and ran out before I could stop her, Grandpa. It was all my fault!"

"No, Sonny. There was nothing you could have done. You were smart to stay alive. Alive to help me figure out who did this. Don't ever think again it was your fault! It was not, Sonny," Israel emphasized.

"Lieutenant, do you know for sure what tribe this war party was from?" Israel asked as the Taylors came out to greet him.

"Not really. I heard Crows, but both the Sac and Fox tribes have been acting up a bit. They raid up here and disappear into the unassigned Indian country below the Kansas border."

"And, you tracked them there and had to turn back due to lack of jurisdiction?" Israel asked.

"Can I say something which will go no farther than just us?" the officer asked.

"Of course."

"I read the Act. I believe we had proper jurisdiction and the major at the head of the column did not know what the hell he was doing."

"Yes. I would think the US Army could pursue hostiles anywhere they need to, Lieutenant. I will not ever mention what you said, but I believe you are correct."

"Are you going after them?"

"Would it be legal, Lieutenant?" Israel asked.

"Probably not."

"Then, I probably won't go after them," he said,

winking.

"Good luck, sir. Whatever you do or don't do."

"Thank you. I'll need it. For sure, I'll need it!"

The Taylor's invited him in. He wanted to thank and question them anyway.

"First off, thank you for taking care of my grandson. Second, I'd like to know all I can about the raid. Who, how many, maybe if you recognized the tribe. Those sorts of questions."

"Wal, I can't tell you the tribe. They weren't too well armed. A couple old muskets and mainly bows, lances, and tomahawks. Them fellas looked real fit, though.

You can be real proud of your son. He had a Henry rifle and killed four or five. His wife had a fowler and must have had buckshot in it. I found some bodies which was tore up something fierce.

Once all the shooting started, me and the boys jumped on our horses and rode hard. I figured if we let 'em know we was coming, they might stop killing and retreat.

They did once we fired shots at them from a long distance. They didn't expect a group of armed men riding fast on them.

They didn't have time for scalping. Your boy was killing them with a couple arrows in him. Mr. Pope, could we send the boy outside. He don't need to hear this," Taylor said.

"Grandpa. I saw it. I need to know everything so I

can help you track them down and kill them. Please let me stay. I can handle it," the little boy said.

Israel Pope had bonded with his grandson who followed his every step around the ranch from the very first. He had never been prouder than at this moment.

"It's your call, John. Mr. Taylor, please continue."

"Just as John's rifle went empty, the leader got him with a lance. The little girl died by arrow. She didn't suffer. It was instant. Your daughter-in-law was wounded but ran at the big man when he killed your boy. He killed her with the same lance. We had already fired some shots and were riding and reloading. They rode off immediately.

I reckoned it was better to check for survivors than chase them. I'm glad about it, because your grandson was there and we were able to get him to safety. John hid the young'uns and the boy came running out shooting a little pocket Colt when his little sister broke out. He was popping the little gun as fast as he could. I sent one of my boys directly to the post to get soldiers on the trail."

"You did more than most, Mr. Taylor. I appreciate it," Israel said.

"I wish we could have saved them. The attack was just too fast."

"Nobody could have done more. And, you protected my grandson. I'll always be in your debt, sir."

"One other thing, Mr. Pope. We might have

winged a couple of them as they rode off. We let go a helluva volley at fifty yards. We had to have wounded some of them."

"I sure hope so. I will let you know when I have dealt with them."

"You are going after them? Leading the army? I know you were a scout and mountain man.

"No army. This is personal."

"You mean you against the whole war party?"

"Yessir. I took on a similar size war party once before. With a single shot Hawken, I had to pick them off one by one. Now, with Henry rifles and Colt revolvers, I will ambush them."

"The previous war party…. did you kill them all?"

"Every single one. The last by my old dependable. My Bowie knife," Israel answered very matter of factly. John looked like he was going to say something, looked at his grandfather and withheld his planned words. They had been able to communicate silently since he was a toddler. It was uncanny, but very useful.

"Oh, Mr. Pope. I have your son's Henry rifle for you. He used it to great effect," Taylor said.

"Excellent!" Israel thought to himself. He and John would have three sixteen shot Henry's for their ambush. His initial plan was to lay down an enfilade of fire on the war party and, hopefully, limit the contact to one skirmish.

"I will make sure it is used again to great effect. Thank you, Mr. Taylor."

"Can I pay you something for looking after him?" Israel asked.

"Yep. Just kill those people who attacked your son, Mr. Pope. Send 'em to hell for me."

Israel nodded solemnly.

Man and boy thanked Taylor again and rode off in the general direction the war party had taken.

"Sonny boy? Remember how we spent time learning about tracking and watching for threats before you moved to Kansas? We are going to use all of those skills for real now. They have a good head start on us. We will spend some time with you practicing shooting a Henry rifle. You can use your pa's as a primary rifle. You and I can lay down a lot of fire up close with three Henry's, John!

I have my two Colt Navy .36's and two old .44 Dragoons. We can pick our spot with some good barriers to protect us, lay out all our loaded guns and open up when they ride into close range," Israel said.

"John, you saw the worst a man can see during the attack. If you ever want to talk about it, just let me know."

"Not right now, Grandpa. Maybe some time, though."

Once they passed the small ranch his son had rented, they veered off the main road and headed south.

There was no traffic in this direction except for two types. One was un-shoed pony tracks. It looked like twenty of them. It was difficult to tell. They were largely obliterated by the uniformly shoed tracks of sixty army mounts.

They had to be the war party and their initial cavalry pursuers.

Israel and John rode until almost dark. Just before they planned to stop for the night, Israel spotted a new grave. It was hastily dug just off the faint trail they were following. The double patrol of cavalry missed the grave.

Using his small trowel, he dug up enough of the grave to identify a brave of perhaps twenty-five years old. He had a bullet hole in his upper chest.

"Good shooting, John!" Israel said aloud.

"Sonny, I'm going to lift his scalp. You can turn away if you want. There'd be no shame in it."

The boy watched and Israel put the first scalp of the hunt in a burlap sack.

Later, they made camp in a rocky area. Israel decided against a fire. They had water and jerky and slept soundly. Israel did his usual circle of the camp before settling to make sure no threats were in the area. He discussed the need to always do this with the boy.

When they stopped for the night the next day, the spot was where the army hoofprints turned and rode back, albeit not on the same exact trail.

"I'm guessing this is the line where the soldiers thought the Indian territory began. I reckon the war party, knowing the pursuit is done, will slow down now. We won't slow down and will catch them within a day or two. I think it would be safe for you to do some rifle practice. First off, did your pa show you how to load and shoot his Henry rifle?" Israel asked.

"Yessir. I know how to load it and how it works. Ammo was scarce, so I didn't shoot it much."

"Well, let's spend half a box of fifty rounds for you today. I will set up some pine cones at ten yards, twenty-five and some sort of larger targets at one hundred yards. Let's see how you do."

The boy blew the pine cones off a log at both of the shorter ranges, which were the ones Israel knew they would need for the ambush. He made his grandson adjust his hold for the longer range and rest the nine plus pound rifle against various rests. He chose trees, rocks and logs. Before the twenty-five cartridges, or "rounds" were gone, the boy could hit each man-sized target at one hundred yards.

"Let's clean her up, Sonny Boy. You did real well. I'm proud of you."

The boy smiled, something he had not done much since the attack on the ranch.

They rode more slowly into the Indian territory for the next several days. Israel did not want to come up on them unexpectedly.

From the way they were heading, he suspected they were after a Sac or Fox war party. Originally two Midwest Algonquin tribes, they were now closely associated. They were originally known as the Sauk and the Meskwaki Tribes. He read about them on the east bound train. They were reputed to be handsome, athletic people and fierce warriors. While some still hid out in Iowa, this band had relocated to the un-assigned territories. They knew they were relatively safe there and could slip out on raids without much fear of being chased back home.

Israel carefully followed signs and showed John each time he made a decision and why.

"Look at the dust and leaf fragments in each track. The limited amount, given our wind and our lack of rain indicates to me we are probably a day behind them now."

They had been following what Israel suspected was the North Canadian River for several days. He did not have any sort of map but based it on his reading on the train.

"I suspect they are going to a village. We will follow them there and ambush them just before they arrive. We will have to catch up, give them a look-see, then circle around unseen, and get ahead of them for the ambush.

They will be careful. While there are plenty of rock formations in this damn red dirt country, they will avoid any place where someone could ambush them. The unassigned lands have warring tribes in 1865, as well as crooked whites. And, there is virtually no law here," Israel told his grandson.

He focused on teaching John listening and smelling skills. He thought the boy had tracking down well.

"Your pa grew up until almost your age as an Indian. He started refining his sense of smell from the very beginning. I was in my late teens before Jed Hunt, the man for whom you and your pa were named, taught me about it.

You have, ingrained in you, the capability to smell far more than most white men use. You need to use your brain and nose together. Blow stale air out of your nose and concentrate on the air coming in. Over time, you will be able to pick up man. Human beings have a smell about them. Horses do, too. Part of human smell may include smoke. Smoke from a campfire or tobacco. Think about when your ma cooked. Fish smelled different than beef or bacon, right? So, on the trail, a cook fire will smell different than one for warmth.

Indians and woodsmen like you and me make smaller fires. We often use a fire pit with an air hole and tunnel. The main pit fire sucks in air through the air hole, pulls it through the tunnel and feeds the fire in the pit. The fire in the pit then burns better and is hotter with less fuel and less smoke. Both are good things on the trail, especially in country where there may be hostiles about."

"You mean Indians, Grandpa?"

"Not always. Hostiles can be anybody. It can vary from place to place. There are hostile, evil people of every color and description. Depends on where you are," Israel said.

"What are we going to do tomorrow?" John asked.

"I'm thinking we are going to make a wide half circle around the party we are trailing and get 'way ahead of them. We want to find their village and see who's there. Lots of warriors to reinforce them when we ambush? Or, are these the primary men in the village? This is called intelligence. And, we need it to make our decisions. It's the kind of thing your pa did in the war.

Then, we will carefully ride back towards the men we have been behind. Along the way we will look for a good place to stop and set up. We have to be real careful to not ride plumb into them. Good warriors or not, I reckon they will be getting a little less cautious as they get closer to home, don't you?" John thought about this, then nodded at the logic.

They did their wide half circle. At the top, Israel smelled a fire.

"Do you smell it?" he asked John.

"Yessir."

"What kind of fire is it?"

"I think it's a cooking fire, Grandpa."

"It is. We are nearing the camp. Let's leave Bear and Amos here. We can sneak over, take a hidden position and watch and learn for a while."

The boy slid off Amos and withdrew his pa's Henry rifle from the scabbard.

"Always take a few magazine tubes full of ammunition with you. Also take your canteen. Never know when they might come in handy," Israel said as he did the same.

"Bear will stand, reins down. So will Amos. No need to tie his reins over a branch, alright?" Israel said.

They crept towards the village. They walked through red dust and rocks. It was uncommonly hot.

There was one tree offering shade. Israel passed it and laid in tall broom straw.

He stuck his finger in his mouth and raised it to feel the direction of the breeze. Unfortunately, it was blowing their scent and voices directly to the village. Israel shared this with John in a close whisper.

"Wouldn't the tree have provided more shade and hidden us better, Grandpa?"

"It would have. However, the Indians in the village would already know about the shade and additional hiding it gives. So, they will watch it and listen periodically.

We will lay here without moving and see what we can learn."

They laid an hour. People, mainly women, moved about the village doing a variety of chores. Israel closely watched a big teepee. Its position and large fire pit reminded him of Lone Bear's. He thought this would probably be the chief's teepee.

Presently, a large man walked out. He was probably seventy, but still looked strong and capable. He clearly was, or had been, a warrior.

He spoke with a woman and returned to the teepee. There did not seem to be any other men above the age of fifteen in the village.

Israel tapped John on his shoulder. The two backed away, still on their bellies. After fifty yards, they turned and crawled out of sight. They mounted up and rode slowly away.

An hour later, Israel found his battleground. The shots would not be heard from the village. There was a dip in the faint trail. Several large rocks were beside the trail. There was a heavy growth of juniper near the rocks.

They unloaded canteens, the three Henry rifles and the heavy Colt Dragoon .44's.

While John took the mounts to a stand of trees several hundred yards away, Israel used the butt of his rifle to roughly brush through the juniper for snakes. There apparently were none. He cut some juniper with his tomahawk to pile on them once they laid down.

Israel looked up at the sun. He reckoned the war party would be nearing within half an hour.

Weapons, ammunition and water at hand, the two laid down in the juniper. Israel took the cut juniper and put a big piece on his grandson's back and head. He virtually disappeared from sight. He laid a new Russell Green River knife on the trail where they would see it and stop. Stop exactly where he wanted them to stop. And, die.

He laid down under the juniper thicket beside his grandson and dragged a big cut bough over his head and shoulders as he had done for John.

"When the time is right, I will touch your shoulder and stand up. You do the same. As soon as we are up, we will commence firing. We are close, so let's not shoot each other. At such close range, just hold the butt of the Henry under your armpit. Turn your body to aim. There's no need to shoulder the rifle to use your sights on big targets from six feet.

Fire as quickly as you can pull a trigger and lever your rifle. I want our fire to be devastating and overwhelming, John. As soon as a gun is empty, pick up the one at your feet and start firing it. We have sixteen rounds in the Henry's, and twelve in each pair of Colt's. Which gives us fifty-six shots for around twenty men."

"Sixty-one, Grandpa. Pa gave me this just before the attack," John said. He produced the small 1848

Pocket five-shot .31 Israel had given his son when he was about his grandson's age. He flashed back to a very similar looking young boy so many years ago. Hopefully, today vengeance will be dealt for his death. And, the deaths of his wife and tiny daughter.

They laid motionless and silent under the juniper growth. The wind moved the leaves. Israel could hear and, indeed, feel insects moving around.

In the silence, Israel could hear the muted hoofbeats of unshorn horses on the trail.

The hoofbeats became louder and stopped. They stopped and there were guttural questions in a language unfamiliar to Israel. They had spotted the new knife in the trail.

He knew they were speculating about how it got there.

Israel Pope, and to a slightly lesser extent, John Pope, could feel them beside where they lay. The mountain man touched his grandson's shoulder and both came up shooting.

Even to experienced warriors, it was as if demons had risen up from hell. The surprise gave the Pope's several seconds of target confusion to multiply the advantage of their repeating rifles.

Men and ponies were falling.

Israel dropped his rifle and drew the two Colts and kept shooting without a pause. He felt, as much as heard, his grandson drop the first Henry rifle and grab his second one. The boy shot immediately upon raising it.

An arrow flew between them and Israel shot the warrior in the face with his Colt Navy.

They were not watching the scene unfold. They were in the middle of it.

A warrior aimed his musket at one of them. Israel was not sure which. Before the warrior could fire, John shot him in the gut and folded him up. He was still a danger and Israel shot him again, this time through the neck.

Targets were any part of the enemy's anatomy which would take him permanently out of the fight.

The hammers clicked on the cylinder nipples of the Navies without firing. He was out. Israel dropped the two revolvers and reached down for the massive Colt Dragoons at his feet. He started firing and only one man remained standing in the trail.

He saw the brave with the scar on his face—the leader—draw his bowstring back on an arrow. It was aimed at the boy.

Israel barely had time to step in front of John and catch the arrow in his shoulder to save the boy. His urgency worked. Israel did not know about adrenalin, but he knew some power had infused him with speed as he felt the burning agony of the flint broadhead sink into him.

He grunted and cocked his right hand Dragoon. It

was opposite the shoulder with the arrow protruding.

John fired the rimfire Henry, not as powerful as the fifty-five grains of powder loaded in each cylinder of the big Colt.

John's conical bullet hit the warrior in the navel. Israel knew it must be an excruciating wound.

The man flashed a look of pure malevolence at them both and staggered towards them. He had his knife in one hand and a tomahawk in the other.

Israel dropped the Dragoons and drew the Bowie.

The two warriors, one a Sac and the other a white Kiowa met in seconds.

Israel let out the victory cry of the Kiowas and slashed the twelve inch clipped point blade.

The warrior tried to fend off the slash with his tomahawk. The Bowie severed the wooden handle of the 'hawk. The man with a hole in his gut and the man with an arrow in his shoulder crashed into each other.

Israel felt the warrior's knife stab him in the side.

Israel returned the pain by sinking the Bowie deep within the warrior's chest.

It was over.

Over, except for the pain. Excruciating pain. And, the scalps.

Israel put one moccasin on the lead warrior's chest. The man who had killed his son.

He looked up at the blue sky and emitted the Kiowa victory cry again.

There was silence on the trail. By some miracle, the boy was unscathed.

The world spun and Israel Pope fell on top of his foe. His Bowie was still deep in the warrior's chest.

******

Off in what seemed to be a great distance, Israel heard the intermittent "crack" of a small caliber revolver. He opened his eyes and the world spun again.

Israel shook his head and tried to refocus. He got it right after a few seconds.

His grandson had the small five-shot Colt .31 in his hand. He was walking around shooting each fallen brave in the head. Five braves, reload. Another five, reload. Several cylinders later and there was no chance of a wounded foe arising to do harm.

The boy came to his grandfather and knelt on his knees.

"Grandfather, you are not going to die are you?" he asked.

"Not right now, Sonny Boy. One day maybe, but I got to get you raised up first. You did better than anyone alive could have done. I'm not surprised. But, I'm real proud of you, John.

We still have some work to do. You just did the first thing I'd have done. There's more.

Take this arrow in both hands and pull it straight

out of me. Breaking it off and cutting it out would be better, but we cannot do surgery here. Just hand me a stick to hold in my teeth and pull 'er out. No matter what noise I make, it has to come out. First, get the folded linsey-woolsey cloth out of my possibles bag to put on it and press down as soon as the arrow is out."

Israel clamped a bit of juniper stick between his teeth so he wouldn't break them grinding with the pain he was getting ready to feel.

The boy did as he was told.

The pain of the arrow coming out was geometrically worse than when it went in.

John placed the folded cloth on the wound.

Israel spit the stick out and said, "now press down hard and just hold it there. I might pass out but keep holding it until it stops bleeding."

Both things happened. He did pass out and John obeyed him.

When Israel came to, his side hurt almost as badly as his left shoulder. He had forgotten about the stab wound. He found it was not deep, but more of a glancing blow. It seemed more a surface wound than a penetrating one. Black walnut salve should handle it. He had John retrieve the screw top can of salve and he put a copious amount on each wound.

John was sent to recover Bear and Amos. While he was gone, Israel crawled on all fours to each warrior and scalped him. They had nineteen new scalps. No one had escaped to attack another family. The sack now had twenty scalps in it.

They left the bodies where they had fallen and rode half an hour closer to the village.

It was too close for a fire, in case a young brave was out hunting and smelled it and alerted the village. They cleaned and reloaded all of their guns. Israel sharpened his razor sharp Bowie out of habit. His side hurt but was tolerable.

His shoulder throbbed, but compared to his first bear fight, it was nothing. He just needed to make sure it did not get infected. He planned to ride to the fort up in Kansas and have the army surgeon stitch it up.

They were ready after three days. Henry's over their saddle horns, they rode into the Sac village and straight up to the chief's teepee.

Using plains sign language Jed taught in the first winter in the Wind River Range, Israel identified themselves. He said he was the father of a family the war party had killed up in Kansas. And, the boy was the son and only survivor. He dumped twenty scalps on the ground at the chief's feet and once again emitted the Kiowa victory cry.

It was the last time in his life he planned to voice it and he gave it all he had.

The chief did not have warriors left to get even with the two. He just looked at them with hatred. If looks could kill, they were in big trouble.

Israel looked at the boy. The young warrior who had gotten even for the death of his family. There was an almost imperceptible question in his eyes. Just as imperceptibly, Israel nodded.

John Hunt Pope shot the chief under the chin with his Henry rifle. The man was dead, a .44 bullet in his brain, before he hit the dirt. The boy bent, and using his Green River knife, scalped the chief and threw the scalp on the pile.

He then faced upwards and emitted the cry his grandfather had used.

Israel's blood ran cold hearing the young voice telling the world retribution had come and his family avenged.

On a thought, Israel put the scalps back in the burlap sack, including the chief's. They rode off, leaving the depleted village stunned.

He looked at the ten-year old riding next to him. He was not a child. He was not just a man. He was a warrior.

As proud as he was, Israel wondered, "Dear God. What have I created?"

******

They rode back to Kansas and the army post.

A sergeant got the lieutenant, who got the colonel.

Israel dumped the bag of scalps much as he had

at the Sac village.

"My son. His family. Your scout. They have been avenged," Israel said.

The officers were speechless, as where the gathering crowd of troopers.

Finally, the colonel asked "This happened before you got to the unassigned lands, right?"

Israel Pope looked him directly in the eye and lied.

"I am pretty sure we were still in Kansas when we caught them and killed them."

"Mr. Pope, did the boy see all of the mayhem?" the colonel asked.

"Colonel, the boy wreaked about half the retribution himself. He is not one you would want to rile up."

The army surgeon stitched both of Israel's wounds and gave him some sort of white powder to put on them.

Eschewing the powder for his salve, Israel dumped it on the trail.

"Where are we going now, Grandpa?" John asked.

"I was thinking about heading towards a train depot. Ever ridden a steam train, boy?"

"Nossir. Sounds like something I'd enjoy."

"Let's give her a try and ride back to California. You can help me raise horses and maybe get some schooling."

"I studied McGuffey's Reader."

"Good! But, we'll get you into a school. Mainly, I

want to introduce you to literature. I spent my nights trapping reading Shakespeare and anything I could find on the frontier. I believe it made a more knowledgeable man and it will you, also," Israel said. The boy nodded, ready to do anything which would make him more like his grandfather.

CHAPTER 7

They rode to the nearest depot and put Bear and Amos in a stock car. The two Popes climbed onto the train and found seats. Israel could feel the boy's excitement and watched him, smiling. The mountain man had one arm in a sling and his midriff tightly bandaged. He said nothing about the extreme pain. The boy was a child again, wide-eyed with excitement over riding a train. He would now move faster than the fastest horse.

The steam whistle blew and the train slowly pulled out of the station. The trip back to California was three days, each one more of a joy than the previous to the boy. He watched the different terrains—mountains, plains, forests, deserts flash by. If he was suffering any trauma from what he had seen and done, it did not show. He was just a little boy thrilled with his first train ride.

Israel's first priority upon arriving at the ranch was to check on P'ahy. The horse was in a far pasture and a bit overweight from lots of grazing and little riding. He would keep John on him until he was back in shape. He needed to retire Amos. The mule had been a wonderful partner for so many years. He deserved to spend his final ones eating sweet grass and not carrying loads over long distances.

The two rode P'ahy and Bear to Oakland to see Alameda sheriff Harry Morse. The sheriff's office was where Israel had started this quest from what seemed like long ago.

"Sheriff Morse, this is my grandson, John," Israel said. The sheriff proffered his hand as to an adult, something Israel appreciated.

"Son, I'm sorry about all you have had to go through," he said to the boy.

"Thank you, sir. My family's deaths have been avenged. My grandfather and I are going to raise some horses now," the boy said.

Harry Morse raised his eyebrows at the statements. He would delve into the story later with Israel. He knew there was quite a story and he wanted to hear every bit of it.

"You know, Harry, I came to you to check on warrants when you gave me the fateful telegram. Anything interesting I can help with now?"

"I just got one in beyond my jurisdiction. There

has been a consolidation of three stage and express companies into Wells Fargo and Company. They just issued a five hundred dollar dead or alive wanted poster for a stage robbery in Sonoma County. A passenger was killed and a jehu was injured by the robber."

Morse saw the confusion on the boy's face and explained, "A jehu is what they call the stage coach driver. It's a biblical reference."

"When did this happen, Harry?" Israel asked.

"Four days ago. For a wanted poster, the ink is hardly dry yet," the sheriff said, handing the poster to Israel.

"My sister and brother-in-law live in Sonoma, so I'd have a good base of operations. We'll leave today. I reckon it's about sixty miles or so around the east side of the Bay," Israel said.

"It is, more or less. It's getting so fewer ferry's carry stock across, so if you want your own mounts, riding around is about it."

"One last question, Harry, is there a good school here in Oakland I could sent John to?"

"There are several. Reverend McClure just opened California Military Academy. It's residential, but John could come home on weekends."

"Thank you. We will look into it after our trip up to Sonoma."

They rode back home and packed for the ride around San Francisco Bay to Arthur and Maude's farm.

******

It was just after dark when Israel and John rode up the lane to the farm. They hailed and his sister ran out, followed by Arthur. One child remained home. The other two had married. Arthur looked as fit as ever and Maude looked no different than she had fifteen years ago, but for a few strands of silver.

"Israel, you look like Wild Bill Hickok!" was Arthur's greeting.

"No, he looks like me. I looked like this, but with a beard when he was a little boy in Illinois. Say hello to your grandnephew, John."

Both Arthur and Maude had flashbacks of an almost identical meeting over twenty years ago with a little boy named John who looked exactly like this one. Later, they whispered to each other, the father did not have the steely look in his eyes the son had. They chalked it up to what the boy had seen and lived through. Both knew the story from Israel's letters.

"Howdy, John. Welcome to our farm!" Arthur said.

"Israel, are you home for a while?" his sister asked.

"Pretty much, except for day trips after fugitives. Have made a fair amount of money chasing down people who committed a crime, then left the jurisdiction. It's banks and express company's footing the bill, so the money is dependable."

Israel's unmarried niece was the spitting image

of his sister, which he thought was a good thing. The married niece was Mary after Arthur's mother, this one was Alma.

While Alma gave John a piece of apple pie, Arthur took him out to see the crops.

"Israel, can we mention the boy's father and family?" he asked.

"I think so. He seems to have taken it all in stride. What worries me is he has not talked about it with me. He's holding something in. He feels it's his fault the baby sister rushed out in the middle of the fight and died. I told him it absolutely was not his fault, but he still thinks it is. Maybe if you get a chance to talk about it, Arthur. You are better dealing with young ones than I will ever be...."

"Maude and I will speak about it and see what we can do. No promises. Just our best efforts, Israel."

"It's all I could possibly expect. So, you have two married children. Where are they?"

"Arthur Junior has a small farm about four miles away. He's doing well. Mary, named for my ma, married a shopkeep. They live in town and do just fine. You are going to be a great uncle yourself. Twice over, my friend."

"I hope I live up to the title."

"Your fame precedes you wherever you go, Israel. You are known throughout the West. As a brave man, fierce fighter and a good man. You have done well, despite having rotten luck losing those you care about."

"It has been tough, Arthur. I never said so before. But, it has. You just have to put one moccasin in front of the other and plod along."

His longtime friend nodded in agreement.

"Changing the subject, do you think Maude has any more of the apple pie left? We've been on a long hard trail and it might sooth the belly of the savage beast."

"I'm betting she does. I had some after dinner. It's pretty darn good."

They went in. On the way, Arthur said in a low voice. "We both want to hear the details of the vengeance ride. What you did and how young John dealt with it all."

"I'll tell you both once John gets asleep." He did and neither were surprised. Maude asked a question which had been worrying Israel and he admitted it.

"Israel, the boy has seen so much horrible violence and now has committed it. How do you think it is going to affect his brain when he grows up? Do you think we all have to watch him closely?"

"It's been uppermost on my mind, Maude. I plan to watch him and hope, in my absences, you all will too. The absences will be shorter and less frequent. Maybe a few days several times a year. Otherwise, he and I will be together. He's sharp as a tack. He picks up things immediately and generally understands the reasons behind them. I never expected such from a ten-year old. I worry about what he's going to do with his life. My callings of being a trapper and a guide are fading rapidly. You heard Kit Carson and me talking a while back. I don't see young John as a shopkeep or a farmer or rancher. He might follow the cowboy trail for a while. He rides well. Maybe a lawman where his logic for killing would work in his favor? I just don't know. But, he's growing and doing adult things so fast, we'll sure as dickens find out soon. I have to get him some schooling. Is there one here he can go to for a while?"

"There is. Our children went to it for the last of their education. It's alright. Your typical school marm and six grades in a one-room school. But, our children can all read, writer and cipher well," Arthur said.

"You care if John stays here with you for a week or so while I go after this stage robber? If I catch him, the reward will cover us for half a year," Israel said. They agreed. Just as Arthur loved to build and grow things, Maude loved to raise children and was good at it. They were the perfect Western frontier team.

The next morning Israel asked John to stay at his aunt and uncle's until he brought the stage robber in. He told him it was for two reasons. He needed to get to know them and he could attend school for a while. John clearly wanted to go on the trail with his grandpa.

"Sonny Boy, there will be plenty of trails and fugitives for you and me. I suspect you will be chasing fugitives long after I am retired and riding a rocking chair. Now, I have another plan, too. Once I get the money for bringing in Bill Toomey, we'll go out and get you a horse. Amos has been a wonderful mount for you and me. But, he deserves a rest and a retirement. And, you deserve a horse. Think about what kind you want and we'll get it."

"I want one like yours. A paint. A black and white paint," John said.

"Well, then. We'll look for one just like mine for you!"

Israel rode out around lunch time. He carried his Henry rifle and twin Colt Navy revolvers, a copy of the poster, and his iron nippers to slap on the wrists of Bill Toomey as soon as he was captured. Or, killed.

******

He rode to Santa Rosa. Israel's first stop was the sheriff's office. The head deputy was there and told Israel as much as he could about Bill Toomey.

"We only know his name because a passenger recognized him under his mask. He then shot and killed the passenger. He's not from this area. Our deputies checked one end of the county to another. No Toomey's here we could find," he said.

"Where was the passenger from?

"I don't know. Wells Fargo will know where he left from, but it may or may not be his home," chief deputy said.

"Was Toomey alone?"

"Yep. Seemed to be. He did not threaten about somebody being out of sight who would shoot them or anything."

"What was the description they gave?"

"Like most witness descriptions. 'A tall, short white or black man with a shotgun pistol,'" the chief deputy said, tongue-in-cheek.

"Chief, was there any agreement beyond him being a male?"

"When you put all their blather together and sort it out, we got a vague picture of a fella who was middle aged, medium height. Kinda stocky and had shaggy brown hair with some gray in it. We think he was armed with a sawed-off shotgun. May have had a revolver stuck in his belt, but we're not too sure about it. Rode a gray mule."

"Where, exactly, did the robbery occur?"

"On the road up to Hot Springs, or Agua Caliente. Some folks are starting to call it Calistoga. Don't know if such a made-up name will stick though."

"Chief, were there any memorable landmarks on the spot where the robbery occurred?" Israel asked.

"No. It's gonna be hard to identify now. The road

is used a lot. Are you the mountain man and scout named Pope?" Israel nodded.

"You might be able to find some signs. The other bounty chasers who came through the last couple of days won't have a clue. I never saw such a couple of dumbasses in my born days, Pope."

"Well, maybe we'll luck out and they'll shoot each other."

"They sure didn't have the brains to ask your type of questions." Israel nodded again.

"Chief, I think I'm going to walk over to the Wells Fargo office. I take it was their stage he robbed and their driver he winged."

"It was. The driver might be able to help. Except he already was sent back to San Francisco to the head office. Joseph Montalbano is the manager. Tell him Chief Deputy Moses Parson sent you."

"Thanks, Chief. I sure will." They shook hands and he left for the Wells Fargo office.

He walked in the door and waited patiently a few minutes while the manager finished with a customer.

"Mr. Montalbano? Chief Deputy Moses Parsons sent me over. I'm following up on your wanted poster on Bill Toomey. My name's Israel Pope."

"I thought he was an old time mountain man," Montalbano said. Israel nodded.

"You're not a kid. But, you don't look old enough for those days," Montalbano added.

"I was late starting in the beaver trapping, but was at several rendezvous, including the last one in 1840."

"Hmmm. I see. How can I help you?"

"Any markings on the site where the robbery occurred. Moses Parsons was not aware of any. I wondered if someone from Wells Fargo had been there looking for clues."

"Not yet. We might have a man coming up from San Francisco in a day or two."

"The man who was killed. Where did he get on the stage?" Israel asked.

"He got off the ferry and got on in Marin County. Came over from San Francisco. Don't know where he came from originally."

"Can you share the amount he got away with?

"He broke open the green treasure box by shooting off the padlock. Took a thousand in bills and three thousand in gold dust. The bills were strapped and the dust was packed in six small brown leather bags."

"So no gold or silver coins?" Israel asked.

"No. Not on this run."

"I understand he fled on the road to Hot Springs?"

"Yep."

"What was his robbery method. Just stop the stage at gunpoint?"

"No. He laid a log across the road. Shot the driver and disarmed the shotgun messenger when the stage stopped. The shooting of the passenger came about late in the robbery."

"I was told he used a short-barreled shotgun. Did your men see a revolver?"

"The messenger did, the driver did not. I'd go with the messenger's recall. The driver had just been shot."

"Makes sense to me, Mr. Montalbano. Thanks for your help. Oh! Anybody else been asking around?"

"Not here. Moses told me a couple of low-life bounty hunters were asking questions of him and some barkeeps." Israel touched the brim of his hat and left. He picked up some sandwiches to add to the camp food Maude sent with him and left town.

He rode towards Hot Springs. After seven miles, he knew he was approaching the halfway point to Hot Springs and began scanning closer.

He rode another three and knew he was past the halfway point. The road was well-used. Apparently the messenger had picked up the green box and destroyed padlock. He did not see any shotgun shells on the road or the side of the road. Either Toomey had picked those up or was using a muzzle loading shotgun.

Israel dug out a sandwich from his saddlebags and munched thoughtfully as he rode.

At Hot Springs, he asked around. Nobody had seen anyone with Toomey's name or description. There were a couple of roads out of the village. He knew he could choose exactly the wrong one. He had to choose one, so he stayed on the road upon which he rode in.

The road surface was sunbaked and cluttered with tracks. Israel was unable to cut sign at all. He followed carefully. Toomey may be camped in the woods on either side, or may have ridden on. It had become a game of chance.

After four hours, he came upon a small mining camp along a creek.

Men were building sluices to direct stream water into collectors easier to pan than standing in a stream. The take had dwindled significantly from the original 1849-50 level. Even a few flecks of color a day exceeded the annual income of a laborer, shop clerk or teacher. So, the hot work and primitive life were worthwhile.

Israel rode into the camp and dismounted. With his dark suit and wide-brimmed hat, and twin Colts, he did not look like a miner or a drummer.

"What's the law doing here?" a surly miner demanded.

"I'm not the law. I'm a bounty hunter after a murderer."

"Same difference, mister," another man said.

"Not to the innocent man's family. They want justice. I'm gonna deliver it. You see a fella ride through here in past several days? Shaggy brown hair with some gray in it. Medium height man on a gray mule."

"You just described about anybody," the first miner said.

"It's all I got from the witness reports. Carried a sawed-off scattergun and maybe a pistol. Should have a bag hung from his saddle."

"What's in the bag?" one asked.

"His takings from the stage robbery. Shot the driver and killed a passenger who recognized him," Israel continued.

"Know his name?"

"Passenger called him 'Bill Toomey' before being killed to shut him up."

Israel saw two men look at each other.

"I see the name means something to you two. What can you tell me?"

"What's it worth?" one said.

"Depends on how good the information is," Israel responded.

"There is a man up in Ukiah City. It's about twenty miles up the road."

"Did you just meet him there one time, or do you think he lives there?" Israel asked.

"Ok, the whole family lives there. He's got three brothers. The oldest, Tom, is the meanest. Bill is next and the kid brother is wild. I ain't sure he's right in the head."

"Where do they live?"

"I don't know. The three of them are in the saloon most of the time."

"As I remember, Ukiah City is the county seat. The

sheriff is there. Is he close with them?" Israel asked.

"Ha! More like terrified of the Toomey brothers."

Israel reached in his vest pocket and took out four five-dollar gold pieces and gave them to the two men who had given the information.

He spun Bear around and trotted off to the road, then north.

Three mean brothers and a weak sheriff. This was going to be trying. Very damn trying.

Israel knew he would make it to Ukiah City by dark. If he waited long enough, the three ought to be well into their cups. The liquor should slow them down. He reckoned the sheriff would be home and of no help. Perhaps there was a town marshal or night marshal.

Part of his problem was a man in black with two guns and a flashy horse could not ride in without attracting notice. He had to chance it and gain some intelligence about the Toomey's.

Without knowing more about the other two, he would be riding in blind.

Israel rode down the main street and tied up at the sheriff's office.

The sheriff was in. He was a balding and pot-bellied man with a .22 Smith & Wesson spur trigger revolver stuck in his belt. Carrying it was hardly worth the effort.

"Howdy. My name is Pope." Israel handed him the

wanted poster. It was clear the sheriff had never seen the document before.

"I'm after your resident, Bill Toomey. Know where I can find him?" Israel reckoned it was better to play a bit dumb and see what answers he received.

"He and his brothers are sleeping last night off. They will come in after dinner and do it all over again.

So, one of them finally killed somebody? I can't arrest him without a warrant," the sheriff said. It was obvious he had no interest at all in going up against any of them.

"Well, I can. And, will. You want to get a shotgun and back my play outside the saloon door?"

"Nope."

"When I take him into custody, will you certify it's him in writing?"

"Nope. Not as long as there is one Toomey standing. Any one of them could and would kill me."

Neither Israel's face nor words reflected the distaste he felt for this cowardly so-called man of the law. The sheriff needed to go back to working in a feed store or something.

"Will the jail be open around nine or ten tonight if I need to hold a prisoner overnight?"

"Nope."

Israel frowned at the incompetent lawman.

"I'll handle this on my own, Sheriff. Since you won't back my play, keep the hell out of my way. I mean it. Stay clear!"

Israel turned and walked to a café and had dinner. It was filling but otherwise tasteless. The general store across from the saloon was still open. He bought a long, thin cigar and took a match to light it. The store had a couple of rocking chairs outside. Israel chose one and made himself comfortable.

He watched silently, only nodding politely at anyone who looked his way in passing.

Israel did not carry a pocket watch but guessed it to be around seven when three men rode up to the saloon together.

The resembled each other enough to be brothers. The oldest was late forties and the largest. The next was probably Israel's fugitive. Israel could feel the craziness of the younger one from his fifty foot distance. All had revolvers. Bill Toomey carried his stuck in his belt. The older one wore a left handed holster. The younger one had two holsters, worn down low. He seemed to fancy himself a gunfighter. He was in his early twenties.

Israel reckoned he would practice his craft more than his brothers. They were real. He was a wannabe. Israel had to kill him first, if it came to gunplay. And, it would surely come to gunplay.

He let them go in without making his move. It was not time yet. Two hours later, he got up and walked behind the store. He put fresh caps on all the cylinders of his Colt's.

Israel resumed his rocker and waited.

Close to midnight, he saw some people coming out. Maybe the saloon was closing.

He got out of the chair, loosened his Navies in their holsters and walked slowly over to the saloon.

The three Toomey's came out in the next group.

"Bill Toomey! You are under arrest for murder!" Israel yelled in a stentorian voice.

Before he finished the word "murder," the younger brother grabbed for both guns.

Israel drew and shot him dead.

He swung his guns toward the other two.

The older Toomey was in the act of drawing when Israel shot him in the gut. Israel turned on Bill Toomey and winged him in mid-draw.

"Don't die like your brothers, Bill!" he yelled as he cocked his Colt Navy again.

Bill Toomey had his revolver in his hand. It was pointed downwards. He dropped it in the dust of the street and slowly raised his uninjured arm in surrender. Israel had no idea whether he realized a hangman's noose awaited him. He put the nippers on his wrists as the older brother rolled around in the street moaning.

Somebody had summoned the sheriff, who lived in town.

"What's going on here?" he asked, as if he was actually in charge.

Israel told him.

"You need to certify from witnesses this was a righteous shoot, wire the Sonoma sheriff and tell him you have the man he wants for murder and wounding, and get some help for the older Toomey," Israel told him. The man shook his head up and down, glad to have a path to follow.

The older Toomey, Tom, had painfully struggled to his feet. He had one hand clamped to his gut. He staggered toward Israel and the sheriff.

As he got closer, he drew a long-bladed Arkansas toothpick knife and gave something akin to an Indian cry.

Israel knew Tom Toomey was too close to depend on an instant kill from a .36 caliber Colt. He drew his Bowie and parried the man's knife.

The parry left an opening and Israel thrust the Bowie into his lower throat. Toomey went down, never to rise again.

The sheriff was sprayed with blood.

"Why didn't you shoot him?" he screamed at Israel.

"He would have cut one or both of us before dying, Sheriff."

The man stood dumbstruck, staring at the dead man at his feet. It was the closest he had ever come to dying. In the line of duty or otherwise.

It was daylight before the paperwork was done. Israel left with a receipt for his prisoner. Toomey would be patched up by a doctor and picked up by a Sonoma County sheriff's deputy sometime during the day.

Israel rode back to Santa Rosa and called on Wells Fargo manager Montalbano. He presented the receipt. Two verification telegrams later and the manager counted out five hundred dollars in coins in return for a receipt.

Israel rode back to Arthur's farm. Time to go horse hunting for his grandson.

******

Israel found John following Arthur behind a mule drawing a plow, learning the commands and how to plow a straight line.

The boy seemed to his grandfather as if he just absorbed knowledge. Arthur later volunteered the same observation.

Westerners did not always speak much around the dinner table. But, these were pilgrims from back East and it was a good time for family discussions. Everyone wanted to know about the capture of Bill Toomey.

Both the boy and his sister wanted details on how he trailed him, who he questioned along the way, and what his questions were. Israel had a strong suspicion his grandson would need this knowledge as an adult. He went into both the detail of his questions and the rationale behind them.

The San Francisco Examiner covered the capture and shootout in detail. Israel was surprised to find the reporting was accurate, lurid headlines notwithstanding.

When one man went up against three and ended the incident with a Bowie knife, it was big news for the greater Bay area. Especially when the single man was a famous mountain man and scout.

Arthur read the story aloud and Israel supplemented it with both corrections and elaborations.

Maude had always been a great fan of his adventures. Now, she had an accomplice in her grand-nephew.

"What did you think when you drew, Grandpa?" John asked.

"Let me turn it around, son. What did you think when the shooting with the Sac war party started?"

"Nothing. I was too busy shooting."

"Well, you just said the answer to your question to me. I was too busy drawing, trying to figure who to shoot first and moving aside to be a tougher target."

"Who did you shoot first?"

"I shot the younger brother. He wore his guns low and fancied himself a gunsel. I reckoned he probably practiced drawing and firing. Most fellas don't. So, speed-wise, he was the first who needed to be eliminated. Of the three, he would get off the first shot. I did not want to be hit by a lucky bullet."

"Israel," Arthur began, "why the old Bowie to end the affair?"

"Wounded or not, the older brother was coming at the sheriff and me. You shoot a man with a revolver and it might take him a while to die. I did not have the time to spare before he got to both of us, swinging a big ole Arkansas toothpick.

I've been in my share of knife fights against men and bears. I knew I could end it quick with the Bowie. So, I did."

"Was it hard getting the reward?" Maude asked.

"Thank heavens it was Wells Fargo. They are organized and honest. I got a receipt for turning Toomey over to the sheriff and presented it to the Wells Fargo office covering the area where the robbery happened. Two telegrams later and the manager was counting out gold and silver coins. He wanted to give me paper money, but I don't rightly trust it as much as gold or silver. Some of the money will go for a horse for John.

Amos deserves a nice rest and long retirement. He has served us long and well. Despite the beautiful P'ahy and Bear, I'll miss riding him everywhere. He's kind of like the Bowie knife. I can always depend on him to get the job done," Israel said.

"Grandpa said we are going to look for a horse like his for me," John volunteered.

"Bear sure looks like an Indian war pony, but bigger," Arthur said.

"Which reminds me of something," Israel said.

"Did Hannah ever mention to you about being part Indian, Maude?"

"No. She kinda looked the part with her dark skin and shiny dark hair. But, she never said anything. Why?"

"She told Chief Lone Bear and White Feather she was one quarter Mattaponi Indian from east of Richmond. They believed her."

"Don't you think they would have known?" Maude asked her brother.

"I do. Lone Bear was not a man you could fool. It had never come up before then though."

"Does it make me part Indian, Grandpa?"

"It does. Just a little bit. But blood you should be proud of. Chief Lone Bear was like a grandfather to your pa. And, White Feather all but raised him until he was almost your age, then your aunt and uncle here took over."

"It breaks my heart what happened to him, Israel. He was your son, but also ours. We loved his wife, too. Just like we do his son. John is a spittin' image of both him and you, Israel."

"Ha! He sure must be a fine looking young man, then!" the mountain man said with a smile. The boy beamed. "And, look at your cousin, boy. She's as lovely as your great aunt, Maude. I remember your boys looking like Arthur.

I'll never forget Arthur handling the sweep oar on our Shenandoah flatboat running through the rapids! Nobody could have done it like him. Those were the first of many of our adventures, including the California Trail to right here. We crossed mountains and deserts. Your great aunt was right there with us. Holding fort while your great uncle Arthur and I were running the wagon train and keeping all those pilgrims safe from themselves and everything else."

The next day, Israel and John visited several horse ranches. They heard a breeder about twenty miles north had a young paint. They rode up the next day. The horse had just been broken gently to saddle. Israel bought him and they led him home behind Amos.

The young horse was a younger, smaller version of Bear. The breeder had told them he would probably grow to fifteen hands, maybe fifteen and a half. Within five years, John might be too tall for him. In the meantime, the paint was perfect.

John rode the horse all over Arthur's fields and the roads near the farm. Much of the time, Israel rode with him, continuing to teach him tracking on different types of terrain. He taught him how to backtrack in creek beds to confuse pursuers, to not only look all around him, but also upwards.

"You could have a hostile or even a mountain lion above you. No direction is safe until you have cleared it as safe."

The worked more on fine tuning John's sense of smell. He had a long way to go to reach his grandfather's abilities. They had been honed over years in danger's way.

After a week, Israel knew he had to check on the ranch and P'ahy. John agreed to stay and help Arthur till fields and prepare to put in wheat. He also attended school.

Israel rode back, strangely lonely for a solitary man. The boy had quickly become almost an extension of himself.

John spent the next several years alternating between the ranch and the farm.

The mid-teens boy, Israel and Arthur built a log cabin on land Israel had purchased in Marin County. It was less than half a day's ride of the farm and wooded. The Pacific was its westernmost border. The hills and tall trees provided a virtual classroom for tracking and hunting.

Israel spent more time there than the ranch. P'ahy and Amos went to their rewards due to old age. Israel was approaching sixty, but neither looked like it nor felt like it.

His diet of fresh meat, fish and either fresh or preserved vegetables from his sister helped. His constant movement and chopping firewood with his Hudson Bay pattern axe and a maul splitter maintained his corded muscles.

By his late teens, John was well over six feet and lean like a rider. He had worked for several ranches in Alameda as a cowboy for roundups and driving cattle to the railhead.

Within the decade, trains and telegraph were almost everywhere. Cartridge guns had replaced loose powder, percussion caps and balls. Both Popes wore Colt's .44-40's introduced several years previously in 1873. Like his grandfather, the grandson was never without a Bowie knife nearby.

A few days after John's eighteenth birthday, the two Popes rode into San Francisco armed with a letter of referral from former Alameda Sheriff Harry Morse. Over the years, Israel had fulfilled fifty wanted posters from the sheriff and his successors. John had assisted on many.

They went straight to the San Francisco Police headquarters and John applied. He had a diploma signifying completion of secondary school. He had two college courses to his credit, unusual for a SFPD applicant.

The letter from now-famous private detective Harry Morse discussed John's experience as a bounty hunter with his famous grandfather and particularly, as a tracker. It, and the younger Pope's presentment worked. He was hired on the spot. The next day, he was sworn in. Following the swearing, he was fitted for a uniform, issued a Smith & Wesson .44 revolver and truncheon and assigned to a training officer.

John was walking a beat with his assigned trainer the following day. By the end of the week, he went to the range. It became readily apparent his firearms training already exceeded any accuracy standards SFPD had.

The eight years with his grandfather had prepared him well for city or rural policing. The former in how to analyze situations and what questions to ask, the latter in how to track day or night, surveil, and go against uneven odds.

Within a record two years, John Pope turned in his uniform and donned the suit of a detective.

******

Israel and John had tried horse raising and sales and found, while both loved horses, they did not like the business.

Tough as could be in his early sixties, Israel realized bounty hunting, riding in any kind of weather, and sleeping on cold, wet ground was not keeping him young.

He wanted to hold on to the ranch as a legacy for John. However, he did not want to live there exclusively. Israel much preferred the cabin in the woods not far from San Rafael in Marin County. It also put him a quick ferry ride across San Francisco Bay for his frequent visits with his grandson.

Without the horse Lone Bear had given back to him to pursue the war party which had killed White Feather and his beloved mule, Amos, there was no livestock left on the ranch.

Israel locked the door, called Scout, their year old Blue Tick hound, and rode Bear to San Francisco. He found the rare boat accepting horses and effectively moved to Marin County.

He rode, maintained his proficiency with Colts and his Winchester repeater, chopped wood and hiked along the Pacific beach.

His longish hair turned white, as did the mustache which turned downwards at the corners of his mouth. Trim and fit, he was perhaps a more striking older man than he had been earlier in his life.

Detective John Pope solved several related Wells Fargo crimes near the port area of San Francisco.

His actions were observed by James Hume, chief detective for the company and a pioneer in forensics and ballistics. Hume, Allan Pinkerton and Hume's and Israel's friend Harry Morse were considered the top detectives in America. Or, perhaps the world, in the early 1880's.

Israel was thrilled when his grandson, now a star Wells Fargo detective, partnered with the beautiful Sarah Watson.

Sarah was a former Pinkerton detective who John Pope recruited and with whom he quickly fell in love.

******

Israel was returning from a trip to visit Arthur and Maude when a telegram was delivered to him at the cabin.

It was from John. He and Sarah were working a kidnapping case. Certainly not the usual for Wells Fargo detectives.

The sixteen year old daughter of a senior executive at the firm had been taken several days earlier. A demand letter, promising more information to follow, had been delivered the next day. The SFPD was to be kept out of it.

As Wells Fargo probably had a better trained detective force, Hume and the senior leadership decided to not notify the police until young Mattie Lane had been recovered and the suspects were in custody.

John and Sarah were undercover at the executive's home in downtown San Francisco. John's telegram asked for his grandfather to respond to the area and walk the neighborhood at odd hours as part of the surveillance program.

Israel was thrilled. Not only could he help his grandson, he would be actually doing something with the possibility of danger once again.

He rode to San Rafael and stabled his horse. With a valise, dark suit and a black bowler hat, he walked aboard the ferry. Scout was on a leash. An hour later, past Alcatraz Island, they arrived in San Francisco. His hair was cut slightly longer than current fashion, but it went perfectly with the mustache. Upon first glance, he appeared to be a successful older gentleman. Closer scrutiny showed cold blue eyes and an expression of restrained violence one would not want to test.

Israel took a hansom cab to the neighborhood where the Lane family lived.

He found a small upscale hotel several blocks away and took a room. The clerk began to remonstrate about the handsome hound dog, but a stern warning look from the distinguished gentleman stopped him in mid-sentence.

He ate dinner in the hotel's café and with dark suit, white shirt, bowler hat and tie, took Scout for a walk.

Israel passed the Lane residence twice before a raven-haired Sarah Watson came out and began strolling behind him.

He reached a bench in a miniscule neighborhood park and sat down. The hound sat obediently at his side.

Sarah walked up, still in her cover identity.

"Hello. Do you mind if I sit and rest for a few minutes?" she asked.

"No. Please sit down," he said as he stood and doffed his bowler hat.

In a more guarded voice, she said "You must be Mr. Pope. I have heard so much about you from John.

And, from Harry Morse. He says you are a legend!"

"Harry is too kind. Please remind me to buy him a drink in appreciation. I am assuming you are John's Miss Sarah. How can I help the case?"

"I am most definitely John's Sarah! John or I will feed information to you as we get it. For now, please walk this handsome pup around the neighborhood at whatever hours you can. Be observant. We think somebody in the neighborhood may be involved or at least be watching for the kidnappers. Try to identify them and advise us. John says when it's time to deliver the ransom, he will need you to do something called 'cutting sign.'"

She giggled and he looked questioningly at her. It was difficult to not stare at her.

"I'm sorry. You look like a senator. I thought you'd be wearing buckskins."

He gave her a smile which won her for life.

"Even old mountain men need to clean up once in a while. Besides, here, I fit in dressed like this. Imagine if I was riding and wearing a Stetson and Western wear," he said. He handed her a note with his hotel name and room number on it.

"Yes, you fit into this posh neighborhood quite nicely. I have to go. But, I look forward to getting to know you."

"I look forward also. Be safe walking back. I will be a pistol shot behind you. But, I assume you are as well-armed as I am."

"Possibly. But, no Bowie," she said.

"Pity. I will have to buy you one," he said to her back as she walked away.

When she was fifty yards in front, he spoke to the dog.

"Well, Scout. It's easy to see how our John became smitten with her, eh? Let's continue our walk behind her. Keep your eyes peeled, boy."

A block later, he saw a man come out of a house as Sarah approached it. Israel put his right hand inside his suit jacket and touched the handle of the long-barreled Colt Frontier Model. The man picked up a newspaper and returned to his front door without having to be shot.

Israel and Scout returned to the hotel.

He received a message by courier at the hotel the next morning.

"IP, can you meet me unseen at rear of victim residence about noon today? JP"

His white shirt was still heavily starched. He tied his maroon tie, put the gun and knife in place and he and Scout left around eleven forty-five.

Israel had counted the houses on the street on each side of the Lane residence last night.

He went one street over and slipped through the side yards to the house. It was large, as he knew from the front. Three stories. Trees in the backyard. Iron fence encircling. The gate was unlocked.

Israel and Scout slipped in. There was a back porch. The two made themselves comfortable on it. From the sun, Israel knew they were on time.

The door opened.

"Mr. Pope?" a very lovely lady of around fifty asked.

"Mrs. Lane?" he asked.

"Oh, heavens no. I am Millie, the Lane's house-keeper and cook. Detective Pope is still discussing something with Mr. Lane. I came out to see if you would like a sandwich and a glass of lemonade."

"They both sound perfect. Perhaps a bowl with water for Scout?"

Millie had sat beside them on the porch step and Scout unabashedly climbed into her lap and licked her on the chin. She hugged him and began chatting with the dog as if they were old friends.

"I guess I better get what I promised and talk with him later! What's his name?"

"It's Scout. I think you have found a friend for life."

"I hope it's two friends," she said with a smile.

She disappeared and Israel heard a woman with a shrewish voice ask "who's the man with the dog and why are you feeding them? He is too well-dressed to be a hobo."

"He is a detective working the kidnapping under-cover. He is here to meet with Detectives Pope and Watson," he heard Millie say.

"Humph," was the next thing Israel heard. Nice lady. It had to be the woman of the house. The kidnap victim's mother.

If he could hear her, she could hear him, Israel decided. He and Scout relocated to a bench towards the back of the yard.

John came out and hugged him. Sarah joined them.

"So, Grandpa. I hear you met my Sarah. She's as deadly as she is beautiful."

"Sounds like the perfect woman to me. Especially for a Pope," Israel replied.

"Anything new?" Israel asked.

"There is a house I'd like you to pass by a couple times a day. A well-dressed man walking his dog is a great cover, Grandpa." John passed a note with the address to Israel.

"You still want me to keep a watch on this house too, I guess?" he asked.

"Please. When we get the final demand instructions for delivery of the ransom, we will have to move quickly. We have a temporary telegraph set up here. I will wire headquarters and have them contact you at the hotel if it's a time you are likely to be there. Otherwise, we will put a wreath with fresh flowers on the front door. We have you and Harry Morse with a couple of men riding by on horseback or in carriages."

"Does Harry know I'm involved?" Israel asked.

"Nossir. Nobody but you, Sarah and I know you

are involved. At least yet. Now, Millie, I guess. But she seems to think you are a Wells Fargo detective. She whispered to Sarah you and I favor each other a lot, though."

"She's as smart as she is pretty."

Sarah dropped her voice even lower than the conversation had been.

"Millie holds this family together. Mr. Lane is a decent sort. The other daughter is a doll and I understand the victim is too. Mrs. Lane is hard to take on a good day."

Israel nodded. "Just like John nods!" she thought to herself. It wouldn't take Allan Pinkerton to figure out these two were related. At least, she realized looking at Israel, her John was destined to keep his good looks a long time. She was looking at him forty years from now.

Millie brought out a tray with sandwiches, glasses and a pitcher of lemonade. She also had a water bowl and some beef scraps for Scout. He trotted back to the porch behind her. Sarah retrieved the bowl and beef and took it to Millie on the porch where she was playing with the dog.

"I sure like the other detective, Sarah. He is cultured and very handsome," Millie said.

"You probably picked up on the resemblance, so I will go ahead and tell you. He's John's grandfather. He's the famous mountain man and scout, Israel Pope."

"You are kidding! I've heard the name. I just always figured he'd be much older."

"His Indian name is Bear Fighter. He has killed two bears with a Bowie knife at different times in his life," Sarah said. Millie's eyes widened and then, she quickly smiled.

Sarah returned to the Pope's and Millie sat back down on the porch steps. She watched Scout gulp down his beef scraps. He finished almost immediately and soon Millie had a very large blue tick hound asleep in her lap. She scratched behind his ear and he snored.

"He looks more like John Pope's father than grandfather," the fifty-year old thought about Israel. "Get past the white hair, and you realize he's very fit and those sky blue eyes seem to have a glint of steel in them. A bad man to have as your enemy. A good man, though, to have as your friend. Or, your protector," she dared to think.

"I wonder if he has a wife. I sure hope not! Oh, what am I thinking?" she asked herself. It was the first time in several days she had done much other than worrying about young Mattie and how she was being treated. She did not dare mentally question whether Mattie was still alive.

John and Sarah gave all the facts they had to Israel and they worked out how he would trail whoever delivered the money. He would be far enough back to pick up on whether any of the kidnappers were following him to check for police presence. Assuming they were given a destination for the drop off, John would trail the person delivering the money from a parallel street.

"We have to make some assumptions, based on not really knowing anything at this point, Grandpa. We assume Mr. Lane will be required to make the money delivery. If not, I will do it. My cover is as an out-of-town relative. Sarah is portraying my wife. As soon as we hear something, we'll burn up the telegraph. As I said earlier, a messenger will let you know very quickly if you are at your hotel."

"You have already determined there is no chance of an inside job?" Israel asked.

"No chance here at the house. The only non-family member here is Millie. She has been here for years and may as well be a family member. As to the kidnapers, it may or may not be inside Wells Fargo. We don't have enough to go on yet to know for sure. The company's lead detective, our boss, is working on the inside angle. Mr. Lane is prominent in the community as well as the company. He has a high profile. One look at this house would give any passerby a hint at his wealth."

"Israel, you mentioned the possibility of an insider. I agree with John about Millie. She has virtually raised those girls. She is an absolute darling. I really like her.

The mother seems to have some sort of mental or personality disorder. Either an illness or she just has a horrible disposition," Sarah added.

"Millie is certainly an attractive lady...." Israel mentioned, drawing a grin from his grandson. "About time for a second wife, Grandpa?" he asked.

"A third one, Sonny Boy. I guess we need to talk about the wife who actually raised your Pa until he was six or so. Let's wait until all this is over and then talk."

Israel's statement shocked John. He always thought Israel and Arthur and Maude raised his father, much as the three had raised him. His father never spoke about his mother. Any mother. What was the story he never knew?

"I've not thought of another wife. Until meeting Millie. She certainly passed the first test with flying colors," Israel said.

"What's the first test, Israel?" Sarah asked.

"Scout. He thinks she's really special. Scout has pretty keen insight."

Sarah rolled her eyes. John accepted his grandpa's words without question. If there was something about which he and Israel Pope disagreed, he had not found it in his almost thirty years on this earth.

"I better stroll around the neighborhood before dark, then back to the hotel," Israel said as he walked toward the back porch to get Scout.

John and Sarah watched the smiles and body language as the two people on the porch interacted.

Israel and Scout walked back to them and the rear gate. He was smiling. He hooked the leash to Scout's collar for appearances and bid them goodbye.

Unlike the Westerner he was, a man expected to ride off into the sunset without looking back, he turned at the gate.

He and Millie locked eyes and smiled. Israel Pope disappeared silently, as he was wont to do. But, this time, he was walking with even more than the usual spring in his step.

Israel and Scout walked around the neighborhood. Nothing seemed amiss. He passed the house whose address John had given him. He saw a skinny young man enter the front door and made note of it to share with John and Sarah in the morning.

He headed back to the hotel, ever alert. His senses were as sharp as when he was John's age. He gave the credit to the lovely woman he just met.

"Millie Pope. It has a good ring to it," he thought. He caught himself and said aloud "What are you thinking?"

With a silent "Why not?" he proceeded back to the hotel, he and the blue tick hound covering ground at an admirable pace. He had identified his next quest in life and she was awfully pretty. Of course, they had to get the young girl back safe and sound first. He was confident he and John could do it. Especially with Sarah and Harry Morse backing them up.

They located Mattie Lane. Both Pope's and Sarah had to light up their .44's and Israel pulled his Bowie knife. Some of the kidnapers went to prison. Some went into the ground. All of which, though, is another story.

EPILOGUE

The solution of the Lane kidnaping and the careers of John Pope and his partner, Sarah Watson, continue from this point forward in Gun for Wells Fargo. Wyoming Shootout picks up the story immediately after. Shooting for Justice follows in direct chronology in the series.

In each book, Israel Pope and his new wife, Millie, play a significant role in Pope's and Sarah's careers and adventures. Unlike Israel's unfortunate early loss of both of his first and second wives, he and Millie lived in happiness and good health into the 1900's.

Israel Pope's saga ranged from river flat boats, to the Cumberland Gap, the Rendezvous, and the Oregon and California Trails, to automobiles and telephones. He fought bears, hostiles of every description, and experienced danger from the very land he loved in the form of blizzards, deserts, and rushing rivers.

His life spanned a wide and exciting period of American growth and change. Growth and change which would not have occurred without men like Israel Pope and the legends who were his friends.

A LOOK AT: ARIZONA GUNMAN

A WESTERN STORY OF GOOD OVER EVIL, LAW OVER CRIMINALITY.

County Sheriff James Duncan is fast and honorable. An Arizona lawman who rides rough country, often going up against dangerous men and gangs alone. Dealing with bank robbers, kidnappers and rustlers with his fast gun. Much of his tracking ability comes from his Scottish father, who served as an Indian scout. Valuable experience as a Rough Rider with Teddy Roosevelt, then as an Arizona Ranger.

Outlaws and corrupt government tend to stand in Duncan's way, but he manages to overcome all obstacles with integrity and really fast guns.

AVAILABLE NOW

ABOUT THE AUTHOR

G. Wayne Tilman is a full-time author. He retired from the Federal Bureau of Investigation several years ago. Prior to the FBI, he was a Marine, bank security director, deputy sheriff, investigator, and security contractor. He holds baccalaureate and master's degrees from the University of Richmond and has been an adjunct faculty member there, as well as the University of Phoenix, St. Petersburg College and Florida Metropolitan University.

He wrote his first novel over thirty years ago and has now written thirteen novels. Genres include espionage thrillers, mysteries, and Westerns.